Jessica Brawner's first book in the Adventures of Captain Jac is a wonderful opening in what promises to be a great swashbuckling ride, filled with exciting twists and turns. Captain Jac is a woman who rejects the expectations of her family's royal status for the freedom, danger, and open sky of a thief for hire. As the Captain of the airship INDIANA and the leader of a band of well-intentioned rogues, she finds herself taking on one mission that threatens to explode the world's greatest mystery and bring an empire to its knees. A great read!

- *Steven L. Sears*
Writer/Producer
"Xena, Warrior Princess", "Sheena"

Jessica Brawner's *The First Sin* is a rollicking good adventure story with a charismatic and intriguing heroine. Part pirate captain and part French aristocrat, Captain Jacqueline is everything you could want in a steampunk character. Her (mostly) loyal crew remind me of the inhabitants of the good ship Serenity, but these brigands have even more panache. And while the airship Indiana doesn't travel through space, the Earth it explores is no less wondrous. Ms. Brawner's prose is well-written and concise, which is a relief in these days of unedited self-published amateurism, and her characters leap off the page and take root in the reader's imagination. I can't wait to see where subsequent stories take Capt. Jac, and only hope she won't run into any flying sharks.

- *Thunder Levin*
Writer of Sharknado

ALSO BY JESSICA BRAWNER

THE ADVENTURES OF CAPTAIN JAC

Bad Altitude (short story)
Sapphire Eyes Are Smiling (novella)
The First Sin

NON-FICTION TITLES

Booking the Library: A Guide for Entertainers, Musicians, Speakers & Authors
Charisma +1: A Guide to Convention Etiquette for Gamers, Geeks & the Socially Awkward

FIND MORE AT
WWW.JESSICABRAWNER.COM

The First Sin

Jessica Brawner

No part of this book may be reproduced or transmitted in any form or by any electronic or mechanical means, including photocopying, recording or by any information storage and retrieval system, without the express written permission of the copyright holder, except where permitted by law. This novel is a work of fiction. Names, characters, places and incidents are either the product of the author's imagination, or, if real, used fictitiously, and any resemblance to actual persons, living or dead, business establishments, events or locales is entirely coincidental.

The scanning, uploading, and distribution of this book via the Internet or via any other means without the permission of the publisher is illegal and punishable by law. Please purchase only authorized electronic editions, and do not participate in or encourage electronic piracy of copyrighted materials. Your support of the author's rights is appreciated.

Copyright © 2020 Jessica Brawner

Author Photo by Steven L. Sears

Cover design and artwork by Jessica Brawner

Published by Story of the Month Club

All rights reserved.

ISBN: 978-0-9990629-1-3

ACKNOWLEDGMENTS

A lot of love and time went into creating this novel, and I would be remiss if I did not thank some of the people who helped along the way. I couldn't have done this without the love and support of Steven L. Sears who spent hours sitting on our kitchen floor brainstorming new plots and characters, reading drafts, and encouraging me to get back to writing. I would also like to thank Peter J. Wacks who helped flesh out the original idea, though it morphed significantly from where we started; my beta readers who found the plot holes and helped me tighten up the writing, and my fans, who kept asking 'When is it coming out?!'

PROLOGUE

I was born to wealth and power, the second daughter of the Count of Valois in the northern regions of France. My father was the younger brother to the king. Insofar as I knew at a young age, the two of them were not close, but neither did they have any enmity for each other. We would on occasion make the long and difficult trip to Paris to be seen at court, my father more often than the rest of us, but for the most part we remained at home. My mother died when I was very young. Influenza I think it was, but I was not allowed in to see her for fear of contagion.

My sister Marguerite, father's pride and joy, was to inherit and become a countess when he died, and as the youngest I had few responsibilities. I was allowed my mechanic shop, and if I missed my deportment and needle-working lessons more often than not, I made it up with an effort to attend my language and mathematics classes. No one yelled too loudly about my lack of decorum. It was assumed I would make a good marriage and further the family name, though my father assured me I would have the final say on who I married.

A tragic accident. Marguerite was thrown from her horse while riding with her fiancé and broke her neck. My father, convinced there was foul play involved, rode to Paris to demand a trial. He never arrived.

At age 14 I found myself the new Contessa of Valois. I tried. I really did. My sister would have made a splendid countess. I am not suited for that life. At 16 I appointed a steward, donned a disguise, and ran away to join the English air corps.

After a time, the King made peace with my decision, approved my choice of steward, and put about an official story. I had decided to sequester myself on my estate finding court life to be too exciting. He did not wish it known that I was piloting an airship like a commoner, and for the English no less. After my commission with the English air corps was up, I took the monies I had earned, plus a loan from the estate, put together a small crew and purchased *The Indiana*.

JACQUELINE

For our sins are multiplied above our heads, and our ignorances have reached up unto heaven. ~ *Esdras 8:75*

Six Years Later

The Indiana, my pride and joy, limped into the Palermo airfield in Sicily on its last dregs of fuel. The crew looked haggard; the airship was barely holding together; no one had been paid in months. If we didn't get a job, we would be dead in the air. Palermo was new territory for us, but I had some leads.

Today was also my first mate Tyler's birthday, so the crew and I scraped together the few remaining coins we had to take him out for a night on the town.

Even from the street the bar stank of cheap alcohol, sweat and too many drunken brawls. It was perfect. We staggered into the tavern laughing at one of Nina's rare jokes; the sign outside had a picture of a tankard on fire. *The Flaming Mug*.

The crew herded Tyler over to the bar, calling for a round of drinks. I followed, scanning the room to see if my contact had arrived. I hadn't dealt with him before – Zacharias, one of our former clients, provided the introduction. He knew our skillsets – discretion, disguise, misdirection, mechanical genius, procuring the hard to get.

Two men sat in one shadowy corner talking, their voices muted. At another private table a merchant ate his dinner, looking about with tired eyes. A group of young men sat on the other side of the room toasting boisterously and tossing dice. A crowd around the bar awaited drinks from harried-looking bar maids. I smiled and joined the crowd.

When I went back for my second glass of wine a barmaid slipped a note under my glass and glanced towards a man sitting at the other end of the bar. He was younger than I expected, dark haired and dark eyed with a quick smile. I raised an eyebrow in his direction and he nodded. I smiled at the barmaid and slid a few coins her direction, picking up the wine and the note.

11:30 tonight, upstairs, room five.

Chuckling, I rolled my eyes. This was probably my contact, and not some local who hoped for an exciting tumble between the sheets. I had made that mistake once before though, much to everyone's amusement. I glanced at the clock; it was only ten. Looking back, the man was gone.

Joining my crew, I slid the note over to Nina. "What do you think? Job or love note?"

Nina chuckled, "If it's a love note, I'll buy the next round."

I grinned wryly. "And if it's our contact, next round is on me. I wish Zacharias had provided a better description. As much as I hate to pull you away from the party, I'll need a lookout."

Nina grinned. "Of course. And if he is expecting a tumble in the sheets, won't he be surprised to have us both there."

Glancing at her sideways I said, "You're impossible, you know that, right?"

She laughed a deep, throaty laugh. "It's why you keep me around."

Tyler was having a grand time with a willing barmaid on one knee and another who made sure his tankard stayed filled. Marie chatted with the men at the adjacent table, clearly enjoying herself. I'd occasionally hear terms like "overdrive," "inert gas" and "alloy." I enjoyed tinkering with mechanics myself, and I was decent at it, but Marie was a genius. She knew what it took to keep an airship flying, and her miniature clockwork creations were marvelous.

Henri, our ship's doctor, was as out of place as anyone could be at a bar. His button-down shirt and polished shoes stood out among the rough wear of the patrons. He stared at Marie, longing and jealousy flitting across his face. I smiled into my cup. The crew were laying bets on when those two would finally get together.

It took me a while to find Seamus, our security specialist and supply chief. He was standing at the center of a knot of young men, playing darts. I watched as he flung the fletched objects carelessly. To the untrained eye it looked like he was barely paying attention to the game, but each dart hit the center of the subsequent wedge, spiraling from the outer edge to the inner bullseye.

I shook my head with a grin. Those young men would go home tonight somewhat lighter in their pockets.

At eleven fifteen I caught Nina's eye and nodded towards the stairs. She extricated herself from a group of admirers and joined me.

After the noise in the common room, the upstairs was quiet. The hall ran the entire length of the building, with rooms on either side, the wooden floors worn shiny with years of foot traffic. Gaslights flickered along the walls, their cool blue light illuminating the sparse decor.

Room five was halfway down on the right. I took a moment to compose myself before I entered. Nina leaned against the wall next to the door, the one nearest the exit. As I raised my hand to knock, the door swung open.

A small sitting room greeted me. The walls were a soothing green blue, nothing too garish or exciting–there was no bed, only a modest table with chairs off to the side. The gas lamps around the room burned with a warm, welcoming glow.

The man from the bar was sitting on the far side of the room. "Come in *ma belle* please, Captain. My name is Franco." He sat on a small couch, foot resting on one knee, drinking what appeared to be brandy. Several men stood around, looking like they would rather be downstairs in the bar.

"Jac." I said as I entered, Nina a half-step behind and to my right.

The man's eyes crinkled in the corners, and he smiled. "I see you brought a drinking companion for my men. Please, help yourself. The brandy is quite decent."

I nodded to Nina, and she joined the group as I sat on the couch opposite our potential employer, taking him in. Dark hair, dark eyes held a twinkle of humor; he exuded an air of careless confidence as he dangled a brandy glass callously by the tips of his fingers. Another glass sat on the low table between us. He raised an eyebrow at my scrutiny.

"Well Captain, do you like what you see?" He winked.

"I'm more interested in finding out if I like what I hear," I replied coolly. "I understand you might have a job."

He laughed and sat up, leaning forward. "Direct, I like it. Your reputation said as much. Yes, I have a job, if you're willing to take it. It may be beyond even your crew's considerable ability, though." He didn't quite sneer, and his tone wasn't condescending enough to take offense at, but it raised my hackles.

"Try me," I replied. "I'll be the judge of what we take, or don't."

"You have handled jobs involving heads of state before."

It was a statement, not a question, which surprised me. Franco was more well informed, than I thought.

"The job is quite dangerous, and I wish impress upon you the delicacy of the matter and make sure you are capable of completing it, should we come to an agreement."

I raised an eyebrow. "Are you trying to bait me, monsieur? I can't make a fair assessment of the job until I know something about it."

He leaned back hands extended. "I would never bait someone as lovely as you, Jac. Your reputation precedes you, and because my client knows how risky this job is, he is willing to pay a considerable amount to have it done. Your handling of the Stuart Sapphire heist, one of the crown jewels of Europe, is well known in certain circles. That was deftly done. This will require even more ingenuity."

The small hairs rose on the back of my neck. Zacharias had not known about that job. "Ah. So, we will not be working for you." I nodded, making up my mind. "When your employer wishes to meet and discuss the job, please be back in touch. I like to know who I'm working for." I stood to leave, catching Nina's eye and gesturing to the door.

I was halfway to the door when he said, "Captain! At least hear the offer." His voice was tinged with worry. "My employer asked for you specifically, but he deals with no one in person. The rich and powerful do not do their own dirty work."

I smiled to myself. He wanted us. Which gave me all of the negotiating power. I turned back, scowling, pretending reluctance. "Do not waste my time, Franco."

"I have been authorized to pay you a small sum, just to listen to the offer. My employer thought you might be reluctant."

I raised an eyebrow at that. "I will listen, but only because I find you entertaining. You have one minute. Go."

He nodded, breathing a sigh of relief. "Very well. My employer, who wishes to remain nameless, is extremely wealthy and is a collector of rare religious relics. His collection is quite large, but he requires a very special piece, and absolute discretion. The piece he desires is found only in the Vatican. Naturally, given the risk involved, he is quite willing to pay a handsome sum for its retrieval. He is offering two thousand gold pieces."

I looked at Franco with incredulity and started laughing. "You jest. For that sum you could not even convince me to leave port." I narrowed my eyes and leaned forward. "If your employer wishes to hire the best crew for this job then he will have to do better than that."

Franco looked disconcerted and rubbed the back of his neck. "Ten thousand gold," he muttered, just loud enough for me to hear.

My mind went blank for a moment contemplating the sum, as my heart started pounding. Ten thousand gold pieces was enough to buy the ship outright. Deals like this were things you only heard about. It immediately put me on my guard.

I was surprised to hear my voice sounding cool and collected. "That is a more worthy sum, which means he appreciates how dangerous this job is. Make it twenty thousand gold pieces and we will consider it."

Franco didn't even blink when he said, "Done. You drive a hard bargain, Captain."

I understood Franco's original offer then. He had wanted to keep the money for himself. Something was definitely off. No one agreed to that kind of money. I extended my hand to shake his. "I'll let you know tomorrow if we decide to accept."

He did blink at that. "I thought you just…"

I smiled, "I believe I said for twenty thousand gold pieces we would consider it. I will give you my answer tomorrow evening after I've consulted my crew. If we accept, then I will get the details about the item."

Franco's face went through a variety of emotions from surprise to anger, his mouth opening and closing but not knowing what to say. "Captain, I would prefer to get this wrapped up tonight. It is important that I report back to my employer that this has been taken care of."

I nodded. "I'm sure you would, Franco, but I won't do a job this big without the full cooperation and agreement of my crew. As you yourself pointed out, this is not a standard job, and I don't have a standard crew. Shall I meet you back here tomorrow evening, say six o'clock?"

His nostrils flared, and I could see plainly he wanted to refuse me. "Fine. Six o'clock tomorrow. Don't be late."

"And my payment for listening?" I held out my hand and he grimaced. I half thought he had been bluffing, so when he tossed me a small pouch I very nearly missed catching it.

I smiled and tucked it into a pocket in my vest without looking at the contents. "Until tomorrow then. Have a pleasant evening."

Nina followed me into the hall. When we were far enough so I was sure Franco's men wouldn't overhear us, I said, "Round up the crew, get them back to the ship. Now. I need everyone sobered up by tomorrow morning so we can discuss this. I'll settle the bill here."

Nina nodded in her taciturn way. "Aye, Captain. I'll see you at the airship."

At the table I took a moment to open the pouch and spill the contents onto my palm. A dozen tiny diamonds rolled out, one of them falling to the floor. Nina's eyes widened.

"*Merde.*" I carefully poured the contents back into the pouch, hoping no-one but Nina had seen. I didn't want to make a spectacle by searching for the lost one. By the time I got the bar keeper's attention and settled the bill, Nina had the crew out the door and on their way.

Everything was quiet onboard the ship. I took second watch while everyone else turned in for the night. In the small hours of the morning the ship's *grand poche*, the large envelope filled with smaller individual balloons cast shadows on half the deck, creating pools of darkness as a counterpoint to the moon's bright, clear light. The brass vent pipes snaking up through the deck from the engine room below gleamed, winking from the darkness whenever a cloud crossed the moon. Seamus appeared like some mythical creature out of one of his tales, stepping into a beam of moonlight. "I'm here to relieve you, Captain."

I smiled. "I can't sleep anyway Seamus, you may as well go back to bed."

"Jac, if you don't mind my sayin', you didn't look real pleased when you came downstairs from talking to that fella." Seamus leaned against the airship's railing, looking off into the distance.

"You would be correct in your assumption, *mon ami*. The offer is too good, the messenger was too charming, and the job is more dangerous than any we've taken on yet. I can't quite lay my finger on it, but either his employer is an idiot with too much money; good for us, bad for him. Or there is something going on. Did you notice anything unusual about the pub?" I leaned back, elbows propped on the railing, staring across the deck.

Seamus hmphed. "They had painted recently, but that hardly seems suspicious. I dinna see the messenger. Do you want to talk about the offer?"

"Tomorrow when the crew is all together is soon enough," I said, stifling a yawn. "Seems I am tired. I'm going get some sleep. I'll see you in the morning."

Seamus nodded. "Aye. Have a good night, Captain."

I didn't bother lighting the lamps in my cabin, just kicked off my boots and loosened my leather vest enough to wriggle free. The feel of the night air through my thin shirt was chilly but pleasant. Brushing out my hair I tried to pinpoint what was bothering me about the job without success.

JACQUELINE

Everyone agreed on two things: we needed the money, and it felt like a trap. The problem was what to do about it. The crew were sitting around the heavy wooden dining table in the common room.

The catch all room on the ship, the common room was galley, meeting room, workspace and common space for dice or chess. A wide table ran the room's length, with a pantry and cooking area set off to one side. Over the years, the crew had added touches, a hand drawn picture of wildflowers from Henri, a worn rug from Nina's travels in the Far East, Seamus's dartboard, hanging beside the door, brightly colored, misshapen red and yellow cushions, sewn whenever the night watch was too slow to stay awake. These littered the area, giving it a feeling of home.

"If we think it's a trap it's pretty damn stupid to walk right into it," Seamus yelled at the top of his lungs.

Quiet little Marie stood her ground. "But what if it's not a trap? What if it's just a job no one thinks can be done? It's not like we haven't pulled off crazy jobs before. We stole one of the crown jewels of England fer christsake. And no one even suspected us! If we pull this off we can retire. Or have a nice long vacation. Or I can finally buy that little farm for my folks. And I don't know about you guys, but I am tired of having my pay deferred for months on end!" She glared around the table.

I looked at the normally even tempered and cheerful Marie with surprise.

Nina sat at the end of the table cleaning her nails with a knife. "Captain, I agree with both of them. What did Zacharias have to say about Franco? Do we know anything about him?

"He didn't say much. He wrote that he'd recommended us to an agent he knew, and that the agent would be making contact at *The Flaming Mug* in Palermo. I received the letter in Marseille about a month ago."

Henri spoke up from the kitchen, "Is there any way we can contact Zacharias before tonight's meeting?"

I shook my head. "He's been travelling and staying low lately. I don't even know what country he's in right now."

Tyler was holding his head in his hands, nursing a hangover from the night before. "Captain, I think it's a bad job. I mislike not knowing who we're working for. But if you decide we should take it then we will."

I nodded in agreement and paced for a few minutes, thinking. "Here's what I propose," I said at last. "I'll go in this evening, raise our price to thirty thousand gold pieces and demand half in advance. If he agrees to those terms and pays in advance, it's worth the risk. If he refuses, we walk."

Marie and Nina both nodded in agreement. Seamus sat twirling a dart between his fingers.

"Captain I don't like it, but we do need the money. So if they agree to pay us thirty, then I'm in." He threw the dart and it appeared, quivering in the center of the dartboard across the room.

"Henri, you've been very quiet." I turned to the young doctor. "If we are to do this, our decision must be unanimous. "

"I, um." Henri looked startled. "I fix you up after the fact, after you've been injured; you don't normally need my help on the job." He looked around at everyone, eyes narrowing. "And the Vatican? Really? Seems very ambitious. I know we need the money, but I'd rather not see all of you dead. The Catholic Church is a large, powerful, vindictive organization that will not respond well to being robbed. They will hunt us down and kill anyone involved."

Nodding I said, "And that's different from the English monarchy how? We always risk getting caught, Henri."

"That was different. Tyler's life was at stake," he shot back. "This is just for the money."

I rubbed my temples and conceded. We really hadn't had much of a choice on that job.

Marie chimed in again. "Henri, if we pull this off, we could outfit you with a laboratory and surgery like you want. You could finally have the proper tools to work on your research."

"And on us," Nina muttered under her breath. Tyler chuckled and I bit my lip to keep from smiling.

Henri grumbled a bit more, but eventually agreed. After a few more rounds of objections and counter arguments I looked around the table and said formally. "It is time to vote. Those in agreement please raise your hand."

Everyone's hands came up slowly. "We are all in agreement. If they pay half in advance we'll take the job, if not, we'll walk away." Everyone nodded and looked grim.

"Let's get on with our day. Nina, you will accompany me again tonight. No reason to put our potential employer off by introducing someone new."

The crew dispersed to their various tasks, Henri taking his eggs and oatmeal with him. My stomach growled. I told it to hush and headed back to my quarters. My cabin was large and well suited to serve as both office and bedroom. Polished wooden floors gleamed in the morning light. A sturdy wooden desk was bolted to the floor in the middle of the room, and a sternward-facing wall of floor-to-ceiling windows let in outside light. My small dressing table stood against one wall holding what few jewelry pieces of my mother's I still owned. Her hairpins, glittering with sapphires and rubies held pride of place in an ornately carved wooden vase. My hair, when flowing free, reached down well past my waist, and was one of the few vanities I allowed myself. Long hair on an airship was a liability at best, and I kept mine pinned up and out of the way. When it was down however, I reveled in the feeling of the wind lifting it in the breeze. It was lush and thick, brown with highlights of red and gold. I paused for a moment to admire my hair, twisting it up and onto the top of my head and stabbing one of the hairpins through it to hold it in place.

My bunk was built into the opposite wall. Wide enough for two, it had thick heavy curtains to block the light, not that I ever slept past dawn. Wide map drawers covered the wall beneath the bed. I rifled through the middle one, extracting an old map of Rome. Vatican City was a featureless outline in the middle of the map. Taking it over to my desk I set map weights on the corners to keep it open. I knew if I started planning I would want to go through with the job even if our potential employer didn't agree to our terms, so I merely studied the layout, memorizing the major streets and byways. After an hour I put the map away and took out my stationery, jotting a quick note to David.

Mon Cher David,

The crew and I will be out on a job for the next few months and will be out of touch. I miss you. If only I could convince you to do your research onboard instead of in that smelly, damp laboratory of yours then we might see each other more often. I hope you are well, darling. I will send you a telegraph when we return to Marseille.

All my love,
Jacqueline

I blew on the ink to dry it, then sanded the letter, folding and tucking it into an envelope. I set this aside and penned a brief, carefully worded note to Zacharias inquiring about the identity of Franco and who held his leash. Addressing the outer envelope to Zacharias's business manager in Switzerland I put it and David's letter in my side pouch.

Before heading into town to post the letters, I paid Marie a visit in her workroom. She was looking over the scattered bits of tiny clockwork that were her passion. Most of the items I didn't recognize, new inventions she was working on, each with careful drawings laid out beside the half-assembled pieces. Marie looked up. "Is there something you needed, Captain?"

"I was wondering if you had any devices that would allow us to somehow spy on Franco this afternoon." I leaned comfortably against the doorframe.

Shaking her head, she replied, "Unfortunately not. I've been working more on portable weapons and ship improvements than spy devices."

Levering myself up I nodded. "That's okay. I'll do it the old-fashioned way and see if he's known here in town."

Marie hesitated. "Captain. If we get this job, I will need some funds. I have run out of supplies to finish some of these prototypes," she said apologetically.

I ran my fingers over the tiny clockwork of one of the bee shaped prototypes she was working on. "Yes of course. Let me know how much you will need. If we get this job we'll have the cash, and I expect it will require more than a bit of creativity from all of us."

"Thank you, Captain." Marie turned to the nearby workstation and began taking apart one of the projects.

On-deck I let Tyler know that I was going in to town and would be back before tonight's meeting. Posting the letters was a matter of moments before I made my way back to *The Flaming Mug*. The streets were busy. A market had sprung up overnight, and vendors hawked fruit and vegetables from the surrounding countryside. Several booths held clockwork and mechanical aids for kitchens and households – everything from a worrisome looking wind up chopping device for meat, to a series of fans meant to attach to ceilings and to each other to cool houses. I wove through the crowd, avoiding pickpockets and vendors alike. The air was sooty, and a haze covered everything, contrasting sharply to the clean skies that could be seen from onboard the airship. *The Flaming Mug* was just ahead, and I was surprised to see a man on a ladder taking down the sign out front. I watched for a moment and Franco came hurrying out. I ducked behind a vendor's stall where I could watch, but I couldn't hear him over the noise of the market. He gesticulated wildly at the man and the sign. The man on the ladder glared at Franco and gestured back. Taking money out of a pouch, Franco began counting out coins. The man gave a grudging nod and began re-hanging the sign. Franco glanced back toward the market and I ducked behind the stall and out of sight.

The vendor, whose stall I had abruptly entered, was glaring at me, so I asked her, "How long has that pub been there?"

She scowled and shrugged. "My first time at this market – it's not so good as the one on the other side of town. And what are you doing sneaking around back behind the stalls?"

I sidled out of the stall smiling. "Just avoiding an angry lover. I'll be going now."

The woman rolled her eyes in annoyance and I slipped out the front. I filed away what I had seen and crossed the street, ducking into a rival pub. My stomach growled, reminding me I hadn't had a proper meal for some time. I told it sternly to hush. I had only a few coins in my pouch, and plenty of food on *The Indiana*. The bar keeper glanced up. "What'll you have?"

"Just a question if you will – how long has that bar across the street been there?"

A brief look of worry crossed his face, then the bar keeper scowled. "I'm in the business of food and drink. If you're not buying, then turn yourself around and help yourself out the door."

I pondered his reaction and my thin purse, looked around the mostly empty pub and nodded. "As you say then. Have a pleasant afternoon."

He pressed his lips together and glared until I was out the door.

"Seems I touched a nerve," I mused. I stopped in at the other buildings around *The Flaming Mug* and received similar cold-shoulder treatment and wary attitudes. By the time I was done, it was getting on toward mid-afternoon, so I headed back to *The Indiana*.

Tyler was in the galley making his own lunch. My stomach growled again, loudly as I came in. "Oh no! Who loosed a bear in here?" Tyler said in mock horror, turning around. "Oh, it's just you, Captain."

I chuckled, "Indeed. Hand over your berries, or the salmon gets it."

He slid a loaf of bread and a jar of berry preserves across the counter. "Hopefully this will do. Marie found it in the market this morning after you left."

I cut a piece of bread and slathered it with the preserves. "Mmm. She does have a knack for finding tasty things. I'm going to go get ready for the meeting."

In my cabin I finished the bread and jam and carefully considered my wardrobe. Tonight was a gambit, and I needed to appear to hold all the cards. I ran my hands across supple, brown leather pants in my wardrobe. Form fitting, comfortable enough to move in, but tight enough to avoid snagging on shipboard mechanics, I slid them on. Boots followed, slightly heeled, just enough to give me another inch of height. Finally, a high-collared green vest that matched my eyes. It was cut low enough in front that most men stared. Men were easier to manipulate when they were distracted, and I had no qualms about using every advantage I possessed. I pinned my hair up with my mother's jeweled hairpins – an inheritance that I treasured. Two more hairpins followed – gifts from David dipped in Henri's fast acting sleeping serum. They were sheathed so I had no fear of pricking myself by accident. There was a knock at my door and Nina stuck her head in. "Are you ready, Captain?"

I applied a touch of color to my lips and stood to go. "Let's see if Monsieur Franco is interested or not."

JACQUELINE

The crowded streets slowed our progress as we made our way from the airfield to the pub. The market was gone for the day, and the night life was starting to come out. Swirls of humanity ebbed and flowed like a great river, with the occasional brightly bedecked woman in a clockwork carriage carried along like a piece of flotsam. In the distance we could see some of the great builder clanks lined up neatly outside of the half-finished cathedral. These ten foot tall metal constructs moved stone, wood, and other construction materials with ease, each controlled by a team of men. Their dull, non-reflective exteriors made them hard to see in the falling dusk.

The clanks varied depending on their purpose – some had shovel arms for moving earth, others had large claws for holding stone in place while masons applied mortar, and others yet had great pulley systems attached to their body for unknown purposes. The men must have been on break, or gone home for the evening, because the giant machines were still and foreboding.

Pausing, I turned and looked back at the airfield. The clanks used for docking ships and emergency repairs looked different. They were easily twice as tall as the construction clanks. Some had long slender tubes dangling down like snakes; these were for filling balloons with hydrogen, helium or oxygen. Other clanks could join together to form giant cradles for ships in distress. *The Indiana* used a combination of helium and heated air in a dual envelope, multi balloon system. It was much less likely to catch fire than the hydrogen balloons. Smaller contraptions, essentially flying suits with balloons and rotors, each with a man inside, buzzed slowly around the airfield. Most of these were washing or painting airships in the luxury liner section of the field.

The airfield clanks were lined up and easily accessible, a few finishing up repairs on some of the luxury liners, their mechanical arms extending high into the sky. This was an older field – the ships were tethered between two long poles, tied off at the front and the back at varying heights. When the airships were tied off, the tethering poles leaned inwards, hugging the curves of the ship's *grand poche* to add stability. It kept the ships from drifting into each other, unless a storm hit. At the newer fields, giant cradles held the ships in place more securely. When storms hit, all but the oldest airships were equipped with emergency release systems that would cut the cables, allowing the ships to rise at a rapid rate. That posed its own problems but was still better than being stuck in port during a storm. Once upon a time the Spanish had tried building hangars for the airships. This lasted only until a stray spark lit one of the hydrogen ships on fire. The ensuing conflagration took out a dozen privately owned merchant ships housed in the same hanger, and no one was willing to risk repeating that mistake.

To the right, the private cruisers of the rich merchants and minor nobles glittered in the evening sun. Their clean steel rivets and oft-polished brass piping sparked and glinted, throwing rainbows of color. Behind them crews were overhauling several passenger liners. Swarms of construction clanks and workers touched up paint, replaced planking, and re-cabled balloons and *grandes poches*.

My ship, *The Indiana* lay docked to the left of the airfield with the goods transport ships. It was a beautiful ship. Beautiful and sly, with two airhopper docks cleverly concealed in the hull. I could just make out the faint outlines of the doors from here. Objectively, *The Indiana* was much like other ships in her class, but to me she was the most beautiful thing in the airfield, and I knew her every curve. I turned back to the task at hand, but the sight of a full airfield never ceased to amaze me.

At the pub, we bypassed the bar and headed up the stairs to room five. I knocked, and a man dressed for traveling opened the door. I saw Franco standing, looking out the window, a glass of brandy held dangling in one hand.

He turned and gestured to the seat across from him. "Jac. Thank you for being prompt. What have you decided?"

I took a seat on the dainty couch, one of his men looming behind me. "Thirty thousand gold, half paid in advance."

Franco paled. "Thirty thousand? That's absurd."

"Well, as you said, this is a dangerous job, more dangerous than most. Thirty thousand, half in advance."

Franco took a large gulp of brandy and set down his glass. "Even if my employer agrees to that figure, there's no way we can get that much in advance."

"Okay, then we're done here." I smiled and held out my hand as I stood, my stomach clenching. We really needed this job. "If you have another job sometime in the future, please don't hesitate to contact me."

"Wait." I could see a faint sheen on his brow, and his eyes held a look very close to panic. He gulped and said, "Thirty thousand, half in advance. Let me check. I should have an answer in an hour. While we wait, would you join me for dinner?"

I raised an eyebrow, my mind putting some of the puzzle together. There were other thieves that could do this job, but they very specifically wanted us. "Your employer must be close if you expect an answer in an hour. If he finds our terms too high, I can recommend a few others that could take on a job of this nature."

Franco looked startled and wouldn't meet my eyes. "Ah. Yes, close. If you'll excuse me I'll send my message, and have the cook send up something to eat."

Franco stepped out and I caught Nina's eye from across the room. She gave an imperceptible shrug. She strolled towards the door and was intercepted by one of Franco's lackeys. She frowned, but let herself be guided back to the group, glancing at me.

I turned to the man standing behind me. "I believe I will use the facilities while Franco is busy. Can you point me in the correct direction?"

He smiled. "Of course, madam. Luckily this is one of the best suites here, and it has its own toilette." He pointed me towards a small door that was hidden by a curtain.

I smiled a thank you and moved around him to the small door, fuming. *Well that didn't work.* I looked back at Nina and shrugged. This was not good. So far Franco's lackeys had been polite, but they were intent on keeping us here. I took a few deep breaths and rejoined the group, returning just as Franco did, followed by a waiter pushing a cart covered in steaming food. It smelled wonderful.

As the waiter set out a small buffet, I asked Franco, "I must admit, curiosity has the better of me. How do you anticipate getting a response so quickly?"

Franco gave me a wry smile, "As I said, my employer is a collector. Religious items are not the only thing he collects, and he has loaned me some miniature mechanical devices that allow for rapid transmission of information. I'm afraid I'm not at liberty to show them off though."

I nodded, temporarily satisfied as I nibbled on a small quiche. "I'm sure you encounter quite a few interesting mechanical devices in your line of work. It is useful to have surprises up one's sleeve."

We continued to make meaningless small talk and indulge in pastries until one of his men stuck his head in the door. "Boss, I have a reply for you."

"Excuse me for a moment, Jac," he said, as he strode towards the door. I took a moment to admire his trim backside as he paced the length of the room, smiling to myself. Nina snickered quietly behind me. "Could you look a little less like a cat eyeing a fat chicken?"

I chuckled, "It rarely hurts to look."

A few moments later Franco returned. His voice was cool, disapproving. "My employer has agreed to your terms. I will see the monies delivered to your ship tomorrow morning. While we wait, we should discuss the item."

I nodded. "Excellent. What are we acquiring?"

Franco led the way over to a small desk and rolled out a parchment with drawings on it. "The item in question is a hat. A Miter to be exact. This is the hat the Pope wears at all religious appearances and is considered to be a holy relic. The Miter of St. Peter." The drawing showed a slightly conical headpiece, decorated intricately with a variety of precious and semi-precious stones and embroidery.

Franco continued. "The Swiss Guard protects the Vatican; they're legendary in their efficiency and their brutality in dealing with trespassers."

Nodding, I agreed. All mercenaries, thieves or otherwise, knew about the Swiss Guard—the elite force guarding the Vatican. "Do you have a map of the palace and Vatican City?"

"Vatican City, yes." He handed over a rolled-up sheet of parchment. "The Vatican Palace, no. I can sketch a general layout for you, but it will be incomplete at best."

I handed the map to Nina and bent over the drawing of the hat itself. "Anything special we should know about this relic? Don't relics supposedly have powers?"

He laughed, "Captain, don't tell me you're superstitious."

"Just being cautious—I've seen more than a few strange things in this world," I replied.

"No powers that I know of. It is covered in pearls and gems, and the thread for the embroidery is gold. Not to mention its historical value."

Nodding I agreed. "Do you know where it's kept?"

Franco drummed his fingers on the table for a moment. "I do not know exactly where. It will likely be one of three places, on Pope Clément's head, in the Vault of Relics or on display for the pilgrims on the alter in the cathedral."

"I see. Do you know where this vault is within the palace?" Nina handed me the map, anticipating my thoughts. I unrolled it on top of the drawing of the Miter.

"I'm afraid not." He shrugged apologetically.

Studying the map I quipped, "Well, I guess we shall just have to steal it off his head."

Franco chuckled. "I would pay extra to see that."

"What are these buildings here?" I asked, pointing to several large structures outside the walls of the palace.

"Monasteries, mostly, and this one is a cathedral." Franco pointed to a cross shaped building marked on the map.

I nodded, thinking. "When do you want it delivered, and where?"

"One month from now, and meet me here. I will ensure my employer receives his package, and you receive the remainder of your money."

I shook my head. "What hold does this employer have on you, that you protect his privacy so thoroughly, yet disapprove of his choices?"

A slight flush crept up Franco's neck. "My employer is none of your concern."

I nodded, conceding the point, rolled up the drawing of the hat and stuck out my hand. "I'll see you tomorrow. I look forward to receiving the first payment. A pleasure doing business with you."

He shook my hand. "As you say. Tomorrow."

The veil of night loomed over the city as we made our way through the streets. Nina muttered in her native tongue, debating back and forth with herself. At the ship we stepped onto the lift platform. As it rose to the sound of clanking gears, she said, "Jac, this is going to be bad business, I can feel it."

Feeling weary, I nodded.

The crew sat haphazardly around the common room, eagerly awaiting the news. Tyler looked up from cleaning his pistols as we entered. "Well?"

"We have a job, *mes amies*, and they will be here tomorrow with half of the payment," I announced to the room.

Marie looked up from her card game with Henri, shaking her curly black hair out of her eyes with a smile. "That's great, Captain. So what do they want us to steal?"

"It seems we need to steal a hat. Specifically, the Pope's hat."

Marie looked at me, head cocked to one side, gauging to see if I was joking. "The Pope's hat?"

"You heard me. Who wants to have a look?" I waved the rolled up drawings and spread them out on the big table. Nina rolled out the map beside the drawings.

"Now, any ideas? What do we know about the Vatican, Vatican City, the hat, or even Rome?" I asked. After everyone had a chance to look over the drawings, I grabbed a glass of wine and the cheese board, Marie grabbed the bread, and everyone found their drinks and gathered back around the table.

As we sat, I outlined the information Franco provided and laid out the map of Vatican City and the rough sketch of the palace. "What else do we know?"

Tyler chimed in, "The Swiss Guard protects not only the Vatican, but the Pope himself, and reputedly the Vatican clockwork mechanics and research laboratories. It is said they have access to some of the best mechanical designs in the world."

Seamus nodded agreement. "I've met a few of them Swiss Guard fellas over the years. They're a tiny group, not more than two hundred in total I wouldn't think, so they all know one another pretty well."

"So, what do we know about Vatican City?" Tyler asked.

Henri raised a hand. I nodded to him to speak up. "They open the city to pilgrims once a month and the cardinals and priests in residence give blessings. It is the fourth Sabbath of the month if I remember correctly."

Something tickled at the back of my mind. "I heard rumor several years ago," I said. "Tyler, you remember the job we did our last year with the English? Rescuing that nun that wasn't a nun?"

He nodded. "The tunnels. I remember hearing about those, but we never had to use them."

Seamus drummed his fingers on the table then rubbed the back of his neck and glanced up at me. "I canna say as how true this is, but I was in a tavern some years back, drinking with some mates, oh, perhaps twenty years ago now. We met a man at the tavern who spun us this wild yarn about the Vatican."

"Well, let's hear it – at the very least it should be entertaining." I grabbed a chair and the rest of the crew settled in.

"Well, as I said, I don't know if his story was true, but as he told it, back when this old codger was young, he and his mates snuck into the tunnels. They were local kids, just exploring and the like, and one night they were playing in a friend's cellar. They moved some crates and found this blocked up door. So, being curious, they pried the boards blocking the door loose and opened it. They found an entrance to the tunnels. He said it went for miles and miles, full of twists and turns. They got lost down there and came across all kinds of locked doors and barred gates, some what they could see into had great big clanks being built, but when they finally found an unlocked door, it dropped them out in an alley near Vatican square."

I ran my fingers through my hair. "If there are tunnels under the city, this might be easier than I thought. We'd just have to find an entrance. What else have we got?"

Tyler leaned across the table and ran his finger along the outline of Vatican City. "Supposedly the walls are twenty feet high and ten feet thick. I've also heard rumors about the tunnels, though I heard they were in the walls running the length, which would make sense for moving guardsmen around. Might be there are two different sets of tunnels."

"It's a starting point. Anyone know anything about the hat itself?" I asked. I saw blank stares all around.

Henri said tentatively, "The hat of St. Peter, founder of the church as we know it, worn by the Pope for religious ceremonies, miraculously preserved by the will of God... but that's about all I remember from catechism."

I nodded. "We've got a month. Let's do some research. Franco did not like our counter-offer, but he did accept it, and quickly too. I would love to know how he received a reply within an hour."

The brainstorming session went long into the night, as the beginnings of a plan began to take shape. The hat, the tunnels, the Guard, all would require further research. In the early morning hours everyone sought their bunks for a few hours sleep. Gold would mean supplies, and repairs and payday, all of which we desperately needed.

The next morning, Franco arrived with two men carrying a chest. They sagged under the weight of it. The sun was just cresting the horizon. Nina, standing watch, tapped on the door to my quarters. "Captain! Franco is here."

Half dressed, with only a loose shirt and pants on, I swore. "*Merde*. Who shows up this early?" I shook my hair out and tucked my shirt in, then grabbed my vest and threw it on top.

"Have him use the lift," I said, grabbing my boots and stamping my feet down into them. I took a moment to pin my hair neatly and make sure all of my buttons were fastened before joining her on deck.

As Franco's head appeared at the hatch, I smiled. "Monsieur, welcome. Can I bid you join us to break your fast?"

"Captain, that is a generous offer; alas, I must needs be on my way." His words were polite, but his tone was stiff and almost angry. "Here is the initial payment."

His men set the chest down with a thud and Franco unlocked the padlock and flipped back the lid. Sunlight glinted on gold. He frowned, avoiding my gaze.

"Pardon me for being presumptuous, but you seem unsettled this morning Franco. Is all well?" I studied his face, wondering what secrets he kept.

He scowled down at the chest, then lifted his eyes, forcing a smile. "Nothing to concern you, Captain. A minor disagreement with a colleague, no more."

I nodded sympathetically. "As you wish, monsieur. I hope you are able to work out your differences. My thanks for the speedy payment. We will see you in one month."

"Ay, indeed Captain. One month. Do be careful," he said as he strode back down to the lift.

Once Franco and his men were off the airship lift, Tyler and Seamus carried the chest to my office. "Tyler, let everyone know I'll pay out back pay in a hour. A paid crew is a happy crew. In the meantime have everyone update the list of what they need for ship repairs. Seamus let me know what we need to re-supply, and find out if the doctor needs anything for the surgery."

"Aye, Jac," Seamus said, turning to leave with Tyler. "We'll let everyone know."

I sat at my desk and pulled out the giant ledger book. Two hours later, a more cheerful crew went off to do their respective duties while I went down to settle with the Airfield Master. By the late afternoon, all of the supplies were stowed and everyone was back on board.

JACQUELINE

Prevailing winds were good, with clear skies and beautiful weather for our four-day voyage to Rome. Regardless of the pleasant sailing conditions we kept watch at all times. Air Pirates known as 'Rovers' frequented the higher shipping lanes and less travelled routes, preying on merchant vessels and smaller ships alike. Marie made some needed upgrades to the engine. The furnace that heated half the balloons was not producing enough hot air, and the balloons weren't carrying their weight. By the second day she had the furnace blasting at full, and the controls handling the altitude had been taken apart, greased and re-assembled. Two days out of port we swapped out the flags on the ship for those of a Spanish cargo transport. Marie, with her engineering acumen, had devised an ingenious mechanism that would flip between three different name placards at the prow of the ship. *The Indiana* was known, but held a similar profile to many ships of her class. The sleek wooden hull hung suspended by steel cabling underneath the *grand poche*. A multitude of balloons strained under the overarching canopy structure, giving lift to the ship.

Airfield Masters avoided trouble whenever possible. They knew who we were, but with our non-descript profile they could safely record us as whatever name we were displaying. *The Indiana* was registered at three different ports of call with three different names and colors from three different countries. I just had to remember which names had committed crimes at which airfields. It wouldn't do to arrive in on a wanted ship. For this trip, the *Sirena Bellissimo*. We hadn't appeared in this guise for a while, and never in Italy.

By the time we reached the Rome airfield we were back in good condition, and the decks and railings gleamed. The rigging around the *grand poche* still needed some work, but Henri, with his deft hands, had expertly patched the torn and weathered fabric.

The Rome airfield was more modern than the one at Marseille. Each airship hovered inside a giant mechanical cradle. The cradle would hold the airship hull stable in case complete deflation of the balloons became necessary. There was no need for the anchoring procedures or crews the older airfields employed. Row upon row of ships berthed adjacent to each other was a sight to behold. Onboard ship, we were preparing for our first reconnaissance of the city.

"Nina, Tyler, see what you can find out at the taverns. Seamus and I will see if Henri's information about the pilgrim's day is correct," I said, snugging my hat down over my wild hair.

They both looked pleased at the idea of spending the day dicing and drinking. I had to admit, five days shipboard had me ready to climb the walls as well.

Vatican City at the heart of Rome was an hour's walk from the airfield. It gave us a chance to feel out Rome as we passed through the merchant's district, and a few quieter residential neighborhoods. Thankfully the tannery was on the other side of the city, though every once in a while its acrid smell would waft our direction. We passed one building with smoke pouring from the windows, and a smell that would singe the inside of your nose, but passers by looked unconcerned, hurrying past with watering eyes.

Entire blocks were being built along the outskirts of the city. Buildings appeared to be constantly under construction. We passed several cathedrals in various stages of completion, and watched a stonemason carving an angel's face into a future pediment. I shook my head in amazement. I could almost swear the angel was weeping, it was so lifelike.

Streets teeming with the stink of humanity, unwashed bodies, and other fouler smells jostled us. The streets thronged with pilgrims wearing sackcloth and ashes. Many had palm fronds woven into crosses attached to wide brimmed hats protecting them from the sun. Equally conspicuous were the gentlemen in cover suits, loose canvas coats designed to protect nicer clothing, with their hair neatly trimmed or tied back, but with grease under their nails and smudges on their faces. On every corner hordes of beggars accosted the unwary.

By comparison the walls of Vatican City glowed. We approached one of the public gates and marveled at the white marble walls rising twenty feet over our heads. The carved lifelike faces of statuary stared down at us with disapproval. A man in the traditional blue and gold uniform of the Swiss Guard answered various questions in front of the closed gate. Two more stood at the top of the wall, alert for possible intrusions.

The unpolished marble walls looked too smooth to climb. Pulling my hat low over my head I approached the gate. "Excuse me sir, when is the next Pilgrim's day?"

He looked me over with a bored eye. "It's two Sunday's hence, on the fourth Sabbath of the month or, if you are in dire need of confession, you can beg the priests at the monastery outside the fourth gate. For an offering they will take confession from pilgrims." He pointed down the road to the east. "Another three miles or so that way."

I bobbed my head politely. "Thank you, sir; you've been most kind."

Seamus and I turned to go, following the road along the wall to the east, in the direction the guard had pointed.

The walk around Vatican City took hours. The shopping district was delightful, with young women wearing the newest frock designs standing in large shop windows. After that we entered a mixed district; tall houses interspersed with small specialty shops and food vendors. As we continued, the districts became poorer and more run down. All along the road were shrines to the various saints, and pilgrims leaving offerings of food and alms.

Picking our way through the roiling tide of humanity in one of the poorer districts, we heard a commotion. Rounding the corner, we reached the edge of a lower wall, made of grey, rough, base stone, without the same decorations and care that signified the wall of Vatican City.

Two burley men were beating a boy of about twelve with coach whips.

Shocked, I shouted at them, "*Monsieurs*! Stop that!" I ran up with Seamus close on my heels and grabbed the arm of the man about to swing. "What has the lad done?" I asked in the trade tongue that most port city dwellers could understand.

The man looked startled and in fluent Italian told me what he thought of my mother.

Pretending more shock than I felt, I put myself between the men and the boy. In fluent Italian I shouted, "How dare you beat this boy! Why, he is not even half your size, and before the gates of the convent, too!"

Glancing behind me at the boy, I asked, "Are you much hurt?"

The lad shook his head, wincing. "No *signora*."

Seamus had the second man with his arm twisted behind his back. "Let me at him! You've got no right to stop me. The rotten little thief stole a chicken off my cart," the man shouted.

I looked at the boy. He was stick thin and looked like he hadn't eaten in some time. Fear widened his eyes, and a dark bruise stood out along one cheekbone.

"Did you steal a chicken?" I asked, knowing the answer already.

"*Sì, signora*. I was hungry. I haven't eaten in two days." The boy's pathetic eyes widened further.

Turning back to the man in front of me, I asked, "How much was the chicken?"

"Ten denarii," he snapped. "But you should just let me beat him. Otherwise he will never learn."

I counted the money out of my pouch and handed it over. The other man, seeing there was no fight to be had, stopped struggling. Seamus let go of his arm, but kept a wary eye on him. The boy, taking the opportunity to make a break for it, rushed past. I grabbed the back of his collar and held on tightly.

"*Merci*, sirs. We will take care of him from here." I held the struggling boy firmly by the back of his neck as the two men walked away grumbling.

"What are you going to do now, *signora*?" the boy asked, casting a glance back over his shoulder.

"What is your name, boy?" I replied, looking over the sorry state of his clothing.

"Niccolò, *signora*. Niccolò Acconci! Thank you saving me a beating! They don't normally catch me, but a black cat crossed my path as I was making my escape, and as everyone knows, if a black cat crosses your path you must immediately turn around three times while saying a prayer to the Virgin mother."

I raised an eyebrow. "Is that so, Niccolò? I will keep it in mind as I travel the city. Tell me, do you know the city well?" I glanced up at Seamus and shrugged. He rolled his eyes in amusement.

"*Sì, signora*, I know it like I know my own face! Do you need an inn? Some place to stay? The best food in town? I can tell you where to find all of that and more!"

I laughed. "If we buy you dinner, will you tell us about the city?"

Niccolò's eyes lit up at the prospect of food. "Anything you want to know, *signora*! I know people everywhere," he boasted.

"Where is the nearest inn with decent food?" Seamus asked gruffly.

Niccolò looked over the quality of our clothing and sized us up. "*The Goose and Goblet* is the nearest, but *The Cup and Sword* has better food."

"Take us to *The Cup and Sword*. A little more walking won't kill us."

Niccolò led us through the twisting, winding, increasingly dark roads of Rome, talking without taking so much as a breath, it seemed, all along the way.

The Cup and Sword was well lit, and the smells from the kitchen confirmed Niccolò's assertion regarding the inn's fine food. A table near the fireplace opened up just as we arrived. Niccolò eeled his way through the crowd with a practiced ease to claim it.

A harried-looking server swept by, collecting the previous occupants' mugs. "What'll you be having?" She peered at the lad then looked over at me and smiled. "Ah, I see you've been found by Niccolò. Watch out for this one miss, he can get you anywhere you need to go in the city, but oy the tongue on him." She threw a mock cuff in his direction, swinging her hand around to ruffle his hair.

Niccolò ducked reflexively, "Still too slow to catch me! Flora, don't you tell no tales on me! These nice folks are going to buy me dinner! They said so! Didn't you, *signora*?"

"Indeed I did." I smiled with amusement. "Flora, bring us the house special, please. And I'd like a glass of wine."

Seamus and Niccolò ordered, and she went to get us drinks.

"So Niccolò, how did you come to steal a chicken. Are your parents so hard off that you must steal food?"

"Oh *signora*. My parents, may God rest their souls, sold me to a poorhouse. The master there sold me to work for a tanner, but the tanner fell into one of his vats of tanning fluid and died after a month. His wife didn't like me, and wouldn't feed me, and so I ran away. I think maybe she was afraid I would tell the *policia* that she pushed her husband into the vat where he died. She did, but since he beat her regularly, I really thought perhaps he deserved it.

That was last year. Now I have no place to live, and not much to eat, but I am free as a bird." He said all of this without taking a breath, and paused only when Flora arrived with the food. Niccolò greedily accepted the plate and began spooning food into his mouth at an astonishing rate.

I watched horrified and bemused, wondering how much of his story was true. When he finished his first plate of food I asked, "Do you swear you can get us anywhere in the city?" I studied the boy with a raised eyebrow. My expression betokened doubt at his proclaimed abilities.

"Yes! Or if I can't, *signora,* then I know people who can."

Flora returned with another round of drinks and a second plate of food for Niccolò and set them down with a clatter. She ruffled Niccolò's hair with an affectionate hand. "You stay out of trouble."

He mock-scowled at her, "Now what fun would that be?"

I watched the interplay with interest and when Flora went to help another customer I nodded. "I think we could use someone who knows the city well. What do you think a guide would charge?" I knew the answer, but wanted to see how Niccolò would respond.

Turning to me he said, "I think you will hire me as a guide *signora*. I am very helpful. And I don't charge as much as others."

I laughed, "And how much would you charge?"

"For someone as beautiful and intelligent as yourself, a mere five denarii a day." Thinking, he added, "And one meal." He said all of this with a solemn expression of serious negotiation.

Reining in my amusement so as not to damage his young ego, I countered. "I will pay you one denarii and one meal, and you will be available at sunrise each day that you work for me."

We dickered good-naturedly back and forth as Seamus and I watched Niccolò put away enough food to feed three men. When he was done eating we shook hands.

"We are agreed. Two denarii a day plus all the food you can eat." I eyed the empty dishes littering the table. "Which is apparently quite a lot."

"*Signora,* I have learned you must eat when there is food, because there may not always be food."

"Wisely said, my young friend," Seamus replied with a chuckle. "Meet us at our ship, the *Sirena Bellissimo,* tomorrow morning at six."

"*Sì, signore,* I will be there." Niccolò stood and disappeared into the crowd.

I paid the tavern keeper for our dinner. Seamus was silent until we were outside.

"Captain, are you sure hiring a child was a good idea? We know nothing of him. Does he have any other family? Are his parents still alive? Who sells their child to a poorhouse?" The last was said almost angrily.

Sighing I said, "Don't let Niccolò hear you calling him a child. I suspect he would be offended. But as to your initial question, I don't know. I like having options, and at worst, we feed him for a few days, have him run a few errands, and I will pay him out of my portion. Assuming he even shows up. He just looked so very hungry."

I tried not to breathe too deeply as the smell of the thousands of unwashed pilgrims who travelled to the city daily assaulted us. A miasma of sweat, ordure, and coal smoke hung over everything. It was late and the streets were emptying as we made our way back to the airfield. In the distance above us we could hear the thrum of the Vatican airship patrols. The long, sleek airships built for speed and maneuverability protected the airspace around Vatican City from intruders. They were about half the size of *The Indiana* and had directional lights that would occasionally cut a swath of brilliance across the darkness as if searching for something.

The next morning Niccolò, looking hungry and eager showed up right on time. "What are we doing today, Captain?" He bounded on board full of energy.

"Well first, you need to meet the crew." I gave a loud whistle and the crew gathered on deck. Nina and Tyler were both wincing in the light, and Tyler was rubbing his temples. Introductions were made all around.

"This," Niccolò declared, "is a good ship."

I raised an eyebrow at him. "And how can you tell?" I asked with some amusement.

"Everyone is smiling, and no-one is too thin," he replied, poking at Marie. Marie scowled at him and swatted his hand away.

I nodded at this observation. "I believe you are owed breakfast, and then we will talk." He followed me back to my cabin, and a breakfast of oatmeal and fruit. I watched Niccolò tuck into the food like a drowning man gulping for air. *Eat when you can…. He will look healthier with a few solid meals inside him,* I thought.

"So, my young friend, we are doing something dangerous in our endeavors. I do not wish you to get hurt, but I must know if I can trust you. You understand this? If you do not wish to help, I will pay you for so long as we remain in port, three or four days, perhaps a week, and you may do small chores about the ship. But when we leave here you will stay in Rome, somewhat better off, but still on your own. If you choose to help us, you will be in danger, but you can remain on the ship and become part of the crew. I demand a great deal of loyalty from my crew. As crew, we each hold each other's lives in trust. You understand this, *oui?*"

"*Sì, signora,*" he said around a mouthful of apple. "I owe you my life. You shall have my loyalty."

"It is good we understand one another. So then, to business. There are rumors of tunnels leading from Rome into Vatican City. Do you know if they actually exist?"

"Oh *sì, signora*, the priest tunnels are no great secret. Not to those who live in Rome. Everyone knows that's how the priests bring in the Sisters, or their mistresses after dark. The problem with the tunnels is that there are locked gates all throughout, and it is very, very easy to get lost if you don't know where you are going. There are stories too..." Niccolò shivered.

"What stories?" I asked.

He jumped, startled, eyes wide. "People turn up dead down there, bodies mangled with their arms torn off or worse. Last month someone found a head with no body and the brain had been removed. There was hole, a perfect circle in the back of his head. Sometimes, I have heard this myself, you can hear strange clanking and scraping–like a clank, but different, higher pitched and unnerving. If you are not a priest or accompanied by a priest, your chances of returning from the tunnels alive, are not good."

"I see. So if one wanted to, theoretically mind you, arrange to visit someone in Vatican City after dark, and one wasn't a priest or mistress, what would be the best way?" I sipped my coffee.

A dull red blush crept up Niccolò's neck, and he stared resolutely at the table. "I have heard *signora*, if a lady wishes to pay a visit to… a guardsman for instance, that a donation to the convent of the Poor Clares at the east gate will ensure that certain gates will be left carelessly unlocked." Niccolò *tisked* and shook his head. "But that is about the only way to get through those locked gates without a key—the Vatican uses Meridol-84 locks. They are nearly impossible to pick." He eyed the sugar dish with wide eyes and scooped another bite of oatmeal into his mouth.

I filed the information away as I pushed the sugar dish closer and smiled. He reached for it greedily. "And if one wanted to visit the Pope in his chambers?"

Niccolò laughed. "You jest. Who would want to do that? Besides, all of the Holy Father's servants are priests, *signora*, and known to the guard." He took another bite of oatmeal. "Though if the rumors are true he occasionally does call one of the sisters to his chambers for confession. I have never heard of anyone else visiting him—but I do not hear everything."

"*Signora* working for you just for the food would almost be worth it. But," he hastened to add, "since a man must pay his debts then I will stick to our original deal. Do you have my denarii?"

I grinned at the avaricious gleam in his young eyes. "Here is your payment. Now, are you quite done eating? If so, you can clear up your mess while I deal with a few other things."

He looked startled and a little surprised as I pointed him in the direction of the galley. "We all pull our weight here, and you must, too."

I left him working and went to find Seamus. He was in the weapons locker, a small room housing most of the ship's explosives and weaponry, cleaning and oiling knives. Each of the crew members had their own personal favorites. The room smelled of grease, leather and chemicals.

"I have the beginnings of a plan." I sat down on one of the empty benches.

Seamus looked up, "And how many of us will be getting our asses shot off?"

"Probably just me and Tyler. I'll need the rest of you to standby with getaway vehicles."

Seamus grunted. "Well, that's something at least. Let's hear this plan of yours Captain."

"On the next Pilgrim's Day we will gain access to the palace, map out as much as we may, and locate the Pope's quarters. Then we will acquire two nun's habits, one for me one for Tyler, leave an offering with the Poor Clares, go in through the tunnels at night and, using the map, make our way back to the palace. From there we'll have to go aboveground to the Pope's quarters." I paced in the small space, thinking.

"When we arrive at the Pope's quarters, we will have to deal with his personal bodyguards. Marie's bees and Henri's sleeping serum have proven most effective in the past. We will take several doses with us and use those to get past the guards." I stopped pacing to look at Seamus.

"Aye, these bees are a wonder of mechanical craftsmanship." He fingered the one on his collar, held there by a small magnet. I had a matching thumb sized one on my lapel. If he were to pull off the magnet the tiny wings would activate, and it would fly about twenty feet and sting whatever it landed on. Marie loaded the small needle-like stingers with a fast-acting sleeping serum. They had saved us on several occasions and were easy to pass off as jewelry or ship's insignia.

"I would rather not have to kill anybody for this idiocy. The bees will help. With the guards asleep, we will retrieve the hat. We'll try to leave the way we come in." I looked up at him. "Do you think *The Inara* will be able to make it in to Vatican City without being detected by the airships above, or the guards below?" I pondered this as an alternate exit route.

"I dunna think so Captain. Even with all her fancy changes, your little airhopper is bloody loud." Seamus stroked his chin. "We'd have to see where the Papal apartments are, but if they're close enough to the outer walls do ya think ya could shoot a rope from the apartment to the walls and slide down it, Jones style?"

"You mean like Jones did in the fable about rescuing the ungrateful princess from the savages? Do you think we could use such an old trick?" I grinned at the thought. "And they say tradition is dead."

"I would bet Marie could rig something up that would hold both you and Tyler, and we can have *The Inara* waiting right outside the walls to get ya back here again. They will still notice the noise, but they may not spot you right away." He rubbed his hands together and cracked his knuckles gleefully. "This will be fun after all."

I rolled my eyes. "I think we should leave something for Monsieur the Pope in return for his hat." I thought for a few moments, idly spinning one of Seamus's daggers on the bench. "I have it! A pilgrim's hat would be just the thing. A more humble Pope would be to everyone's benefit, and pilgrim's hats are easy to come by."

"With some fine-tuning, this sounds like a fine plan. Simple and elegant. Let's see what the others have to say." Seamus sheathed his knives and put his cleaning supplies away.

"Seamus, gather the crew. I'll see if young Niccolò has finished cleaning up his breakfast."

※※※

"Niccolò, tell me, how well do you know Vatican City?" I asked as he finished cleaning up.

"Not so well, *signora*. I have only been there a few times on the Pilgrim's Days," he said, wiping the last of the water off his plate.

I nodded. "We will have to do some reconnaissance then. The next Pilgrim's Day is in ten days. We will scope it out more fully. Do you know, does the Pope hear confessions of minor nobles?"

"I believe so *signora*. Though they must request an audience." He looked at me with some puzzlement. "Do you know any nobility?"

I put my hand on his shoulder. "One needn't actually *be* nobility to dress and act the part. How would you like to be my page?" I replied.

Niccolò looked puzzled. "Do I have to wear a uniform?"

"Sort of," I responded.

"I do not like uniforms, but you are paying me, so I will do it," he said decisively.

I bit the inside of my cheek to hide a smile. "Come, let us tell the others the plan."

We were agreed; in ten days Niccolò, Tyler and I would attend the pilgrim's day to get a better idea of the layout of Vatican City. I would petition the Pope to hear my confession as a noble, so as to gain access to the palace itself. Niccolò would accompany me as a lady's page – a necessary addition, as ladies of the nobility did not appear in public unaccompanied, while Nina and Seamus would work to acquire two Poor Clare's habits, and Marie and Henri would create a new set of the sleeping bees.

JACQUELINE

"Yes Niccolò, you will come with me to the dressmakers, so we are properly dressed for our audience. Yes, you must bathe first. I cannot have an outfit made for you unless you are there and clean."

"I do not need a bath. I bathed less than six months ago. Besides, bathing is unhealthy." Niccolò glared at me.

"You will bathe, or you will *be* bathed, or you will no longer be employed," I said with steel in my voice.

"I will not," he replied at the top of his lungs. "Bathing was not in our contract."

Tyler came up behind Niccolò soundlessly, followed by Seamus.

I nodded to Tyler and watched with amusement and pity as he grabbed Niccolò around the waist, pinning his arms and lifting him off his feet. Tyler was very strong, having worked airships most of his life. One small boy posed no difficulty. Seamus carried soap and a scrub brush. They dumped Niccolò into a half cask filled with water on the upper deck and held him there, squirming and yelling while they lathered him up.

Twenty minutes later, naked but for a towel wrapped around him, Niccolò stood glaring at me in my cabin.

"Next time you will bathe yourself. Is that clear?" I locked eyes with him and stared coolly back.

After a short contest of wills, he grudgingly said, "*Sì, signora.*"

"Good. Now, here is a dry set of clothing. Put it on, and we will be about our business." I tossed a set of trews and a clean shirt at him. "I need you to look like a respectable messenger boy so you can deliver my missive to the Pope's secretary. Once you have delivered the message, meet me at the dressmaker's shop so we can get outfitted. *Oui?*"

I sanded the letter, folded it, and pressed my seldom-used de Valois family seal into the wax dripped on the back.

"*Sì, signora,* it will be as you say." He still looked dejected, dripping from his bath.

"Cheer up my young friend. A bath is a small price to pay for all the food you can eat."

Mollified, he nodded and took my letter.

When Niccolò had gone, I turned to my wardrobe. I had one dress that might be suitable for an audience with the Pope, and it was several years out of date. The sable crushed velvet was entirely unsuited to the hot climate of southern Italy, though it was perfect for Paris in winter. With a sigh, I donned it. *Perhaps the dressmaker can do something with it.*

The material was still sound, and it fit well. I twined my beautiful, curly, sable hair up into something resembling fashionable and pinned it there with my mother's jeweled hairpins. Two more hairpins, a gift from David, could be twisted to expose a long needle coated in a fast-acting poison.

A woman should never go entirely unarmed, he had said. I smiled at the memory. David understood me better than most.

Looking at myself in the glass I was suddenly a noble again, and not an airship captain with smudges of grease on her knuckles. *Well, only for a short time. Think of it as a disguise Jacqueline. No one will recognize you as the Captain of The Indiana in this getup.*

Taking a deep breath, I stepped out on deck with a resolute look. The crew knew a smattering of my history, but there were details I preferred not to share. Like the fact that the King of France was my uncle, and I was eighth in line to the throne. The likelihood of *that* ever coming to pass was –extremely– small.

When I emerged Tyler and Henri gave appreciative whistles. "Captain, you clean up nice."

I reminded myself to use my Contessa voice. Slightly higher pitched, breathier and more feminine, "Thank you, Henri. Now help me get to the ground in this outfit." I grimaced, holding out a hand. The higher pitched voice was not comfortable, but I had found that men responded to it more naturally than to the tone I used when directing my crew.

"Yes, ma'am," he said handing me over the side onto a swing like platform. When I was secure, he pulled a lever and the swing lowered me slowly the forty feet to the ground.

Holding my skirts up out of the dust I made my way to the Airfield Master's office. His eyes widened when he saw me.

"I require a carriage, sir. Please see to it," I said breathlessly. I smiled, hearing echoes of my sister's voice reminding me to stand up straight and stop fidgeting.

"Yes, madam. Please wait here." He did not recognize me as he hurried outside and spoke to someone in the yard.

Moments later a set of mismatched greys clattered up to the open space before the door. The carriage had seen some wear, but the brass works were well polished, and the cab driver friendly. It was not a full clockwork carriage, those were very expensive, but parts of it had been upgraded for a more comfortable ride.

I nodded politely to the master of the airfield and gave the coachman the address of the dressmaker. As we rattled over the cobbled streets of Rome, I had reason to be grateful for the upgrades. Even with them, I was bounced and jostled as we hit every pothole and loose cobble between the airfield and fabric row.

The dressmakers shop stood along a street of other cloth merchants. There were two attendants busily stitching hems on made-to-order dresses when I entered.

The dressmaker had received my earlier note and was waiting for me. "Madame Jacqueline, I am Mme. Beaufort. Let us see if we can find a dress for your audience. Did you bring your page?"

I nodded at the formidable woman. She was six feet tall and looked like she would be quite comfortable wielding a battle-ax.

"My page will join us shortly, he had some notes to deliver," I said, looking around the shop.

"Very well, we will begin with you. Let's see... that dress will never do," she clucked, shaking her head. "You will roast in it before you even arrive."

I sighed inwardly and readied myself to be poked, prodded, and pinned for the next hour. Mme. Beaufort was quite thorough and within half an hour had measurements, drawings, and sketches of several possible options. Within an hour we had chosen fabric and I was scheduled for a fitting in five days' time. Soon after we were done Niccolò arrived. He gaped when he saw me, and I gave him a stern look. It wouldn't do for him to blow our cover.

Mme. Beaufort sniffed when she saw the ragged state of his hair and hands, and the fresh smudge of dirt along his nose.

I sighed audibly, playing the role of long-suffering noble for Mme. Beaufort's benefit. "He is a new page, and as you can see still needs some polish."

A thin smile fleeted across her lips. As she turned back to her desk to retrieve more sketch paper I winked conspiratorially at Niccolò, holding up a finger to my lips. His scowl at the snub vanished as he caught on to the game.

"Yes, good help is hard to come by. Well, we will work up something sturdy for your young page. Two sets perhaps." She measured him quickly and gave me a basic design for approval. Glancing at it I nodded. "The page's outfit will be ready when you come for your fitting."

"Thank you, madam, for taking on this commission with such short notice."

"Oh, do not concern yourself. It will be reflected in our fee." She smiled pleasantly and we began to haggle. When we had come to an agreement on price, Niccolò and I took our leave.

He fetched a cab and we made our way back to the airship. As we rattled along the cobbles, I looked him over, smiling. "You, my young friend, are doing well, but need some lessons on the appropriate conduct of pages. You did well to follow my lead back there. Not to worry, Tyler and I can teach you everything you need to know. We can't have you giving away our game because of dirty hands." I said the last teasingly, ruffling his hair.

He looked chagrined, then smiled tentatively. "*Sì, signora.*"

"Good. We will begin your lessons when we get back to the ship."

The days passed quickly, and Niccolò's lessons progressed apace. Deportment, elocution, duties, he was a quick learner, and deft in his movements. By the time we returned to the dressmakers shop he was a passable page. I had received a response to my petition for audience, and the Pope would hear my confession in three days' time.

Our return to the dressmaker's shop was a flurry of fabric, attendants, and more pins. The dress would be ready on Thursday and I could pick it up then. Niccolò received his page's uniform with a mixture of glee and dread. "I'm really going to meet the Holy Father?"

I stood on the dressmaker's table waiting patiently for her to return with more pins. "*Oui*. But we must not forget why we are going." I tried not to fidget, I did not enjoy court dresses, and I was certain I looked ridiculous. "We must keep our eyes and ears open and discover all that we may. You must be inconspicuous as we go about our business. As a page you have an opportunity to see and hear much." I smoothed the front of the dress as pins prickled around my ankles and waist.

By the time I picked it up the dress was beautiful. A full skirted summer dress in rose velvet. The modest, fitted top with tiny princess sleeves fell into a full skirt with golden roses embroidered into the fabric. Mme. Beaufort had outdone herself, but I shuddered at the thought of putting it on. Court dresses were part of the life I had left behind, and I preferred to keep it that way.

Tyler and Nina had acquired the nun's habits, and Marie's new batch of bees was almost complete.

CHARLES

Steel rang as two men, shirtless and sweating with exertion battled in the center of the training salle. Light filtered through high windows lining the top of the wall making the well-oiled floorboards glow. Small groups of men watched as the two in the center battled for dominance. Slowly the smaller man prevailed, using his speed and agility to get inside the guard of the larger man, scoring a light gash on the larger man's torso. The training master called a halt. "Charles, Fergio, well done." Turning to the larger man the training master continued. "Fergio, your footwork is improving, but we still need to work on your defense in tight quarters. Charles, thank you for your assistance in training. I know your new duties take up much of your time."

Charles bowed to the training master. "Indeed they do, sir. But I always welcome the opportunity to train. I must, however, be going. His Holiness has a number of delegations today and I must go over the lists again."

"Good luck, Captain." The training master smiled with genuine warmth as Charles took his leave.

Charles sluiced himself off in the bathing chamber, washing away the sweat of training before pulling on his new Captain's uniform. Captain of His Holiness the Pope's personal guard. His reflection still caught him by surprise. It was a great honor to be chosen. Such positions frequently went to noble sons who were sponsored by their wealthy parents, and Charles's promotion had caused a great deal of resentment. Neither wealthy nor noble, Charles had been a member of the Swiss Guard for a half dozen years, rising swiftly through the ranks and serving with distinction on campaigns throughout Italy.

He did not know who had recommended him for the position, and that troubled him. As Captain of his Holiness's guard, he now had to learn an entirely new skillset – court intrigue. Nothing in his previous existence had prepared him for the swirls and eddies and plots laid down by the nobles of the court. He shook his head remembering his interview with the Holy Father just a few days before where he had expressed his concerns.

Kneeling before the Holy Father in one of his smaller receiving rooms he said, "Holy Father, I am not suited for this position, I do not have the qualifications to deal with your court. I am a soldier, not a courtier."

The Holy Father raised his hand, interrupting Charles. "My son. You were chosen precisely because you are not of the court. Your job is to see to the safety of my person, not to please courtiers. Given your background, I did anticipate that you would need some assistance with a few of the more administrative aspects of your new position." He gestured, and a slight, aging man with a kind face stepped forward from the shadows. "You have met seneschal Valero?"

Charles nodded, a spark of relief appearing in his eyes. "Valero keeps the palace running smoothly, he will educate you on the different family houses, some of the intrigues that you must be aware of, and the tone and nature of the different courtiers." The Holy Father paused, deciding how much to share. "I know in the guard it is traditional to trust all of your brothers implicitly – in fact necessary given the situations that you find yourself in. Such is not the case at court. Trust no one beyond myself and Valero."

"I... thank you for your instruction, Holy Father. And thank you for your forbearance as I learn the way of the court," Charles said, still kneeling.

"I expect that you will be up to speed on all matters within the course of the next three weeks. Do not disappoint. You may go," was the only response Charles received.

The intervening days had been spent in endless rounds of lessons on court protocols, family histories, memorizing the sigils of the different houses, learning who was feuding with whom, and meeting with the individual members of the bodyguard to learn their strengths and weaknesses. There were twenty members of His Holiness's personal guard, and as Charles met them individually two things came to light; each member had been chosen for their special skill, and not a single one of them liked him.

Shaking himself out of his reverie, he walked briskly down the corridor to his office. An orderly had breakfast waiting on his desk, and the list of the visiting nobles stacked neatly beside it.

Charles took a sip of the strong coffee, mentally preparing himself. These were the nobles that had audiences today. He checked the list daily to make sure that none of the nobles were currently feuding with another on the list, or if they were, that they were not scheduled in proximity to one another. As he scanned down the list, his stomach clenched. Someone had re-ordered the schedule for today, putting an embassy from the Medici's, one of the most powerful families in Italy, directly before that of the Duke of Modena. The two families had been at war all summer, with the Duke of Modena claiming the Medici's had assassinated his heir.

The remainder of the list contained similar pairings, all scheduled in such a way as to create the most havoc. There were a few names and houses he did not recognize, a Contessa from France, a second son from a Dutchy in

Germany, a Spanish ambassador. Leaving his breakfast, he went to see the Secretary of Audience.

"No... this is the list you sent over to me last night. I did think it a bit strange, but after all, I assumed you had your reasons," the Secretary of Audience said, shaking his head.

"This is not the list I sent over last night. Someone has clearly changed the list," Charles replied, trying to keep his temper.

"Well, it cannot be helped now. The Medici's arrived last night, and the Duke as well. Some of the others are staying in town but are certain to arrive shortly." The Secretary of Audience shrugged his shoulders, dismissing the matter. "It will be a lively day, by the looks of it"

"Is the Spanish ambassador in residence?" Charles asked.

"Yes. His Holiness has kept him cooling his heels for some weeks now. I was surprised to see him on the list at all."

"Can we move him up in the schedule between the Medici's and the Duke?" Charles stared at the list in his hands, thinking.

"Oh, no Captain, that would be a great breach of protocol, changing the schedule after the notices had gone out."

Charles growled in annoyance. "Fine. We will double the guard in the audience chamber to deal with any unpleasantness. And then I will find out who changed the schedule."

The Medici's behaved themselves, much to Charles's surprise. The Duke however had not. The man was distraught at the loss of his heir. Upon seeing the Medici delegation – which had included the younger Medici, about the same age as the Duke's son, he had gone wild, drawing his sword and lashing out. It had taken three guardsmen to restrain him, and he was currently locked in one of the cells reserved for nobles.

During the altercation Charles had glanced over at the Holy Father and was shocked to see that he looked amused. When the Duke had been removed, the audiences continued. The guards, Charles was pleased to note, had reacted swiftly with no hesitation. The Spanish Ambassador's audience was brief – the man wanted only to present himself and greetings from his monarch, Charles V, with a request to access the papal library for research. It was granted with a wave of one hand, and then everyone was dismissed for a short break. His Holiness had exited without a word to Charles, and he didn't know if he should be relieved or terrified. His anger at the changes to the schedule simmered in the back of his mind, as he thought about who would want to undermine him.

JACQUELINE

The day of the audience came. With my hair pinned up, wearing the new dress, and followed smartly by Niccolò in his role as lady's page, I almost felt genuine. The confining nature of the dress, however, served to remind me of why I had left this life.

The Airfield Master hired a coach, and we were on our way to Vatican City. The line of petitioners at the main gate was long, but the coachman took us around to the Noble's gate. There was one other carriage in the courtyard. Two members of the Swiss Guard admitted us with a bow. Nobility has its privileges.

Designed to humble petitioners and make them feel small, a marble staircase descended from the massive edifice in front of us to end in the courtyard. On two sides covered walkways with arches allowed priests and red robed Cardinals to walk in quiet contemplation. Niccolò and I started up the imposing staircase.

A priest met us at the top. "Contessa Jacqueline de Valois you are expected and bid welcome. You are encouraged to spend this day in contemplation of your sins. A private chapel will be provided for you. If you have questions about your faith, please send your page and one of the priests will attend you. The Holy Father will hear your confession immediately after the noon hour."

I curtsied, as was appropriate for a petitioner, and followed him into the building.

"Monseigneur," I asked, using the higher tones of the Contessa, "is there a garden where we might walk in quiet contemplation?"

He slowed his pace through the marble-frescoed halls, where cherubim flitted over scenes of Christ's life, from his birth to his crucifixion, "Yes, Contessa, I will show you the chapel and then the gardens."

"Thank you, Monseigneur." I gave a small curtsey and purposely stumbled, catching my heel in the hem of my dress. Better if they thought me clumsy, and unused as I was to wearing fancy dresses, it wasn't far from the truth. I never had been able to wear dresses successfully, always prone to torn hems, split seams, and awkward moments. Flying pants were considerably more comfortable. Counting to five in my head, I could feel a blush creep up my face.

He held out an arm to steady me. "Are you quite well?"

"*Oui, Monsieur*," I said demurely. "I apologize, I am unused to society, and spend most of my time sequestered on my estate. This has left me clumsy in public I am afraid. It is my abiding curse," I lied.

He nodded, his mouth twitching as he suppressed a smile.

The chapel was a small, plain room with a padded prie dieu for kneeling at prayer facing a silver cross, and the eternal flame in a lamp on the wall. A window on the opposite wall let in stained glass-colored rays of sunlight. I crossed myself and genuflected before the crucifix. Turning, I nodded to the Monseigneur, "And the gardens please?"

He bowed low before the cross and led us off into an an immense, sunlit corridor with large open windows, and doors along one side leading out to the gardens. Frescos adorned the walls, and at regular intervals, alcoves holding delicately carved white marble statues. The Papal palace bustled with quiet, efficient activity. Priests and Cardinals hurried by; their heads bent in conversation. The occasional nobleman or woman, marked by their elaborate, colorful outfits, and followed by pages, walked sedately in contemplation, or spoke in low tones with their companions.

The gardens, it seemed, could be accessed from several points along the main corridor, and the Monseigneur led us through one such outlet. Several other penitents milled about outside, sitting or walking meditatively alone.

"The contemplation gardens, Contessa," he gestured to a small section of a larger complex of gardens. Rising above the garden walls, the dome of the cathedral gleamed brilliantly in the morning light. I gasped at its splendor. The Monseigneur smiled. "It is quite impressive. It will be open to the public after the midday meal today, with several holy relics on display for those who wish to petition the saints for a miracle."

"I imagine there are a great many relics here Monseigneur – which ones will be on display for prayers today?"

"Today is the Feast of St. Peter, and so his bones and reliquary will be on the altar, as well as his Miter, and a section of his staff." Bells tolled the quarter hour, and the Monseigneur looked back toward the Papal offices. "I will leave you now, Contessa. If you need anything, please send your page to the office at the end of the hall. The one with the blue door. I or one of my assistants will be happy to see to your needs." He gestured back the way we had come, inclined his head and turned to go.

I attempted a demure look, and said, "Thank you, Monseigneur, I will."

As soon as he was out of sight I turned to Niccolò. "Okay, change of plans. See if you can locate a way into the Cathedral without being seen, or alternately an entrance to the tunnels and learn what you can of the layout of the palace. This is still a reconnaissance mission, but if the opportunity presents itself... We need to see if the Miter is on the altar yet, or if it has yet to be placed. We have about three hours before my audience. If you get caught, tell them I needed assistance. I will see if I can locate the Holy Father's apartments in this building. I saw several pages in different house colors, so a lone page wandering around shouldn't draw attention."

"*Sì, signora.* I will meet you back here in the garden in a few hours." He bowed, as if I had given him an order, and ran off.

I moved sedately over to one of the benches facing the palace and sat, as if in contemplation. This side of the palace did not appear to be heavily guarded. Those guards that I saw stood out in their blue and gold uniforms, but they were sparse. From where I sat, I counted four on the main level, and perhaps four more visible through the windows of the upper floor.

The flow of foot traffic emanated from a very busy office at one end of the hallway. Clerks moved in and out regularly, carrying letters and papers.

I could not see the other end of the hallway from where I sat. Moving to the edge of the garden, I buried my nose in one of the roses. Looking toward the palace from this angle I could see more of the hallway, though not quite all the way down.

Trying to get a better view I moved towards the palace and up the stairway leading away from the chapel. The dress, fashionable as it was, weighed more than I was used to and made it difficult to move. I missed the last step and went sprawling across the fresco tiles. *Merde! I am not supposed to be here. I will be discovered for certain!*

My heart beat faster as guards began running my direction. I reached for my boot knife but realized there were too many of them. There was no way I could fight or escape, hindered as I was by my court clothing. When the guards came running at me, I did the one thing I loathe. Using what I would call my 'womanly deceptions', I feigned a swoon and prayed that it would be enough.

CHARLES

Charles heard the disturbance before he saw it – priests shouting and running for the garden door halfway down the corridor. *How did an assailant get this far into the Palace?* He thought, instantly alert. Heart pounding, he drew his sword and ran towards the commotion shouting, "Protect the Holy Father! Surround the intruder, men!"

The guards formed a circle around the disturbance. Charles arrived, sword drawn, to find a noblewoman prostrate on the steps, her rose-colored gown billowing out around her. A monsignor was fanning her face, trying to wake her. Scanning the area for a threat he curtly asked, "What has happened, signore?"

"She has fainted, I think. Perhaps the heat? I do not think your sword will be required, Captain, but we must get her inside."

Charles studied the woman but saw no threat. "Men, as you were. I'll handle this."

To the Monsignor he said. "I think I can manage her." He reached down and placing an arm under the woman's shoulders he lifted until he could get an arm behind her knees. She weighed practically nothing, but yards of dress spilled over his arms, threatening to trip him on the stairs.

He thought he saw her eyelids flutter, but they remained closed. "Can you manage the doors signore?" Charles asked.

"Yes, of course, Captain. I think the Rose room is open at this hour. You can set her in there while I call for a physician. This way."

The young woman was light in his arms, and a faint, exotic scent wafted off her. He glanced down as he was negotiating the stairway and turned bright red when he realized he had an excellent view of her gently rising and falling cleavage. While he certainly had appreciated the charms of more than one woman during his career in the guard, he tried always to make sure she was willing, and had not, as other guards had, peeped on noble ladies, or even the maids in their bath. She woke as he was setting her down on a couch in the Rose receiving room. He was instantly captured by her bright green eyes.

"*Qu'est qui s'passe?*" she asked in a high, breathy voice.

Charles, who spoke French passably well, found that language had deserted him when he gazed into those eyes.

The Monsignor replied in kind, shaking Charles out of his daze. The young woman tried to sit up, and Charles, concerned that she might faint again, gently held her shoulders in place, indicating that she should remain lying down. Her hair disheveled by her fall, curled in charming wisps around her face. Charles found he wanted to stroke it gently back. The Monsignor was still speaking to the young woman. Shocked by his own thoughts, he stood abruptly, just as the Monsignor suggested he assign a guard.

Charles bowed, face flaming. "If it please you *signora*, to make up for my lack of manners, I shall stand guard myself."

Scandalized by Charles's suggestion, the Monsignor said, "That would not be appropriate, Captain. You have duties to attend to."

Switching to Italian with apparent ease the young woman said, "I would be honored, Messier, to be guarded by the same blade that guards his holiness. But it hardly seems necessary, it was merely a lightheadedness that overcame me. If it please you, I shall remain here, and you needn't trouble yourself over me."

Charles replied, "I must insist. I would feel remiss if I did not make sure you were properly taken care of."

The Monsignor hmphed, but said politely enough, "If you need anything *signora*, just let the good Captain know."

Charles smiled down at the Contessa with concern. "I shall be right outside the door if you need anything *signora*. My name is Charles, you need but call."

Charles and the Monsignor turned to go. Speaking to Charles quietly he said, "Are you sure this is wise, after what happened? Don't you need to be in attendance?

Charles shook his head. "They've gone into recess for the next hour. I won't be needed for a bit."

The Monsignor nodded. "I'm sure you know best. Keep her here. The Holy Father doesn't need silly nobles disturbing his plans today."

Charles glanced back at the young woman lying on the couch as he closed the door. "Who is she?" he asked.

"That is the Contessa Jacqueline de Valois. She inherited the title at a young age if I recall the rumors correctly. Shockingly unmarried for a woman her age. Rumor has it that she rarely leaves her estate in France–probably why she fainted on our doorstep. Court is not for the likes of her."

Charles digested the information. His list had only noted the fact that she was here to make her confession, not that she was young, unmarried and beautiful. He wondered what a sheltered young woman would have to confess.

"I'll stand guard until the audience goes back into session and then assign a replacement. Her audience is shortly after lunch," Charles said. The Monsignor nodded.

"Thank you, Captain. I find the backcountry nobles far more trying than those trying to kill one another," he said with a wry smile, closing the door.

JACQUELINE

The lushly appointed drawing room had couches and chairs scattered about for visitors. Muted rose and gold colors predominated–a surprising match to my own outfit. The thick carpets would muffle any sound, as would the heavy, red brocade draperies, making it hard to hear what was going on outside the room. There were two additional doors in the room one to the east and one to the west. Lovely, but being surrounded by such opulence made me itch.

I wonder if my erstwhile savior is still standing guard. Probably loyal and fantastic at following orders, so I would bet he is. Although… he is the Captain of the Guard, and that isn't usually a title given to imbeciles so he probably has some skills behind those nicely formed muscles. These thoughts ran through my head as I waited a moment to see if Charles or the priest was going to return. When no one appeared I sat up on the couch and quietly made my way to the door on the eastern wall.

Pressing my ear against the wood and could make out muffled voices. At the door on the western wall, silence greeted me. I turned the handle, and it stuck. *Locked. Damn.*

Bending down I peered at the lock. It was a simple construction. I pulled out one of my hairpins and bent the tip with my teeth, sliding it into the mechanism. Carefully moving the makeshift lock-pick in the mechanism I felt it catch the tumbler and pulled it into place. It clicked, and the lock opened.

The room adjacent was much like the one I left, a lavishly appointed sitting room done in blue and silver. The tapestry on the far wall depicted all the hosts of heaven surrounding the newborn Christ.

A faint sound, loud in the stillness of the room, startled me. I slipped behind the curtains just in time to see a panel in the corner of the far wall open.

Two cardinals, their red robes resplendent in the filtered sunlight, stepped into the room, chatting softly in Italian. "Does the Holy Father seem unduly distracted to you, Pierre?" the one following behind said.

Why would the Vatican be honeycombed with secret passages? I thought, holding my breath. *Well... it's the Vatican – of course it is.*

"I have noticed something seems amiss, but who am I to ask him what troubles his soul?" The portly man wheezed slightly and paused for a moment on the settee, breathing heavily.

"I don't see why Father Michael called a meeting down in the catacombs, it hardly seems worth the trip, and nothing he said warranted that kind of secrecy." The large man pulled out a handkerchief and mopped his red face.

The shorter man continued to the door and opened it a fraction. "The guards are about," he said quietly. "Double the usual number. Best not to talk here." Pausing he said, "Father Michael will do what he will, pay him no mind. He has his own webs to weave."

"Come, I have confessions to hear today."

When I was sure they were gone, I raced over to the wall where they had emerged and searched for the panel. Faintly, ever so faintly, I could make out the seam where the panels joined. I pushed and prodded the wall trying to find the lever. Taking a deep breath, I focused my thoughts and stood quietly in front of the panel studying its design. Tiny, inset roses patterned the wainscot on the wall, carved into the darker wood at regular intervals. One of the roses looked slightly worn, unnoticeable unless you were studying the wall closely. I ran my fingers across the textured panel and pressed. A satisfying click sounded faintly, and the panel slid open and into the wall.

Seizing the moment, I stuck my head through to investigate. The long, surprisingly dust-free corridor lead downward. I set off hurriedly into the darkness, concerned that I might be discovered at any moment.

Dimly lit by the gap in the doorway the tunnel wound down into darkness. After several minutes, my eyes began to adjust. I could make out faint outlines and thought I could see pinpoints of light.

My eyes did not deceive me. Peepholes into several rooms, visible with light streaming through them, and several doors, faintly illuminated around the edges. Undoubtedly the doors were concealed from the outside, but from within the tunnel the mechanisms were easy to make out. Pressing my eyes to the tiny openings, I could hear faint voices. This peephole looked into a personal apartment. Two Cardinals came into view.

Apparently they travel in pairs. I wonder if it's to keep each other honest, or keep each other safe? I mused. I quickly left the peephole and moved further down the corridor. *I wonder how many people know about these passageways. Probably not known or used by everyone, but more a question of who knows and who uses them.* I set the thought aside to ponder on later when I had the luxury of time.

Glancing through a different peephole revealed a similar looking apartment. My internal clock was starting to set off alarm bells in my head. I had been gone from the sitting room for too long.

The next peephole was higher up, and I was forced to stand on tiptoe to see through it. This too was an apartment, only larger and more lavishly appointed, and this door, unlike the others, was locked with a deadbolt mechanism controlled from the other side.

An older man, thin with grey hair surrounding his tonsure, moved around within, muttering to himself. He was alone and wearing robes similar to those the Cardinals had worn, only of the purest white, with a matching skullcap. That gave me pause. The only man I knew that wore white robes in Vatican City was the Holy Father, Pope Clément. This man seemed almost frail; more so than I expected for one of the most powerful men in Europe.

I studied the locking mechanism. There was a keyslot to a very complicated Berger Veritol lock. This was the best lock that money could buy, and ninety-nine out of every hundred thieves couldn't defeat it. Eighty percent wouldn't even know what it was. I smiled. I was one of the few who knew how to open this lock. That thought gave me pause. There was no plan. If I got caught it would be a total disaster, and I had almost been caught once today already. Things seemed to be falling into place very conveniently.

Through the peephole I took a more careful look at the apartment. Though it was lavish, and slightly ostentatious, it looked lived in. The peephole looked in on a small sitting room, with more rooms off to either side. There were several wig stands in the room, holding ornate wigs in the style of the court. This struck me as odd – they seemed to be on display, more like trophies than useable items. Dishes from a recently finished meal sat on a side table, and a cloak lay carelessly thrown across a small couch. The old man was moving back-and-forth between the sitting room and the room on the east wall.

This might be the best opportunity we had, or it might get me killed, and I wasn't sure which.

Taking a deep breath, I went to work on the lock, feeling the tumblers slide into place one by one, each click loud in the darkness. My hand touched the mechanism that would open the secret panel, and there was a soft click. I jerked my hand away and glanced back through the peephole. I saw

Clément pause and look around, then continue into the next chamber. Gulping, I heard a door on the far side of the apartment open and close, and then all was silent.

Waiting a moment to see if he would return, I pressed the mechanism to open the door. My heart fluttered in my chest as it swung open and I stepped into the apartment. I slipped off my shoes and propped the door open, racing to look around the rooms. The sitting room held some unusual objects, a small book in a glass case, artwork, a pair of sandals left by the door, but not what I was looking for. Opening a door on the east side of the room I entered a small office. It was as richly appointed as the other rooms, with thick carpets and artwork by Rubens and Rembrandt on the walls. The small desk was bare except for an ornately carved wooden box. The box opened easily, but contained nothing more than a coiled up, supple looking linen rope, grey with age and handling. I shrugged to myself and closed the box, racing to the door. There was one more room I could check, but I could feel the seconds ticking away.

Opening the door on the west wall I spotted it. The Miter was set within a glass case on an ornate table beside the clothes press with the Holy Father's ceremonial robes. It was considerably larger than I had anticipated. Carefully opening the case I slid the Miter off its stand, closed the case and ran back to the secret passageway. Eyes wide, and palms damp, I grabbed my slippers and closed the door.

What were you thinking? How are you going to get out of here with this?

I raced down the corridor back to the blue sitting room. The Miter was large and heavily embroidered with gold thread and seed pearls surrounding a large crimson cloth cross. A long ribbon descended from the base of the Miter. I tucked the ribbon up into the hat while I walked. Because of the odd, triangular shape of the hat it could be folded relatively flat.

Seeing no other way, I lifted my skirts and tucked the pointed end of the Miter beneath my bodice as best as I could, jamming it up under the front of my corset, hoping it would stay. Thinking quickly I slid the ribbon out of the Miter and wrapped it around my thigh tying it securely. It might still fall but would be less likely to hit the floor. I hadn't planned on more than reconnaissance today and didn't have the normal harnesses I used for carrying items covertly. "I'll just have to make do," I muttered quietly under my breath. I opened the secret door and slipped back into the room.

The Miter pressed under my bodice, poking uncomfortably into my stomach. The ornamentation scratched and dug into my skin and I was very conscious of it as I approached the door. Every time I moved the point stabbed into me. Glancing in the mirror I took in my disheveled appearance. Breathing shallowly, I re-pinned my hair and straightened my clothing.

How am I going to get out of here… I ran through several impractical options and discarded them. *That Captain is probably still standing guard outside the door. Hmm. Wait! That Captain is still standing outside the door! Fantastic! I'll use him as an alibi!*

I passed back into the rose room and went to the main door of the suite. Opening the door and peering into the hallway I smiled. Charles was standing politely at attention guarding the door. When he saw me, he smiled in return.

"I think I will go back to the garden for some fresh air," I said lightly, trying to sound shy and uncertain.

He nodded and offered me his arm with a cheerful smile, and said in heavily accented French, "Yes of course, right this way."

Gritting my teeth, but with a smile plastered on my face, I took his arm.

He gestured and we proceeded slowly down the hall. With every step we took, I could feel the Miter slip slightly. My heart pounding in my chest, I made casual conversation, keeping my voice light and carefree as befitted a young noblewoman.

Niccolò found us strolling in the garden. His eyes widened when he saw the Captain of the Guard.

"Oh, there is my page. Have you come to fetch me for my audience?" I looked at Niccolò and nodded my head hoping he remembered our shipboard lessons.

He nodded once. "*Sì, signora*, the Holy Father requests your presence. We must go now."

Turning to Charles, I said, "Thank you for a pleasant stroll, but I mustn't keep the Holy Father waiting."

"You must be mistaken, young man. The Contessa's audience isn't until later this afternoon," he said to Niccolò. "I feel certain that the Holy Father will send one of the Monsignors when he is ready for you, Contessa," Charles said politely. "But I can escort you back to the chapel that has been set aside for your use. Or we can continue our stroll in the garden."

The Miter jabbed into my stomach, an uncomfortable reminder. The chapel had only one entrance and could only too easily become a trap. "Perhaps we should stroll for a few more minutes then," I simpered, batting my eyelashes up at him. "Certainly, you will protect me from the Monseigneur's wrath if he thinks I have ignored his summons." Let him think me the silly noblewoman then – it would be easier to escape from the gardens.

He bowed crisply over my hand. "As you say, *signora*. May I show you the rose garden?"

Wide eyed and uncertain, Niccolò watched me. "Yes, Messire, that would be delightful. Niccolò, follow along please." I laid my hand lightly on Charles's proffered arm and made light conversation as he guided us toward a large rose garden. In other circumstances, I would have found his banter delightful, and his golden eyes, staring down into mine a challenge worth pursuing.

As we entered the rose garden, a priest came running at a most undignified pace. "Captain! Captain, I must speak with you."

Charles turned, a flash of annoyance crossing his face. "Father Michael."

"Captain Durstain, my apologies, but I must speak with you immediately." Father Michael glanced in my direction. "Alone. It is urgent."

Charles grimaced, his irritation at Father Michael apparent. "Contessa, forgive me. If you will wait here, I will return momentarily. It seems my duties intrude."

Relief flooded me. "A man of your rank must have many important things that demand his attention. I look forward to the next time we meet, Monsieur." I bowed my head slightly, a curtsey being out of the question.

Speaking urgently, Father Michael took Charles's arm and turned to go. Looking back over his shoulder at me, Father Michael mouthed the word 'Run'. Surprise hit me like a cold wave, but I nodded. Waiting until they were around the corner, I grabbed Niccolò's shoulder.

"We must be going." My voice was calm, but my body thrilled to the adventure, heart beating with excitement. I knew how ill-advised my hasty theft was however, and risk of capture was high. Niccolò, needing no encouragement, began walking at a brisk pace.

"We must get out of here," I whispered to Niccolò, hand on his shoulder. "Now. I have Pope Clément's hat hidden under my skirt."

The boy paled. "How?... If they catch us now they will kill us."

"Go and fetch the coach as if nothing has happened. Do you understand?"

He nodded eyes wide.

"Remember, so long as you act like a page, that is all they will see." My own hands were shaking and I clasped them together to hide my trembling.

Seeing my hands tremble, and taking it for distress, Niccolò calmed. "Do not fear, *signora*, it's an adventure remember?"

I chuckled, "Very well, lead the way my gallant knight."

Adventure or not, there was a disturbance behind us and it was getting louder. I gritted my teeth and continued at a sedate pace. Niccolò walked ahead of me. When we reached the chapel, I ducked inside while he called the carriage. As I waited for Niccolò, the Monseigneur returned. My heart hammered in my chest, and I felt the Miter shift and start to slip.

The Monseigneur wrung his hands. "Contessa, I am afraid I have bad news. Something has come up and the Holy Father will not be able to hear your confession today. I'm afraid your visit has been in vain. I do apologize. Would you like me to arrange for one of the Cardinals to hear your confession instead?"

He doesn't know I have it. I'm just some silly noblewoman to him. This was an entirely unplanned theft. I repeated this mantra in my head, controlling my expression as my heart pounded. I looked demurely up through my lashes, "*Non, merci* Monseigneur, I will petition the Holy Father for an audience at a later date."

"Of course, Contessa, if such is your decision." He looked relieved, the look of an administrator who had been forced to deal with too many nobles and their foibles. The Monseigneur looked around. "Where is your page?"

"I sent him to fetch me some water," I lied. Niccolò popped his head into the chapel. "And here he is now. Perhaps we should be going if the Holy Father is indisposed." I clutched Niccolò meaningfully by his shoulder.

"Let me call you a carriage, Contessa." The Monseigneur started towards the doorway.

I reached out to stop him and remembered myself. "I am certain my page can handle that. And an important man like yourself must have better things to do than to wait on a silly noblewoman like *moi*."

"Nonsense. Come, my child. I will see you safely off." He gestured for me to proceed him out of the room.

I replied in a soft voice, "Of course." The Miter scraped and rubbed against my skin, as we walked, becoming more painful with every step and the trip down the hallway was agonizingly slow. I felt the tip slide out from under my bodice and gasped, clutching at my stomach. Turning the Monsignor paled. "Are you quite alright, *signora*?"

Niccolò, playing his part well, said, "She has spells, sir, and is easily overwrought."

"*Signora*," Niccolò said, "lean on me. You will be alright. We will get you to your carriage and call your physician."

Seeing that Niccolò seemed to know what to do, and that a carriage was becoming more urgent, the Monsignor hurried ahead to the carriage yard, giving me a chance to re-adjust the Miter.

Clutching my stomach to hold the Miter in place, we made it to the carriage yard. The Monseigneur was startled to see a carriage already waiting and the disturbance I heard earlier seemed to be coming our way.

"You must have a secret system of communication to have the carriage here so fast." I let amazement tinge my voice, hoping he would choose pride over curiosity.

Pride won. "Um. Yes Contessa, something along those lines." He tried to hide his confusion, smiling and gesturing to the carriage.

As I stepped up into the carriage, I felt the Miter slip through my fingers, sliding along the front of my leg, held and hidden only by the hem of my dress. The edge of the Miter peeked out under my dress, dazzling to my eyes. I nudged it further into the carriage with my foot and slammed the door quickly. "Well, thank you, kind sir. We will be going now," I said with as much grace as I could muster, fanning my face.

Niccolò hopped up beside the driver and we started moving.

Breathe. Keep facing forward as if nothing has happened. How did that priest know, and why did he help us? What did Charles call him? Father... Michael.

I pulled this thread, running back through where I had heard that name before.

As we were driving out the gate, I heard angry voices behind us. I did not turn to look out the carriage window and I heard Niccolò direct the coachman to take us to the airfield.

The further away from the palace we got, the easier it was to breathe. I closed the carriage curtains and picked up the Miter. With some awkward gyrations, I repositioned it securely under the front of my gown. We reached the airfield and the carriage dropped us off at the Airfield Master's office. Niccolò ran for the ship, and I followed at a more sedate pace, still praying the Miter wouldn't slip.

Niccolò climbed the ladder and had Seamus lower the platform for me. When I was safely on board, I asked Seamus, "Is everyone here?"

"Aye. Henri and Marie just returned."

"Excellent. Nina!" I shouted. "Take off. Now."

Seamus's eyebrows climbed further towards his hairline.

"Aye, Captain. Running hot?" she called back as she climbed the ladder to the steering deck

"We'll know soon. Let me get out of this gown." I held the skirts up and strode across the deck, kicking layers of petticoat out of my way. In my cabin, I shouted into the communication tube that could be heard throughout the ship. "Prepare for take-off."

With my door closed I quickly untied the ribbon holding the Miter and set it on my desk, then unlaced the over garments and tossed them onto the bed and slid out of the corset with relief. When I could breathe again, I took a moment to examine the Miter. Beautifully crafted, the gold stitches were so close together and so even that the fabric looked like woven gold. Hundreds of seed pearls, each as tiny as a grain of sand, covered its surface. A cross, emblazoned in crimson, edged in diamonds, adorned the front.

I allowed myself a moment to revel in our success as I felt the ship launch toward the sky. We had succeeded with no advance plan, going strictly on intuition and circumstance, on what was supposed to have been a reconnaissance mission only. And Niccolò and I had done this with no backup, and no escape plan. Niccolò's performance was brilliant, and I looked forward to telling the tale to the crew.

Several map drawers lined the wall under my bunk, and under those were deeper drawers for clothing. Pulling out the third drawer I ran my fingernail under a nearly invisible seam. A thin sheet of wood popped out revealing a hidden compartment about four inches deep. I flattened the Miter and pressed it into the depression. Replacing the contents of the drawer, I felt my shoulders loosen a little.

Changing into my everyday attire of leather pants, a vest with one of Marie's golden bees, and daggers in my boot tops, I tucked a pair of leather gloves into my belt and went back out on deck. The ship was just clearing the cradle, and Nina had things well in hand. Eyes wide, Niccolò stared out over the airfield as it receded slowly.

"You did well today." I leaned against the railing, watching him. "Would you like to join the crew?"

Still focused on the retreating ground he nodded his head once, emphatically. I smiled, enjoying the look of wonderment on his face. "Okay, report to Seamus, he will show you where to sleep and what your duties are."

Taking out my spyglass, I scanned the airfield and felt my stomach clench. A mass of distinctive blue and gold uniforms had appeared at the main gate and were creating a disturbance.

CHARLES

"Holy Father!" Charles barked; he was angry. Yelling at Monarchs is never wise, but Pope Clément's revelations were infuriating. "Holy Father," Charles said more calmly. "If you knew that there was a plot, why did you not alert me of the possible threat? We could have prevented this."

A slow rumble rolled through the palace, vibrating the soles of Charles's feet. He looked around, startled at the small earthquake. Faint concern passed across Clément's face in time with the distant rumbling. This region was not known for earthquakes.

Charles brought himself back to the moment. Clément loomed over him, all the might of his papal authority and anger ready to bring down on his new Captain of the guard. After the fiasco between the Medici's and the Duke, the subsequent audiences had gone smoothly – until this. Charles was altogether disgusted with today and stood his ground. The guards posted around the edges of the room remained expressionless, watching.

The ground shook again, stronger this time. Strong enough to rattle the stained-glass windows.

Clément paused and re-considered, becoming again merely mortal. "Charles, you are right, we should have brought this to your attention sooner, as Captain of the Guard you should have been informed of this potential threat."

Charles started, surprised. The last thing he expected from this Pope was an apology. Clément wasn't known for his humility; he was known for his temper.

They were in a small audience hall, devoid of courtiers with only the additional guards as witness. Clément paced back and forth on his low dais, white robes swirling with every pass. "Our spies have told us that someone was plotting to steal a relic from the Cathedral, but we had no further information. This group moved faster than anticipated, and somehow managed to penetrate the palace – they must have had help. We planted a decoy in the Cathedral but somehow they must have divined this. The thieves must be returned here and put to the question. I had hoped that the story we put out about the Miter being on display would have led them into a neat little trap, but they seem to have found the real one."

Charles nodded. "Is it possible that they had help from someone within the palace?"

"It is always possible. There are many within the court who would be happy to see me fall. Rumor also says that the Pirate, Captain Jac, may be in the area, but that has not been confirmed." Clément smiled and continued, "Investigate all avenues, but find the Miter. As a relic of the church, it's value is well beyond that of the gold and jewels encasing it."

Descending from the dais he put a hand on Charles's shoulder. "And know, my son, if during the course of finding the Miter you or your men are forced to kill, or to do things that go against the teachings of the church, heavenly Father above has already forgiven you." He sketched the sign of the cross above Charles's brow. "I feel that this is an excellent opportunity for you to show me that

I was correct in my selection of Captain."

Charles was uncertain as to what had just happened. He had expected a dressing down, possibly dismissal from his new-won post. But instead he had been ordered to pursue the criminals and given carte blanche to do what was needful.

He bowed low. "Your eminence, I will not fail you. We will bring the criminals to justice."

Pope Clément looked him in the eye, "Bring them to me in chains if you can. I will pass judgement on them myself. If that proves impossible, dead if you must...."

Charles nodded, gestured to three of the guards to join him, and strode out of the room with new purpose. When they reached the corridor, he turned to two guardsmen, "Find my second in command, have him meet me in my office, and put together three teams of air squadrons. Have them gather with their supplies, enough for a few days, in the courtyard in a quarter hour." Charles grabbed a fourth guardsman. "Send couriers to the city garrisons to secure the exits. Lock down the Vatican. It's more likely that the thief is already outside the Vatican walls and will be leaving by air, but we will cover all contingencies."

Gesturing to the fourth guard he said, "Take a horse and ride to the airfield as fast as you can. Have the Airfield Master engage the ship restraints on all ships currently docked. As soon as the squadrons gather we'll be right behind you."

The four guardsmen saluted and ran off in opposite directions.

Charles was shoving two clean uniforms into his pack when his second in command, a tiny man stuck his head in the door.

"Come in Dupaul. The Holy Father has tasked me with bringing these criminals to justice. I'll be taking three air squadrons with me. Should this go past a few days, in my absence, you are in charge of the Pope's guard."

Dupaul saluted. "I'll keep everything in line while you're gone, Captain. You've got nothing to worry about. Did you feel the earth shaking today? That's got the people more worried than this theft."

Charles did not know Dupal as well as he would have liked. Of all the Pope's guard, Dupal seemed the most inclined to work with him, but they were still feeling each other out. "I did feel it. Perhaps God is not pleased about today's events. Do not let anyone into the Holy Father's section of the palace who has not been thoroughly investigated."

He shook his head and clapped Dupaul on the shoulder. "I'll send word if we find anything. Double the guard in my absence and keep a sharp watch."

Three squadrons of Swiss Guard, Charles at the head, arrived at the airfield in Rome within half an hour of his audience with His Holiness. They were close enough to the airfield that they heard the docking clamps clang into place, anchoring the ships in their berths.

Three ships floated free above airfield docking mechanisms, each with their turbines engaged, making haste away from Rome. Charles swore. "Airfield Master – which ships are those, and what are their home ports? Did any register their next destination with you?"

Waiting for the Airfield Master to find the information he studied the airship outlines. One was a hauler, fat bellied and slow, used for long distance transport. They were hard to maneuver but could withstand the worst hurricanes. The other two were lighter, more maneuverable ships. Pulling out his spyglass he studied the rudders and sails on the two vessels. "Fire the cannon!" he barked at his squad leaders. "Aim between those two ships."

"Captain?" the guardsman standing beside him said in confusion.

"Fire. The. Cannon. Are you deaf, man? Before they're out of range. Don't try to hit them. We just want to see which of them drop ballast to gain altitude quickly."

"Yes sir!" The guardsman saluted, and shortly there was the loud boom of cannonade.

Charles watched, but neither of the ships dropped ballast. He swore softly to himself. The ship on the left – the *Sirena Bellissimo* – had some subtle but unusual modifications, and the outline, base model ship fit at least one known pirate ship, so he made his decision.

"Squadron one, you have been briefed on the item in question – search the ships still in port. Once your search is complete, send a messenger with a status update. Squadron two, get in the air immediately. Split into two cadres, catch and board those ships and search them from stem to stern." He pointed at the hauler and the other, lighter ship in the distance. "Squadron three, you are with me. We are going after that ship." Charles pointed at the ship headed west. "The *Sirena Bellissimo* resembles a known pirate ship. Captain Jac and her crew are known for high-profile theft. We do not know for sure if this is her work, but I have a strong suspicion it is. This Captain Jac, is known to prefer the lower lanes, and she is very good a disappearing suddenly. I suspect she will jump to the upper lanes."

The Airfield Master popped up at his elbow suddenly. "The *Sirena Bellissimo*, Captain, out of Milan. The other two are English: *The King's Grace* and *The Enterprise,* none of them filed their destinations with us." Charles digested the information while directing his remaining troops.

"I need two volunteers to stay here to run messenger duty and relay the results of the search here." Turning to the Airfield Master he said, "Thank you for your assistance – my men will handle searching the ships."

The Vatican owned a section of the airfield and had row upon row of docked vessels. Sleek blue airships with white crosshatching, built for speed, were docked beside larger airships used for carrying supplies and more ornate airships used for transporting Vatican passengers. A smaller section had vessels known as 'airhoppers' – single or double passenger vehicles intended for short journeys. Charles and his squadron took one of the smaller airships – a crew of six could easily man the ship, and he had double that. He saw the other squadrons splitting themselves between one of the small airships and several of the airhoppers and nodded with approval. Here on the ground the blue and white coloring of the airships made them stand out and looked faintly ridiculous, but once in the sky they were near invisible from the ground. From below the ship would look like blue sky, and from above it would look like a passing cloud. It made them hard to see from the deck of a moving ship.

The *Blue Raven,* rumbled underfoot as they took to the sky. Charles was surprised to see how much distance the ship ahead of him had gained as they carefully navigated out of the airfield. Once clear, they deployed the turbines, great, large fans that would propel them forward in pursuit.

JACQUELINE

"Nina, running hot." I yelled over my shoulder. "Take us out low, and then raise altitude to the upper lanes as soon as we're out of sight. They won't expect that."

"Running hot, aye!" she called back, and pulled a lever beside her console. I heard the flame jets roar into the balloons above us, and the ship gained altitude more quickly. "Niccolò, give Marie a hand in the engine room."

Taking one last look at the receding ground, he scampered below decks, moving nimbly down the ladder. I joined Nina on the steering deck and pointed out the mass of guardsmen.

Rome had a busy airfield and a host of other ships were departing as we were. Nina maneuvered *The Indiana* skillfully between two passenger liners, using their bulk to temporarily hide us as we cleared the airfield. "What happened, Captain? Why are we leaving before the job is done?"

"An unlooked-for opportunity. The Miter is onboard. I'll tell everyone the story once we're clear. Someone in the Vatican was helping us."

Nina raised an eyebrow and nodded. "I look forward to hearing the tale."

I heard the docking mechanisms lock down and clang against the ships in berth. The lockdowns were controlled by the Airfield Master and would prevent any of the ships still in berth from taking off. It was intended of course to prevent criminals from escaping, or people who hadn't paid their airfield fees.

A contingent of the Swiss Guard, tiny from our vantage, ran to the docks of the departing ships, one squad of six for each ship, swarming like ants, shouting for us to land. Nina, ignoring the drama below, engaged the propellers. We sailed out of the airfield just as the announcement closing the city came over the loudspeakers. Swinging my spyglass around towards the Vatican, I could see the air patrols massing. Cannon fire rang out and I pressed my lips together in a thin line. He was trying to get us to drop ballast and reveal ourselves. Smart. The ship that did would be the one they chased, and pursuit wouldn't be long in coming.

I stood at the stern looking behind us. I had been watching for some time. The lack of Vatican ships was beginning to unnerve me. There was nothing but blue sky, a few clouds, and the vast ocean. Nina was at the helm and Tyler watched beside me. "Nina, find us a safe altitude and maintain course. Tyler, gather the crew."

"Yes Captain," they said in unison.

I retrieved the Miter and joined the crew in the common room. "My apologies for our abrupt departure, but we got what we came for." I set the tall ornate hat down on the table and related the story of the day's adventure.

Tyler looked shocked. "But... you just walked out with it? How does that even happen?"

"It doesn't. And it shouldn't. And this priest, Father Michael, seemed to know what I had done and helped us. It makes no sense. The patrols were massing as we left. They will be coming after us." I prowled around the confined space. "They will start by sending out small patrols to pursue all of the ships departing with us—but they only have our name, not our description. Tyler run up the English colors. Marie, put out the *Bessie Quinn* name plate. It won't fool anyone who knows what the ship looks like, but it might throw them off if they don't. How far until we are out of Rome's airspace?" I asked, chewing on my thumbnail.

"Another hour at least," Nina replied.

"Then let's stay on the move and hope they pass us by. Be on the alert, people. Remember, we're a perfectly honest crew, flying from Naples to Corsica looking for work." I grinned, and despite the tension around the table I saw answering grins on most of the faces. Adventure was adventure, and we were good at those.

"Also, we have a new crew member. You've all met Niccolò. He'll be our new ship's boy."

The crew took turns slapping him on the back in congratulations, as they left to swap the colors. Marie beckoned to Niccolò to follow her, "I'm going to show you the mechanism for the nameplates so you can help change them," I heard her say.

Seamus pulled me aside as they filed out, "Ye took great risk stealin' the hat that way, Captain," he said.

I leaned against the wall, watching the crew. "*Oui*, I know, but it was too good an opportunity to pass up. That's why I had to bring Niccolò along with us."

He nodded. "The lad will do just fine with the crew."

"If we've got pursuit, there will be plenty of fun to be had." A welter of emotions ran through me as the adrenaline surge wore off, and I smiled. "For now let's get back to France and lie low for a week. The Airfield Master at Marseille always treats us well, and keeps his mouth shut.

We should be safe there. We don't have to be back in Sicily for another two weeks at least."

He scratched behind his ear and was silent for a moment. "Ay. That's sensible. Italians won't be happy about losing their fancy hat."

I grinned at him. "No, they won't. And I do wonder why that priest helped us out, and where the pursuit is. It almost feels like it isn't a proper robbery without a chase. Let's get to Marseille before we start celebrating, though."

JACQUELINE

Two hours that felt like eternity slipped by, and we were nearly out of Rome's airspace. They slipped over the horizon just as we passed the invisible border of Rome's territory. I counted eight, studying them with my spyglass. The patrol rode sleek, black airhoppers, small airships designed more for short distances than long journeys. They were followed by a Vatican airship with contours built for speed and endurance. The *Blue Raven*. The presence of the ship meant the airhoppers would be able to re-fuel and travel longer distances. If we ran, they would suspect us. If we didn't run, we would be boarded.

On the deck of the *Blue Raven*, one man caught my eye, and I raised the spyglass to get a better view. *Merde*. It was the guard Captain from the palace, Charles. I gathered the crew.

"We have a problem. As expected, they sent patrols out after all ships that departed with us. I recognize one of the members of this particular patrol—he is the one who helped me when I 'fainted' at the Vatican this morning. I feel certain he will recognize me."

"Tyler, you will have to be the Captain. The papers for the *Bessie Quinn* are registered to one Bethesda Peterson.

You know where they're kept. I'll hide up in the *grand poche* with the Miter.

Tyler and Nina nodded, calm. "Just like Perin-noir, eh Captain?" This wasn't the first time we'd had to do this.

"*Oui.*" I chuckled. Perin-Noir was a chateau on the border of France and Switzerland. We had 'borrowed' the castle, and convinced a visiting lord that Nina was a duchess, whilst we liberated certain documents from his possession.

I looked over to Marie. She had a wide smile on her face. She loved this part, the chase and the escape, but was not good at dissembling in the slightest. She was really not suited for crime but was such a genius mechanic that we had found ways to work around her particular weaknesses. "Marie, stay down in the engine room. Keep Niccolò with you. No need for you to pretend to be anything other than an excellent engineer." She gulped and nodded, scurrying out. I looked to Nina and Tyler. This con depended on them, but I had great faith in their talents.

"Captain, you best get that hat and get out of sight." Nina winked, and I rolled my eyes. Trust Nina to think being boarded was fun. I raced to my quarters and retrieved the hat from its hidden compartment, shoving it in a satchel that I tied across my back. I heard the ship being hailed, and Nina's reply. *Merde.* They arrived faster than I had anticipated. If I exited my cabin by the door, I would be seen right away.

Three of the four floor to ceiling windows on the back wall of my chamber were fixed in place, but the fourth had a small section that opened to allow for airflow on hot days. I opened the casement carefully and looked out. Peaceful clouds floated beneath us, but I shuddered at the drop. A small ledge ran the length of the window, not more than eight inches wide. I could hear the propulsion fan whirring and rumbling under the ship, its blades rotating at an incredible rate. On either side of the window, following the line of the ship up and out, was a decorative post carved with mythical creatures of the air: sprites, winged fairies, the

North Wind. These helped hold the window in place and ran up the outside of the ship to the upper deck. Steeling myself, I crouched down on the interior window ledge and slid through the open window, pulling it nearly shut behind me. Pausing for a moment to get my bearings I noted just how small eight inches really was as I slid my feet carefully to the left, inching my way to the carven post, my nails digging into the casement around the windows.

I am going to have a ladder installed here as soon as we get a chance.

I reached the post and dug my fingers in, trying to find a stable grip. It was as wide around as my two hands, and the carvings left ample purchase, but I would have to lift myself by my arms, hand over hand to get to the top. A sudden brief gust of wind flung my hair about wildly, and I clutched at the post as the world spun below me. Clinging to the outside of *The Indiana* like a sea barnacle for more than a few minutes wasn't an option. My fingers would tire long before Charles departed my ship.

Taking a deep breath, I swung out, my fingers grasping and straining, my entire body dangling for a moment with nothing but clouds and sea beneath me before my feet found purchase. If I thought about what I was about to attempt, I would fail, and I would die. Taking a leap of faith, I unlocked the fingers on my right hand and launched myself upward, seeking my next handhold. I repeated this over and over, inching up. My arms burned. The Miter grew heavier with every passing moment. I heard a 'thunk' a sound no Captain wants to hear. Grappling hooks hitting the wood of the railing. The entire ship lurched and my left hand slipped, leaving me dangling, holding on by only a few fingers, my legs dangling free. Trying not to panic I pulled up with all of my strength, the grasping fingers of my left hand finding railing instead of carven post. I breathed a sigh of relief.

I hauled myself up, scrambling over the railing and lying flat on the rooftop deck. Feeling the solid wood beneath me

I curled into a ball and began to shake as a delayed reaction to terror and adrenalin took over. The sway of the ship calmed me, and slowly I uncurled from the fetal position.

The *grand poche* was another fifteen feet above me. I crawled over to the edge of the platform. The ship's main deck spread out below me. I could see Tyler and Nina talking with the patrol, but I couldn't hear them. I backed away from the edge of the deck and considered my options.

Waiting until the patrol headed below decks, I climbed the ladder that led up to the envelope above. Quietly I opened the trap door leading to the maintenance platform. This led directly to the balloon itself and was not easily visible from anywhere else on the ship.

The vast interior of the *grand poche* opened above me. Narrow rope bridges ran from one end to the other, attached to the interior balloons containing the gasses that kept us afloat.

When I purchased *The Indiana*, I upgraded her flotation system to the double-walled German construction we currently had. The ship was kept afloat by a combination of helium and hot air. The overarching *grand poche* formed an envelope that contained a series of smaller balloons grouped into sections and then tied off to the rigging. If something were to happen to one section, or one series of balloons, it wouldn't be a total disaster.

I heard voices below me, coming from the upper deck of the ship.

"Captain Peterson, thank you for your cooperation. I'm sure you understand our need to be thorough. We will be done shortly." It was Charles's voice, growing closer, speaking passable English.

Merde. What now? I thought silently. Lacking a better idea, I stood on top of the maintenance platform's trapdoor, holding on to the handholds to either side, hoping to weigh it down. I'm not a large woman, but nine stone is a fair bit to lift straight up when you're not expecting it.

"It seems to be stuck." I heard Charles growl.

"Aye, yes. It's been stuck for a while now. I keep meaning to have it fixed, but it hardly seems worth the money they want to charge me to do it." Tyler said smoothly. "Why at the last port, they wanted one hundred pounds just to unstick it, not even to fix the mechanism."

"Here, Sam, you try. Put your shoulder into it," I heard Charles call out. I never did see Sam, but he had quite the shoulder on him. I willed myself to be heavier, and felt the trapdoor give underneath me with the force of Sam's blow. A sudden gust of wind and a crackle of electricity made the hair on the back of my neck stand on end. I instinctively flattened myself on the platform, trying to make myself small.

"Hey now, I'm happy to be cooperative and help you find your criminals, but kindly don't break my ship to kindling!" Tyler said in dismay. A giant crack of thunder crashed out of the clear sky.

I heard cursing and swearing as Charles called Sam down. "You're right of course Captain."

"It looks like we're about to get a big blow..." The rest of Tyler's words were lost, carried away by the noisy gust of wind. The trapdoor below banged shut, and faster than I believed possible the sky was pitch black around us.

I peered over the edge of the platform and saw the patrol scrambling to re-assemble under Nina's watchful eye. Strangely, the acoustics from the platform were much better than from the deck. I could hear what was spoken clearly, but as if from a great distance. Charles and Tyler emerged quickly from the lower decks, still talking. Lightning struck off the stern, back towards Rome. Charles flinched and even Tyler, accustomed to sudden storms, jumped at the sight. Another gust sent one of the patrol's airhoppers careening out behind *The Indiana*, straining its tether until it broke free. And then the rain, in one magnificent burst, obscured everything. Sheets of water poured from the sky, coming in sideways along the edge of the *grand poche*. The platform bucked and rocked and I took a firm hold, looping the satchel carrying the hat across my body. I grabbed my gloves out of my belt and using my teeth slid them on over my wet hands, never letting go of the platform railing. Looking up into the *grand poche* I could see the narrow rope bridge bucking and writhing.

Lightning arced down, hitting the lightning rods, rivulets of blue flame running across the wires from one end of the *grand poche* to the other. It was magnificent. I felt the hairs on the back of my neck start to stand up again. Teeth chattering with cold I decided it was better to brave discovery than be fricasseed by lightning. Gathering myself I prayed Tyler hadn't locked the trap door behind him. I wrenched open the door on the upper platform and held on to the ladder as the ship tossed beneath me. Rung by rung, blinded by the rain, I made my way down to the top deck. Taking hold of the ring embedded in the door I yanked. The door came flying open with a crash. *Merde. I forgot I had that fixed. Definitely not locked though. Hopefully they just thought it was thunder.* Jumping through the hatch I pulled the door shut behind me.

The hatch led into a small, enclosed room used for storage, and from there into the heart of the ship's communication system. Pipes and tubes ran the ship's length, in every room, meeting at this central location. I reached up and touched one of the cold, brass pipes and followed it along the wall to the next room. Sound from this room could carry through the entire ship, and in the darkness the sounds of the crew shouting and the storm raging outside made an unsettling combination. An honest captain would never refuse another shelter in such a storm, and it would have been inhumane to turn the patrol out in any case. Likely Tyler would settle them in the common room while the crew kept the ship from flying apart.

Dammit. I had to assume Charles and his patrol were still on the ship. I had to stay out of sight.

Sitting in the dark listening to the sounds of the ship and crew I felt like a ghost in the heart of everything. I wanted to be out there helping them. After a while the sounds of the storm became a dull roar in the background and I found I could make out various conversations by pressing my ear to the pipes.

Nina, up on the steering deck, was having a conversation with the storm itself, shouting into the winds. "You will .... devil... fight you all the way," I heard her yell, her words indistinct and faint.

From another pipe I heard Marie's surprisingly colorful vocabulary as she worked on the engine, and the occasional shocked sound from Henri. No surprises there.

I tried a third pipe and was rewarded with the sound of unfamiliar voices. They seemed to be praying.

One voice, clear and strong said, "Holy Father, protector of your servants, guard us and guide us in the search for those who would profane your holy objects."

I shook my head. My spine tingled with foreboding as the prayer continued and the hairs on the back of my neck rose. Fanatics. Of course they were fanatics, they were the security service for the representative of God on Earth. I pressed my ear back to the piping.

"...awful storm. You three, go see if the captain needs any extra hands. Make sure you clip in to the harnesses when you go above decks. We don't need anyone being blown overboard." There was a pause, and a door closed. The voice resumed, but the tone had changed, as if he was speaking to someone in confidence.

"Daniel, while the crew is busy, see if you can poke around the ship discreetly. I want to know what was behind that trap door, and what else they're hiding. This ship's profile is similar to what we know of *The Indiana*. If they're hiding something we need to find out, and if they're not, no harm.... Oh, and Daniel..., don't get caught."

Merde. There were plenty of other things onboard besides me and the Miter that would mark us as 'not quite legal' to anyone looking. And no hope that Charles was just a pretty face filling that uniform.

Thunder crashed overhead, and the ship shuddered. I jumped as the metal tubing hummed against my ear, stinging. It would be tricky to get down into the hold without being seen.

I pushed open the trapdoor and water poured in, slapping my face. The wind tried to yank the handle from my hands. I scrambled up the ladder as fast as possible and closed the door. The rain sheeted so thickly I could barely see the lower deck. Pulling myself hand over hand along the railing I found the stairs down to the steering deck. "Nina!" I shouted as I came up behind her, my voice barely audible above the howling wind. She turned and grimaced.

"We're holding together okay, Captain, but we've still got those buggars from the Vatican on board," she shouted against the wind.

"I know! I've got to get down to the hold. They've decided to do some exploring on their own. Can you keep everything together up here?"

"We're good for now, but we've been blown way off course," she replied. Her muscles strained as the wheel tried to escape her grasp, and she wrenched it back into the heading she wanted. The storm had come in so fast she hadn't had time to fasten her safety harness. I grabbed it and clipped it to the back of her belt.

"Where's Tyler?" I shouted.

Nina gestured towards the prow, and I could make out figures fighting with one of the cables. "One of the cables slipped and they're trying to tighten it back down."

I nodded, pushing wet hair out of my eyes. "I'm going below to find our visitor. Hopefully this lets up soon."

She nodded back, concentrating on the storm. I grabbed the handrail and inched my way to the ladder as wind and rain continued to slice across the ship. There were two ways down to the main hold from here; one through the common room, the other through the loading hatch. Going through the common room wasn't an option.

From the main hatch it was a fifteen-foot drop to the floor of the hold. I put my foot in a loop of rope attached to a belay pin, secured there for the crew's convenience, and started to step over the side. Pausing, I grabbed one of the other belay pins and shoved it in my belt. The arm length of wood would do nicely as a weapon if needed, and I certainly didn't want to fire a gun in the hold.

Letting the rope slide slowly through my gloved hands I stepped over the side. I sped down quickly and landed at the bottom with a soft thump. Letting loose the rope I stepped into the deeper shadows. The hold was dark at this end, lit only from the open hatch above. At the far end, towards the steering column, was the engine room, and Marie's workshop. Breathing deeply for a moment I calmed my heartbeat and listened to the sounds of the hold.

My eyes, accustomed to the darkness, spotted a faint light moving along the cargo racks. It looked no bigger than a firefly but moved in an unnatural, halting way. I let my brain puzzle on the source of the light while I slid silently through the clear spaces, ghosting towards the telltale pinprick.

As I got closer I could make out the outline of a man, holding a small light. He was muttering softly to himself, looking for something. Pulling the belay pin out of my belt I moved up behind him and cracked him on the back of the head. He toppled like a felled tree. The tiny light went bouncing from his hand and rolled through the hold.

Checking his pulse, I was pleased to find it strong and steady. He'd live, though he'd have a good lump when he woke up. I searched around on hands and knees until I found his light. I used it to locate a small length of rope, then slipped it in my pocket. Tying the guardsman's hands behind him I rolled him over, dragging him by the collar to a post, I tied him tightly to it.

With the storm above I knew Marie, would be in the engine room. I was surprised to see Seamus, Niccolò and Henri as well. The engine was loud. The clanking clamor of steam in metal piping and pistons and gears working their hardest drowned out the noise of the storm above. Marie was hanging from a harness using a giant wrench to tighten a joint on a large steam pipe. Seamus and Niccolò were on the belay line keeping her up near the ceiling. Henri was off to the right, standing by a table covered in tools, looking like a nurse in an operating room ready to hand Marie any tool she needed at a moment's notice. Marie signaled Seamus to lower her and smiled at Henri as she touched down.

"Marie, how is the storm doing out there?" I asked.

She looked startled. "About what you'd expect for this kind of sudden squall, Captain! What are you doing out of hiding? Those bastards from the Vatican are still on board."

"*Oui. Je sais.* I am aware. Can you spare Seamus? I caught one of them sneaking around the hold."

"Aye, yes, we are done here for the moment." She looked through a viewfinder that allowed her to see above decks. "The storm seems to be slowing. I can see daylight again, and it's not raining quite so hard."

Turning to Seamus I said, "There's a man tied up in the hold. He was sneaking around uninvited. Can you let Tyler know?"

"Aye, no problem. We'll handle him," Seamus replied, voice grim.

As quickly as it had started the storm ended. The skies cleared, and Mother Nature said she was done with us for the time being.

An hour later we met in the common room for dinner. Taking meals together made us feel more like family. Henri passed out steaming mugs of chocolate, and Tyler filled me in. "So Seamus comes barreling up the stairs dragging that young guard behind him yelling about thieves and god only knows what else," Tyler continued.

Seamus chuckled. "You'll make an actor of me yet, Jac," he said, sipping his chocolate.

Tyler laughed. "Well of course this gave me the chance to play the angry captain. 'We gave you shelter and you betrayed our hospitality! How dare you send men sneaking around!'" Tyler put on a stern, mocking face and Marie giggled as he waggled his finger in her face.

"Charles demanded to finish their search, though he left the young guard tied up on deck at mine and Seamus's insistence. I took him on a brief tour of the hold and allowed him access to the crew quarters as any honest captain would." Tyler paused for a moment. "I will say, he kept his men in line. They searched the rooms efficiently but didn't damage anything."

Niccolò burst out laughing. "Tell her... tell her what happened when they searched her quarters..."

I raised an eyebrow in Tyler's direction.

"I was wracking my brain, Captain, on how to explain your quarters, what with me being the 'Captain' and your quarters being most definitely those of a woman. Then I remembered some of the fancy lady houses I'd been to in England. So I show Charles my regular quarters, then I take him up to yours." Tyler chuckled, remembering.

"He walks in, and says, 'And how do you explain this Captain?' wandering around picking up jewelry and stuff and I say 'This is my entertainment room – for when I bring ladies on board. They love it. They like to feel pampered and it pays its own dividends.' I elbowed him in the side, and winked, and I kid you not, Captain, he blushed scarlet. One of his men picked up something on your dressing table and held it up – 'whot's this?'

'I have no idea' I replied, but the ladies love it. One of my mistresses left it here, and I forgot to remove it before the next one came over – and she nearly swooned with happiness when she saw it."

"At any rate, they packed up and left quickly after that. Charles, the young captain fellow, seemed pretty upset that they hadn't found anything." Tyler set his mug down and stretched.

"Marie, I took this off the young guard when I hit him over the head." I handed over the small metal cylinder.

Marie took it from my hand and examined it, tapping it against the tabletop. With a quick twist of her hands she split open the tube. "I've not seen this particular construction before – it may prove useful." She rejoined the two halves and slipped it into a pocket on her work vest.

"Jac, we took damage in the storm, several cables snapped to the aft, and we may have lost some of the face boards on the hull." Nina said.

"Given the size of that blow, I'm not surprised," I replied. "Show me."

I followed Nina out to inspect the ship. The cables were a serious issue, those held the *grand poche* in place. As we contemplated the necessary repairs, I scanned the horizon, noting the position of the sun.

Doing a few mental calculations, I said, "We're a day off course, maybe two. If we're where I think we are, there should be a few small islands around. We can hole up for a day and fix the ship, then be on our way."

CHARLES

Back on board the *Blue Raven*, Charles untied the young guardsman and allowed the surgeon to look at the swollen purple lump that was forming on the back of the young man's head. His second in command for the mission, an unimaginative, solid guardsman named Yusef, a man he didn't know well, and didn't entirely trust as yet asked, "Is he going to be alright?"

"Well, he was hit with some sort of heavy blunt object. He'll have a headache for a few days." The surgeon examined the swollen knot on the back of the young guardsman's head. "Tell me if you start seeing spots, or if your eyes won't focus. You should rest for a few days before you go back on duty."

Charles nodded to the surgeon. "Thank you, my good man." Turning to the guardsman he asked, "What happened? What did you find?"

The guardsman shook his head, winced and replied. "Not much, Captain. I'd wager that the ship has been used for smuggling before. The way the hold is set up would make it easy to hide stuff down there, but I didn't find anything specific before someone walloped me."

"Did you see who it was?" Charles ran a hand through his hair, thinking.

"No. Wish I had though. They walloped me good. Didn't even hear them coming." He thought about that and added, "Of course, with the storm I probably wouldn't have heard a whole troop coming, and it was dark."

Charles nodded. "You rest. If you think of anything else, let me know."

Yusef followed him back to his cabin, as Charles pondered the situation. The storm would have hindered any messengers with news of the other ships, and the story that the Captain of the *Bessie Quinn* told – of sleeping in crew quarters and having his main cabin made up to please his mistresses – did not ring true. He also judged that his guardsman was telling the truth about the ship. It was a class of ship frequently used by smugglers.

"Captain," said Yusef, interrupting Charles's thoughts. "Captain, why did you let them go? I do not see the sense in it."

He didn't care for Yusef overmuch, but if Yusef was asking the question, then it was certain that the rest of the crew was too. Right now Charles couldn't afford the appearance of incompetence and he was extremely conscious of that fact, so he entertained Yusef's question. "Besides the fact that we didn't find anything you mean?" Charles replied.

"Well, yes. Besides that. It was obviously a smuggling ship, we certainly could have brought them up on some charges, even if we didn't find what we were looking for," Yusef replied.

"This is true," Charles conceded. "And I am nearly certain that this is the ship we are looking for. However, if we arrested them now we still wouldn't have the missing item and we would have no chance to find out who hired them."

Charles paused for a moment. "It seems to me that while our first priority is finding the Miter, it would be nearly as important to find out who paid to have it stolen."

Yusef nodded. "I see. Thank you for sharing your plan with me Captain."

They had searched the ship, and they hadn't found anything, but something was niggling at the back of his mind. Following the *Bessie Quinn* for a bit longer might provide some clues. The ship was limping in the direction of Marseille and would be down for repairs for some time. Stepping out on deck he beckoned the pilot over. "Follow them out of sight above the clouds at a discreet distance. I would see where they go and if they continue on to Marseille."

The pilot saluted crisply. "Yes, Captain."

The *Blue Raven* hadn't suffered any damage in the storm, and Charles had no doubt they would be able to follow the English ship.

JACQUELINE

Nina found a small, protected cove while it was still light out and we stopped for repairs.

"Niccolò! Keep watch – I do not trust that they just let us go. If they are smart, they'll send someone to follow us. If you see any ships in the sky, call out." I instructed, as I tied my hair up and out of the way. "Their ship will be hard to see at this angle, they paint them blue on the bottom to look like part of the sky, and the *grand poche* is white to look like a cloud. If they are watching, they will likely be very high up to try and stay out of sight."

"But why did they let us go? Do you think they are working with Father Michael who helped us at the Vatican?" Niccolò asked.

"I doubt Charles would be working with anyone that way. He struck me as much too honest and straightforward for that type of deception." I chewed on the side of my thumb, pondering. "That does bring up the question again of why Father Michael helped us at all though. How does he fit?"

As I was pondering this, Nina brought the ship down near the shoreline, half above solid land, half over the water, and deployed the land anchor to keep us in place. We lowered the loading hatch, and I stepped out to assess the damage.

THE CREW

The hull was an easy fix, though it took time. The tiles for the hull snapped in to place through clever interlocking slats. Seamus would snap one into place, then Marie sealed it with a heat torch.

"What keeps you in this game, Seamus?" Marie asked as they worked.

Seamus looked up and blinked. "Come again?"

"Well, I was just thinking about the crew the other day. We all know Tyler just follows the Captain around out of some sense of loyalty. He'll be with her forever. Nina's pretty closemouthed about her reasons. Henri – well, less said the better there. Why do you follow the Captain?" Marie asked.

"Oh. I'm just in it for the money." Seamus said shortly. "I've got a figure in mind. Once I save up, I'm going to go buy a castle in Scotland and retire."

Marie paused and held the heat gun away from the tiles. "Really? Just for the money?"

Seamus grunted as he snapped a new tile in place. "Really. Jac's the best there is, and she pays the best. Our recent dry streak excepted. Look at this job we're on right now. Thirty thousand gold – there's not another ship out there making that kind of payload."

"What if there was?" Marie asked. "Or what if someone offered you money to sell out?"

"Well, then that would be a very interesting conversation." Seamus replied. "I'd have to weigh my options."

Marie looked horrified. "You wouldn't."

"Maybe. Maybe not." Seamus looked up at Marie. "I'm just keeping my options open."

Marie resumed sealing the tiles with the heat gun. "What if something happened to the Captain? You'd bail?"

"Probably. I'd certainly not be taking orders from anyone else on board this boat." He chuckled in amusement. "What, do you see yourself as Captain? I'd jump overboard before I took orders from you."

Marie aimed a playful kick at his head. "You wouldn't have to. I'd likely push you," she chuckled.

"Well, see, then we're in agreement. You should not be Captain." Seamus laughed. "What about you? What keeps a slip of a girl like you here?"

"Oh, I like the travel. And working on engines. And Captain gives me leeway to build my little clockworks." She smiled. "It's hard for a woman to find a job as a mechanic on an airship. Lots of crews still think it's bad luck to have a woman on board. So long as the Captain keeps flying, I'll stick around. I've no desire to settle dirtside."

"You're young yet. I expect you'll change your tune." Seamus replied.

JACQUELINE

Seamus and Marie had finished the hull. The cables were more challenging. I attached the end of a splice cable to my belt and slung a tool vest across my back. Seamus and Tyler hoisted me into the rigging using a sling. The heavy splice cable pulled at my belt, dragging behind me. As I came nearer to the *grand poche* I saw the broken cable swinging free. Splicing the cables took several hours of hot, exhausting work. The back of my neck itched with the feeling of being watched, but I could see no ships in the sky. When the last one was securely re-attached, we called it a day.

Tyler built a bonfire on the beach while the rest of us brought out bread and cheese from the ship. While we had been splicing cables, Niccolò, currently learning to cook, had fished off the stern of the ship while keeping watch. He had a nice catch of anchovies, and Henri showed him how to skewer the fish. Bottles of wine passed around the fire while we picked steaming hot fish off the skewers with our fingers. When darkness fell, I could feel some of my tension ebbing. We had not been followed or had provoked no new interest from Charles and his men.

Nina offered a toast, "To good friends, and a good caper."

"*Salut!*"

Seamus started singing a low sweet tune, the story of a sailor led to his death by the sea. I joined in–it was an old song, meant to be sung as a duet with a descant, the female's part, calling to the wives of the lost sailors. Nina followed the song with a slow, powerful one of her people. The unfamiliar language, and tempo invoked the exotic heat of the Sahel, the desert borderlands, and the unfamiliar. It sent chills tingling across my spine.

We sang long into the night with the deep sky and a million diamonds smiling down from above. The fire sent crackling sparks dancing in a counterpoint to the soothing crash of the tide. Towards midnight, yawing, I looked around the fire at my friends, pondering how very fortunate I was. Nina eyes half closed, ebony skin dark against the night, leaned up against a piece of driftwood. She caught my eye and smiled. I raised my glass in her direction. Seamus stirred the fire meditatively, glancing now and again at the sleeping Niccolò, shaking his head in his gruff way. Henri and Marie were cuddled up under a blanket, and Tyler was sprawled, looking up at the stars. There was nothing I wouldn't do for these people. I fell asleep on the warm sand, happy to be surrounded by friends and crewmates.

Dawn was hard to ignore with the tide rolling in. There were cheerful groans all around as we climbed the ladder back to the ship.

"Niccolò, change the ship name and colors back to *The Indiana*. Nina, let's get her in the air!" I said exuberantly. "Let's get back to Marseille."

CHARLES

The Bessie Quinn limped in to a protected cove on an island so small it wasn't even on his navigation charts. From the deck of the *Blue Raven* Charles watched the crew for an hour, and the only mystery so far was the appearance of two crew members he hadn't seen during his search of the ship. He judged them to be women from their slender forms. He and squadron leader Yusef kept a close eye on the group throughout the day, taking turns watching.

The crew below spent the remaining daylight making repairs and doing what any normal crew would do after a hard storm. Once night fell, Charles ordered the airship closer and assigned men to take turns monitoring the crew throughout the night.

In the morning he watched from far above as the crew of *The Bessie Quinn* ran up the French colors and changed the nameplate on the ship.

Calling for his squadron leader and handing over the spyglass, Charles said. "We've got them now."

"Look there, Yusef. They've changed the name back to *The Indiana*. One of those two women is most certainly Captain Jac."

"Likely to slit your throat, that one is. Bloody pirate. I bet she'd do it from behind and in the dark too."

"I don't think so, Yusef. She understands people. That's probably why she excels at outthinking her opponents, but she has a code that she lives by. She likes to laugh, and wants to know the why of things. Why people do what they do, why the world works the way it does."

Yusef hmphed. "The stories about her…"

"Are probably wrong." Charles interrupted. "Because if they were right, then she'd have a hook nose with a wart and other distinctive features, and we wouldn't have nearly so hard a time finding her."

Yusef conceded the point with a shrug. "Captain – what's your plan?"

"Now that we have confirmation on who they are, they will most certainly be heading for Marseille. It's close, *The Indiana* is known to berth there, and they are still in need of repair. We can beat them to the port and see who they contact when they arrive. I'll want a close set of eyes on that ship."

Yusen nodded. "Aye, Captain. I'll inform the pilot to put on some speed."

The pilot caught the wind and they arrived in Marseille in record time. That's where things began to go wrong. The pilot was a surly fellow and overconfident in his approach to the busy airfield. Misjudging the distance between two ships, he scraped the side of a rich merchant vessel in an adjoining berth, tearing off several hull tiles. While trying to correct course and avoid tangling the cabling of the two ships, he navigated into the path of another ship trying to dock.

Charles watched, horrified, as the second, larger merchant vessel bore down on them. Pushing the pilot aside, he pulled the lever to increase the helium in the *grand poche*. The *Blue Raven* rose to the next lane above them, missing the merchant vessel by inches. Tapering off the helium and checking to ensure that no more mid-air collisions were imminent, he turned to look at the pilot with an icy stare. "I would expect a pilot in His Holiness's service to know how to dock a ship."

"You said you wanted us here fast. We're here. No reason for us to bother about that merchant vessel, they can't do anything to us. We're here on Rome's business," the man said with a sneer. "I would expect you to know that, Captain."

Gesturing to Yusen, Charles said, "Confine him to quarters. Once we are docked, five lashes for impudence, another ten for causing an unnecessary accident. I will guide us into berth. Once we are tethered, have the men draw tarps up over the ship to hide our appearance and see if we can somehow change our outline a bit. Drop the colors as well. We don't want to spook *The Indiana* and her crew."

Charles's stomach roiled with anger and frustration as he took the helm and guided the *Blue Raven* into another free berth. He had no rapport and no trust with these men, and he knew it. The thought sobered him. And then he remembered that he was going to have to see the Airfield Master to pay for berthing and sort out the damage to the merchant vessel and he groaned again, dreading the upcoming encounter.

JACQUELINE

Chaos reigned at the port of Marseille. A fleet of small air transport ships were trying to leave port just as several large airships arrived requesting berths. Looking through my spyglass I could see several Air Controllers on the ground waving flags directing the incoming airships.

A particularly animated ant caught my attention. The Airfield Master was gesticulating wildly, the large, feathered plume of his official hat bobbing madly in my spyglass. Though I couldn't hear him, he appeared to be yelling at the captain of another ship. I saw him jab the man in the chest with his finger and the man stepped back a few paces. *"Must remember to bring the Airfield Master something pleasant when we pay our airfield fees,"* I thought.

"Nina, signal a request for berth. It looks like we're going to be stuck in the air for a while."

Niccolò stood next to the railing, watching the scene below him in fascination. I pointed out the airfield controllers, and then the sights around Marseille through the heavy haze of smoke and soot. To the east giant clanks lifted stones to the cupola of a half-built cathedral. In the bay, the Chateau d'If was visible on its solitary island. The entire city was spread before us, bathed in the afternoon light. He was practically vibrating with excitement. "I've never been outside Rome before, Captain. Who knows what might be out there!"

I smiled. "You'll see a lot more than just Rome. We'll be docking soon; you'll want to see how it's done."

When the glut of airships thinned, the Airfield Master cleared us for docking. Nina lined us up with the large clank the Air Controllers directed us to and slowly lowered the ship into the cradle.

The clank, moving slowly below the ship, lined us up with a causeway attached to stairs leading to the ground. When we neared the causeway, Tyler at the fore and Seamus at the aft threw ropes to the airfield workers. They tied us off and cranked a gangplank out from the causeway to the ship. Niccolò stood wide eyed, taking it all in.

"Would you like to come with me to meet the Airfield Master?" I asked.

He nodded, looking around, pretending to be worldly.

The office clerk sitting behind a counter in the Airfield Master's office looked up as we entered, a harried expression on his face. "Yes?"

"Just here to pay our fees—and a gift for Eugene. Is he in?" I asked, holding out the monies and port papers first.

The clerk rolled his eyes but took the money and made a cursory check of our papers, writing us down in the ledger. "He's in. I'll get him for you. Fair warning though, he's not in the best of moods. Some crazy airship out of Rome nearly caused two collisions today."

"Ahh, so that's what was going on. I wondered." My heart skipped a beat, and my pulse quickened. Had Charles beat us to Marseille? Had he figured out who we were and what we were about? Had I underestimated him? I clasped my hands behind my back, instead of chewing on my thumbnail like I wanted to. The thought of Charles figuring out our plan was both exciting and worrisome. I had no desire to be caught with stolen goods, but a worthy adversary was always diverting.

The clerk slid off his stool and stepped into the back room, murmuring briefly. When he re-appeared, he said, "You can go on in, Captain. But he has another meeting in twenty minutes."

"Eugene!" I said heartily as I strode across the worn carpet. "I brought you a gift from Spain." A smallish man with a large presence, Eugene looked up at the sound of his name, his posture screaming annoyance at the interruption. On seeing a familiar face, he relaxed. His large hat marking him as the Airfield Master sat beside him on the desk.

"Jac! I see you're back in town." He took the bottle of brandy. "Oh, this will be most welcome. Join me in a glass? Who is your young friend here?" The Airfield Master took out two brandy snifters and worked the cork out of the neck of the bottle.

Niccolò, staring at one of the maps on the wall, jumped at the question. "Oh, um. Hello," he said, trying to make a bow.

"This is my new cabin boy, Niccolò. He wanted to meet a real Airfield Master. And since I wanted to drop off the brandy as well, I brought him along."

Eugene poured two glasses of brandy, paused for a moment and brought out a third, pouring a smaller amount for Niccolò. He passed the glasses around with a smile. "Well young man, you've now seen one. What do you think?"

"Well, you're shorter than I thought you would be, looking down from above," he replied candidly.

I bit my lip in amusement, and Eugene let out a hearty laugh. "Well, he's honest at least."

Eugene lifted his brandy snifter in toast. "*Saunte!*"

We all took a sip. I enjoyed the smooth richness of the drink. It had aged well. At the first sip, Niccolò gasped and coughed.

"The trick, my young new friend, is to take small sips with your lips almost all the way closed. Let the brandy trickle in, rather than gulping. You will find it easier to swallow that way." Eugene chuckled and took another sip.

Still coughing, eyes streaming, Niccolò nodded. "I will keep that in mind next time, sir! Thank you."

"Any news or excitement hereabouts?" I asked.

"Nothing too exciting. Some idiot from Rome trying to command a prime berth 'on order of the Pope' and then nearly causing an accident."

I shook my head in commiseration. "Some urgent news out of Rome?" I asked, keeping my face smooth, while my brain spun out different scenarios.

"Gossip says some Vatican relic has been stolen. They're sending Papal Agents to all ports apparently. He wouldn't tell me what it was or who stole it, though. Apparently, I'm not important enough." Eugene chuckled. "You wouldn't happen to know anything about it?" He raised an inquiring eyebrow.

I smiled serenely at him.

"Fine by me, the less I know the better." He shook his head.

We chatted for a few more minutes, then Cal knocked and poked his head in. "Your next appointment is here, sir."

Niccolò and I rose and took our leave. "*Bon saunte*, Eugene. I'll come by to chat again when it's less busy."

He grimaced at the impatient noises coming from beyond his door. "Any time Jac. It's always a pleasure."

Outside, I pointed out the telegraph office to Niccolò. "I need to send some messages off. Head back to the ship. I'll be back shortly. Tell Tyler that a ship from Rome has been seen in port, and to be on the lookout. He and Nina will know what to do. We may have to change our plans."

Niccolò nodded and took off at a trot across the airfield. At the telegraph office I wrote out a short message to David in our secret code.

PORT OF MARSEILLE FOR A FEW DAYS STOP CAN YOU COME VISIT STOP ALL MY LOVE, JACQUELINE

I sent it off to David's flat in Paris. With luck I would have a response by tomorrow.

JACQUELINE

The next morning a familiar, cheerful male voice called out from the deck. "Permission to come aboard, Captain?"

My eyes widened in surprise and I stuck my head out the door of the common area. "David? How did you get here so quickly?"

My lanky, dark haired, sometimes lover stood on deck. "Well, my dear, I had been planning a trip to Marseille already. I was supposed to leave Paris today, but came down early when I got your message." His eyes twinkled, and his thick Colonial English accent warmed my heart.

"Come in," I said, grinning brightly. "We were just about to have breakfast. You are welcome to join us. Nothing fancy I'm afraid, just croissants and fruit."

When the crew saw David they elbowed each other, and Marie giggled. I shot her a look promising mayhem if she didn't behave. She swallowed her giggle and concentrated on her breakfast, darting gleeful glances in David's direction, much to Henri's chagrin.

Nina, far less impressionable than Marie, smiled in welcome. David greeted each of the crew in turn, taking a moment to catch up and visit. He spent most of his time pursuing scientific and alchemical research in Paris, and I couldn't tempt him away from his laboratory for more than short stretches of time. His visits were a pleasure for everyone.

"Captain, I'll be taking care of that errand you wanted today, so I'll not be onboard for most of the day." Nina said.

I nodded. "Be careful."

"Always am."

After breakfast I held out my hands to David. "Come, I have something I want to show you." We made our way up to my cabin. After the door was closed I turned to him, happy laughter bubbling out. "You are a good sport. That is the phrase, is it not?"

He laughed and wrapped his arms around me. "It is good to see you, Jacqueline. I won't ask what you've been up to, as I'm fairly certain I don't want to know."

I nodded. "You would probably find it interesting, but I don't think you want to be involved. Though we did acquire a new crew member."

"Well, is she cuter than you?" he asked teasingly.

Pretending to consider this question seriously, I replied, "I think *he's* a bit young for you. But I can call him in and we can find out."

David chuckled, "I think if we are going to try another *menage a trois*, then we should find someone of the appropriate age."

He scooped me up and carried me to the bunk, nibbling on the side of my neck. "Shall we do things that would make your crew blush?"

"Mmmm, yes. Let's."

<hr>

An hour and a half later, fully clothed, David ran his fingers through my hair loosening it as I worked to pin it back up. "You have such beautiful hair, darling. One would almost think you a noble."

I froze as he tweaked an errant lock playfully. Forcing myself to breath I said through a mouthful of hairpins, "Oh, I'm just lucky. Nothing noble about me." David knew some of my history, but not that crucial bit. Stabbing the last hairpin in hastily I stood. "Can I pour you some coffee? He smiled fondly and released me.

Chatting over coffee in my sitting area I continued talking about the crew.

"Niccolò needs manners, and quickly. I like the lad quite a bit, and he has made significant progress, but I'd rather he learn when it is a more-than-friend I am dealing with and not a potential client." I chewed on the edge of my thumbnail. "He is a good lad. Very bright. I'm more than happy for him to stay with us, but should he choose at some point to leave us, I'd like him to have the skills necessary to make a good life somewhere." Pausing, I smiled at David as I idly stroked the back of his free hand. "You haven't met him yet, but I think you will like him too."

David nodded and sipped his coffee. "Has he shown any aptitude for mechanical workings? That's a skill you can take anywhere."

"I should check with Marie. I know he's been spending time in the engine room with her."

David paused, considering me for a moment, then continued along a different line of thought. "While I'm here, do you mind if I look over some of the upgrades I've made to the ship and make sure they're functioning properly? I want to check on the heat booster I installed last time and see if it's performing as expected."

I smiled. "You know you have full run of the ship anytime you're on board. Do you want to take my airhopper, *The Inara,* out later today? Test out the upgrades on the steering system for yourself?" I wanted to spend some time with David but needed to do some reconnaissance as well. Biting my lip, I hoped that David would ignore the fact that he had already tested the upgrades and come along for the ride.

"That would be great. I have a couple of ideas for additional modifications for the rest of the ship as well, if you want to look over them. I've come up with a burner system for the heated balloons that Marie could control from the engine room. It would allow her to inflate specific balloons instead of doing all of them at once and risk overfilling some and under-filing others."

"I'll take a look. We'll be in port at most a week. Probably less, due to some unforeseen circumstances. Can I tempt you to come with us this time?" I took a sip of my coffee and raised an eyebrow inquiringly.

"We'll see." He smiled. "For now, let me look over the ship."

I spent two hours discreetly studying the other ships in port. The Rome contingent, when I found them amongst the sea of other docked airships, was mercifully on the far side of the airfield from us, with at least five large ships between us. Even so, it had only taken me two hours to find the sleek blue and gold Papal air cruiser, and they were looking for us too. It looked like Charles had tried to disguise his ship, but the distinctive colors made it stand out in port. Why hadn't they found us yet? Or more to the point, why weren't we swarming with Swiss Guard yet?

David found me on deck pondering options. Without speaking, we made our way down to the hold. My airhopper, *The Inara*, was built to carry two. As David slid into place behind me, I fired the propulsion system, opened the launch hatch and we went sailing away.

David slid his arms around me and cuddled up close enough to be able to talk into my ear. "Did you have a place in mind?"

"Not really, just somewhere away from the ship," I replied, navigating around the berthed behemoths in the airfield.

"There's a little cafe on the edge of the city that we should try," he replied. "Head north and I'll show you where to set down."

I nodded and turned the airhopper away from the bay and back towards the city. We flew in silence for several minutes enjoying just being together. Our rendezvous were infrequent and our time completely alone even more rare.

The cafe was on a quiet side street. We parked *The Inara* in the field reserved for public parking in this quadrant of the city and walked hand in hand. It was nice having a moment of normalcy. I smiled and looked over at him. "Come join us, David. It would be wonderful to have you onboard."

He rubbed his thumb across the back of my hand. "Jac, you know I can't do that. My research doesn't lend itself to your lifestyle. Some of the chemicals I work with are very delicate and do not react well to altitude, and you simply don't have the space for my mechanical research. "

I sighed ruefully. It was a conversation we'd had before. "Travel with us for a little while? I miss you, *mon chéri*."

He smiled. "Now that I can do, at least briefly. I was coming down to Marseille for a conference on antiquities when I got your message. I would love to stay onboard while I'm here. Perhaps I could even convince you to come to one of the stuffy academic parties one must attend at such events."

The cafe had floor-to-ceiling windows looking onto the street. We sat in the back corner shielded from view by the high booth walls. The waitress came with menus and brought a carafe of chilled white wine.

"Oh, I don't know," I said teasingly as I poured a glass of wine for each of us. "With that kind of party recommendation, I'll just have to go."

"I was coming down for the conference because one of my old schoolmates will be here. I haven't seen Abraham in years. He is a professor in America specializing in ancient religious garments."

I choked on my wine, coughing and sputtering. David jumped up, and the waitress rushed over. "Is Madam okay? Can I get her anything?"

Coughing I waved them both off and dabbed at the front of my vest with a napkin. David looked at me quizzically. I shook my head, glancing at the waitress. "Later. I'll explain. Tell me about this friend of yours. How well do you know him?"

David raised an eyebrow at me. "Well, as I said, we're old school mates. We were close back in the day, and have kept in touch, but our lives have gone in different directions." He paused as the hostess returned with a glass of water. A waiter followed with our lunch. He set the tray down with a flourish and passed out salad plates, setting a bowl of chilled tomato soup in front of each of us, and a basket of fresh bread on the table. I smiled my thanks and dipped my spoon in the thick red soup.

"He was, as I recall, a fair student, and has managed to secure himself a tenured position at the University of New York. When we were in school he was a loyal friend, and never told the Deans when our pranks got out of hand. All in all, he's a decent chap. I'm looking forward to seeing him again."

David dipped a piece of the bread into his soup distractedly and pondered. "Not really much else to say. He's devoted to his research, and his scholarship. I had a bit of an interest in those topics myself during our University days, but I rather suspect it was just because he was so enthusiastic. Abraham can make the dullest of subjects sound interesting."

I nodded, pondering, tearing bits of bread into small pieces. My face must have given something of my thoughts away, because David raised an eyebrow. I smiled serenely in return. "Ah. It's like that," he said, chuckling. "You're on a job right now." He paused.

"Jacqueline, you know I would never actually want you to be more like conventional women… but sometimes I wish you were more like conventional women."

I chuckled. "David, if I was a more conventional woman, we never would have met, or if we had you would have grown instantly bored, and I would have been appalled with your profession. Have we decided on a title for you yet? Mad Scientist, perhaps."

David pretended to look offended. "Mad Scientist, indeed. I am of quite a mellow temperament, thank you very much. And what of yourself, Captain? Privateer? Pirate?" He waggled his eyebrows at me menacingly and I burst into laughter.

"Oh stop. When you do that it looks like two fuzzy caterpillars have come to life on your face and are trying to tango."

He smiled roguishly. "Let's finish lunch and then you can take me back to your ship and show me your treasures."

My laughter drew disapproving glances from our waitress and a few other patrons. I bit my lip and stifled my giggles.

We finished up at a leisurely pace. David settled the bill and we strolled back to *The Inara* hand in hand. "When you come to Paris next, you could maybe stay for a week or two?"

I smiled, aching inside. My connections to the nobility in France, and my role as an airship Captain rather than a Contessa, made staying in Paris uncomfortable. I had to keep a low profile to avoid drawing the attention of the King, or his advisors, lest I find myself married off, my crew murdered or imprisoned, and my ship grounded. Staying in Paris for long periods of time wasn't an option for me. "I'll see what I can do."

Back on the ship I took David to my quarters. "So, *mon chéri*. I have something to show you."

He waggled his eyebrows at me again and said, "Your treasure box perhaps?"

I chuckled, "Yes, but perhaps not the one you want to see." I turned him so he faced the wall. "No peeking," I warned, as I tweaked the end of his nose playfully.

"On my honor as a gentleman," he said.

Standing in front of my bed, I opened the secret compartment and removed the Miter. Closing everything up, I turned and set the hat in the center of my desk. "Okay, turn around."

Still smiling he turned around and glanced at what was on the desk. His expression showed curiosity, nothing more. "It's a hat, religious by the look of it, not cheap certainly, with the beadwork and thread. That's what you wanted to show me?"

I nodded. "The ceremonial hat of the pontiff, Pope Clément. And someone paid us a handsome sum to acquire it."

David gingerly touched the peak of the hat, as if afraid it might bite him. "This is the actual Miter…? How long have you had it in your possession?"

"Five days," I replied. "Why?"

"Jac, how on earth did you get this?"

He picked up the hat and examined it closely. The outside was decorated with thousands of tiny seed pearls, and the cloth below was stitched with gold thread so fine it looked like it was the fabric itself. A crimson cross adorned the front, edged in diamonds. Running his fingers over it he said, "Abraham used to talk about the Miter of St. Peter. Legend, or rumor at the very least, holds that the Miter is the key to the final scripture. Naturally this makes it a highly guarded …"

"Do you really want the details?" I replied.

"Perhaps not." David continued examining the Miter, turning it over in his hands. "Jac, you know they'll be coming after you."

"The meeting with our buyer is next week. I only have to keep it hidden until then."

"Then for God's sake why are you sitting in port and not hiding on some remote island somewhere?!" David's face was pale, eyes searching about as if he expected the Swiss Guard to burst in at any moment.

"It was a mistake to show you this," I said, taking the Miter out of his hands. "David... this is what I do. You know that."

David scrubbed his hands over his face and took a deep breath. "I know that. I just... I'm not usually confronted with it quite so openly. This is dangerous Jac. The Vatican – if they catch you, you'll likely hang, or burn. And the crew with you."

I nodded. "We all know the risk. What I want to know is, can you get information from your friend about the Miter? Or is there some way you can arrange for me to meet him to ask him a few questions?"

David *hmmd*. "So this is why you were quizzing me about Abraham." He paced back and forth for a moment. "I'm sure I can set up a meeting with him, but Jac, I do not want him caught up in this. He's a friend, and an academic. If any hint of scandal came back on him he could lose his position at the university. Not to mention of course if Rome found out."

I nodded. "I understand. Perhaps a casual meeting at one of those oh-so-boring receptions for the conference you told me about. Surely discussing his topic of expertise at an academic conference wouldn't cause much of a stir?"

"Jac – why do you even want to know about this? I thought the motto was 'do the job, don't ask questions'. The job is very nearly done. You aren't acting like yourself with this one." David studied me out of the corner of his eye, troubled.

"It's... I am having doubts about the job, like we shouldn't have taken it in the first place. The pay was too good, it was too easy to get in to the Vatican, the job went too smoothly. It's like everyone was looking the other way all at once. One of the priests, Father Michael, helped me to escape. Even now – there's an air cruiser out of Rome sitting at the other end of the airfield, and they haven't found us yet. It's like they're waiting for something." I looked up at David from the other side of my desk. "The Swiss Guard isn't known for being slow or stupid, and yet they board us, wander around for a few hours and leave? It doesn't make sense. There is something about that item," I waved in the general direction of the Miter. "I mean to find out what is going on."

David nodded, face still troubled. "I see what you mean. The opening reception for the conference is tonight. I will arrange that you and Abraham have a discreet introduction. Be ready to go by five o'clock."

CHARLES

Charles was fumingly angry. The Airfield Master in Marseille was an insufferable bureaucrat. Yes, the mid-air near collision had been his pilot's fault. The man had been disciplined, and Charles had already agreed to pay the fine for endangering the other ship. To keep his ship on lockdown however, seemed beyond what was reasonable, and refusing to answer his questions about the ships in port without a direct authorization from the Vatican was nothing but a delaying tactic.

From the deck of the *Blue Raven* Charles could see *The Indiana* on the far side of the port. Every time he tried to get near it, or any other ship, he found himself accosted by the Airfield Master, or one of his employees. He was shocked that the ship, a known privateer, was allowed to dock so openly. When questioned, the Airfield Master shrugged. "*The Indiana* has no open warrants out against it in France, the crew pays their port fees, and they don't cause trouble in Marseille," was all he would say.

In addition, Charles was shocked to find, Rome held very little sway here.

He could not search the ship with impunity, he must seek permission from the head of the city – something the man was loath to give. Charles cursed his luck – either everyone in power was protecting *The Indiana*, or his association with Rome was hindering his ability to get the warrant he wanted.

While he didn't want to use the carte blanche that the Holy Father had given him, it was looking more likely by the moment. Pulling Yusef aside he said, "Who amongst the squad has experience in surveillance and following people?"

Yusef named off three men, detailing their strengths and weaknesses. Charles nodded, annoyed with himself that he had not yet had time to learn this for himself. "Excellent. Assign them to watch *The Indiana*. Get as close as they can without arousing suspicion and follow anyone from the crew who leaves the ship. I want to find out who their buyer is. Privateers like Captain Jac don't work for free, and it seems to me that knowing who is willing and able to pay her fees to rob the Vatican would be almost as valuable as the item itself. For now it seems the Airfield Master is protecting them, and until I receive word from the Mayor of Marseille we cannot move against the ship."

Yusef nodded. "Aye, Captain. I believe you're right about finding the buyer. I'll have the boys report back if they find anything."

Charles nodded. "In the meantime I'm going to send a message back to Rome informing the Holy Father that we will be going after the buyer as well."

JACQUELINE

I was waiting for David outside the airfield gates dressed in a well-cut women's suit of heather grey. The skirt, divided for easy walking, did not require a corset, and one of Marie's golden bees decorated my lapel. David's carriage stopped, and the driver jumped down to help me in. It was a carriage for hire, and the red cushions had seen a great deal of wear, but it was clean and serviceable. David's suit, an older style, showing wear, had a small grease stain on one cuff. The brown tweed had seen better days.

The hotel, near the university district, was lit up with chandeliers and glowing like a jewel box. The carriage stopped in front of marble steps worn smooth by countless feet. The driver handed me out and David offered his arm, a roguish smile on his lips. "You my dear, will make me the toast of the party."

I smiled and gestured for us to proceed.

The hotel interior was well kept but worn. The fresco painted ceiling was in need of repair, and years of use showed in the décor. One of the hotel's employees looked us over and gestured down the hallway. "You will find the academic's reception at the end, on the left."

The room was large, well lit, and comfortably full. Our entrance caused a brief stir in one corner, when a gentleman raised his glass and waived at David. Conversational groups had already begun to form, and servers with trays of wine and small finger foods circulated through the crowd.

"Come. That's Abraham in the corner. I sent him a note earlier letting him know we were coming." David guided me through the crowd with his hand on my back. I plucked a glass of wine from a passing server, just as we arrived at Abraham's cluster of friends.

A sandy haired, slightly portly gentleman, clapped David on the shoulder and his face split into a grin. "David Scheherazade it's been eons since we last saw each other! I'm so glad you were able to come to the conference. Who is this delightful creature you have brought with you?"

"Abraham, may I present my companion, Jacqueline." David held out his hand to me, and I nodded to Abraham, smiling.

Stepping forward I said, "I have heard so much about you. It's a pleasure to finally meet you in person. David tells me you study the history of religious garments? That sounds like a fascinating area of expertise."

Abraham took my hand and bowed over it. "Indeed madam. I find religious haberdashery is fascinating and helps us to learn about the early Church."

"Tell me sir, something I have always wondered, why are Miters such an odd shape?"

This launched Abraham into a detailed explanation of Miters in general but did not enlighten me on the Miter of St. Peter. "You seem very knowledgeable on the topic," I said. "Have you ever had the opportunity to examine the Miter of St. Peter?"

"Oh! No, I'm afraid that one is very closely guarded. It has a most fascinating history though." He snagged a canapé from a passing server. "I've made quite a study of it over the years, but the Vatican has never allowed anyone to examine it. I've sent several petitions on behalf of the University, but they are always declined. Did you know, for instance, that the Miter of St. Peter is the oldest garment in the church's possession that is still used regularly? Or that it is supposedly guarded by demons? There are even stories that it holds the last scripture. Something so powerful that it could bring down the church, or give it absolute world dominance." Abraham laughed. "There are many, many stories about the Miter of St. Peter, but I'm afraid without examining it, separating fact from fiction is nearly impossible."

I laughed in return and glanced at David. "There are really stories saying it's guarded by demons? I would think Angels would be more in keeping with the church."

"Perhaps Lucifer has sent his demons to guard it so that the Holy Father cannot use the last scripture to ensure the absolute dominance of the church. And the church guards it to keep Lucifer's demons from using the last scripture to end the church," David offered. "Something to maintain the balance of the world."

"Perhaps. Or perhaps it is a fanciful story the Church has put out to keep thieves away." Abraham sighed wistfully. "But, as I doubt they will ever agree to let me, or anyone, examine it, we will probably never know. Unless someone steals it and demons come after them." He chuckled at that, dismissing the idea.

"Where do you think the scripture is hidden?" I asked, the question coming out awkward and forced in the brief silence that followed Abraham's last statement.

Abraham raised an eyebrow. "I have no idea. It could be patterned into the beadwork, or written in code, or stitched on the inside. Or the Miter itself could merely contain clues leading to the actual location...you seem rather interested in this topic. Perhaps you should attend one of my lectures."

I cursed myself for appearing too eager. "I'm afraid I do not get to the Americas often, but I do have a passing interest in the topic."

"Ah well. You would make a charming student. But I'm afraid, as I mentioned, without the physical object to hand, there isn't much more known about the Miter of St. Peter other than the various embellishments and which Pope had them added and their symbolic value. It's a pity. I would risk my life against these demons for just an hour to examine it."

"I imagine such a thing would make your career as an academic," I commented.

Abraham looked around the gathering and chuckled. "Indeed, it would. Half the fellows here would want to kill me, and I would most certainly be made a dean at the University."

I liked him. David glanced at me, eyebrows furrowed, as if he could read my thoughts. I had the basic information I needed – a collector would be interested in the Miter of St. Peter, but it had more potential value as a political object that could be used to bring down the church. The question was – which was it? A collector, or a political power or someone with an interest in both. And should I pursue this beyond just the job. And was allowing Abraham an hour to examine the Miter worth the extreme risk? All of this flashed through my mind in an instant. I smiled charmingly and said, "Well, perhaps you will one day get an opportunity to examine it then." I saw David's shoulders relax.

"From your lips to God's ears, as they say." Abraham saw someone else he knew and waved. "David, I presume I'll see you during the week for the conference. Jacqueline, it's been a pleasure. If you'll excuse me, I've been trying to corner Dean Devlin for some time, and he has just walked in."

David clapped him on the back and turned to me, letting the increasing crowd swirl around us. "Did you get the information you wanted?"

"Yes, but as with many things, it has merely raised more questions." I tapped my fingernail on the edge of my wine glass. "Your thoughts on the guarded by demons aspect?"

"Well, after we learned that the Stuart Sapphire held the

spirit of the Bonnie Prince, when last you visited Scotland, I'm a little more open to believing in demons, but I am decidedly not happy about it. It offends my scientific mind." David drew me further into the corner, using the crowd for privacy.

"It can't be that all such tales are true, or we would be infested with elves and goblins as well." I laughed but felt the hair on the back of my neck rise uncomfortably.

"Thank you for not bringing Abraham further into this." He kissed the side of my neck. "Now, let us circulate for a few minutes more, so I can show off my handsome companion and be the envy of my peers, and then we can depart."

Chuckling I took his arm. "Anything for you *mon chéri*."

While David led us from group to group of academics, my mind swirled on the question – is the knowledge worth the risk? Is lying to David about it worth the risk? Would Abraham even accept such risk, and would he tell David? What would I do with the knowledge if I had it? The last question didn't trouble me as much as the others. Knowledge was always useful, sometimes how it was useful didn't come to light until the proper moment.

Making a decision, as David introduced me to yet another small group of academics, I excused myself. At the hotel's front desk, I asked for a pen and paper and penned a brief note.

If you would like to significantly advance your knowledge in your field of study, meet me here at three o'clock in the morning. Come alone. Do not tell anyone.

I left the note unsigned and folded it up to fit in the palm of my hand, sliding it inside my glove for safe keeping. As the evening wore on, and the various professors began to depart, Abraham found us again, as I thought he might. Saying our goodbye's, I slipped the note into his palm. He raised an eyebrow, but gallantly slid the note into his pocket without otherwise reacting as he turned and shook David's hand. David's hired carriage came for us at eight o'clock as most of the academics were filtering out to dinner engagements. We joined the exiting throng and bumped and jolted in the carriage back to the airfield.

"If I know you, Jac, you're immediately going to go back to the ship and spend hours pouring over it based on what Abraham said." He twirled one of my curls in his fingers. "I am guessing your mind is lost to me for the rest of the night."

I chuckled, acknowledging the truth. "You do know me very well, *mon chéri*."

"Shall I have the carriage drop you off, and come join you for breakfast in the morning?"

I leaned in and kissed him. "You are a gem among men. Thank you for understanding." I quashed the feelings of guilt coiling in my gut. His kiss turned heated, and I responded in kind, my face flushing as I pressed against him in the narrow confines of the carriage. The carriage arrived at the airfield much sooner than either of us wanted, and we emerged, disheveled, but fully clothed. The carriage driver studiously stared down the road as David bid me good night.

JACQUELINE

Tyler had the watch when I arrived. "How goes it?" I asked. "And what has Nina learned about that ship out of Rome?"

"It's the same one that boarded us on the way here. It is definitely a Swiss Guard ship. I've seen that Charles fellow on the far side of the airfield. My guess is that they don't want to cause too much of a ruckus. They're watching us Captain," he said in a low voice. "But they're being very discreet about it. A 'mechanic' has been working on the clank berth next to us all day, but he doesn't look the part. And there has been more foot traffic than I would expect on that airship there." He nodded toward the ship off our port side.

"They're as curious about our benefactor as we are," I murmured. "Are we prepped for an emergency launch?"

Tyler nodded again, scanning the other ships around us.

"I have to go out again this evening. Late. If there's need, leave without me. I'll meet you at the bookstore in Aubagne to the east. Hopefully there's no trouble. We will be leaving tomorrow afternoon."

Tyler glanced at me inquiringly. "Out, Captain?"

I nodded, sealing my lips.

"Okay. Out." Tyler didn't pry, but his eyes looked wary. "Seamus is keeping an eye on the incoming ships. I'll double the watch as well."

"Good man. Thank you, Tyler."

In my cabin, I stripped out of my clothes and donned a set of dark flying leathers. They would raise no comment onboard ship and would be harder to spot in the darkness.

Lighting the lamps in my cabin, I closed the shutters to avoid prying eyes and took the Miter out of its hiding place. At my desk, I examined it closely with a magnifying glass, not sure what I was looking for. The seed pearls that encrusted the outside were tiny, irregular shaped beads, but I could find no pattern to them. The soft hempen rope, affixed the way one might affix a ribbon struck me as odd. It was old, and it was clearly rope. Not the sort of decoration I would have expected to see, as it held very little aesthetic value. The crimson cross was stitched and the diamonds held in place by fine gold wire. The outer fabric was linen, with some sort of thicker, sturdier backing that smelled faintly of wool and incense. The lining was also linen, but newer, with tiny stitches of white thread visible where it had been attached.

With a deep breath I took a pen-knife out of my desk drawer and slid it to the edge of the first stitch. "Knowledge for knowledge's sake."

The knife was sharp and parted the small stitches with a pop. I worked my way around the edge, careful to leave the linen undamaged. Setting the lining aside, I peered into the dark interior. Angling it so that the light penetrated deeper into the Miter, I thought I could see faint sparkles, but whether it was simply backstitching, or something else, I couldn't tell in the light of my cabin.

I pressed on the pointed end of the Miter experimentally. It was firm, but as I applied pressure, it slowly sunk inward. With some careful maneuvering, I was able to turn it inside out. There, in front of me, in gold stitches on a background of silver thread were an elaborate set of slashes and curls. A language, but not one that I could read. A rust colored stain was smeared across half of it.

I drew a deep breath. Abraham had been right about a hidden message. I hoped he wasn't right about the rest. Hastily I drew out a piece of paper and copied the script, mimicking the letters and line breaks. Double checking my work, I sanded the paper and slipped it inside my desk drawer for later study.

I turned the Miter right side out, pearls on the outside, wrapped it in a dark cloth, and put it into a satchel. Slinging the strap over my shoulder, I checked my boot knives, grabbed a hooded cloak and headed for the rendezvous, hoping Abraham was intrigued enough to show up.

A quick journey by horseback put me at the front of the hotel a few minutes before the rendezvous time. Sliding past the front desk, I slipped into a side room, leaving the door slightly ajar so I could see down the hallway. When I saw Abraham down the corridor, I beckoned for him to come in. The room was windowless, with a meeting table and a few comfortable chairs. A side table sat against the far wall, intended for small buffets or drinks.

"I must admit, your note intrigued me. A beautiful woman, a secret meeting, the chance to advance my career…" He closed the door and lit the gas-lamps in the small meeting room. "I almost didn't come, thinking David was perhaps playing a prank with your help."

"David must not know about this meeting." I said emphatically.

Abraham looked surprised and started to say something.

"How much has he told you about what I do?" I had positioned myself on the far side of the room with a table between us.

"Ah. Not much. He mentioned that you travel a lot, and that you don't see each other often."

I nodded. "I captain a ship. My crew and I transport specialized items for high-value customers, and we are known for doing so discreetly."

He blinked a few times, digesting that bit of information. "So why are we meeting?"

"I have in my possession, something that I think you would have great interest in, and I need more information about it. There is some personal danger to you, but, knowing academics as I do, I thought you might be persuaded to tell me what you know of the item in return for being able to examine it to further your research."

Abraham's eyes lit up with understanding and excitement and his demeanor changed. "Yes, such an arrangement might be beneficial to both of us. The advancement of research through illicit means is by no means unusual. Rest assured, your name will not be associated with any findings I release, and it takes months to write up such papers."

I nodded. "I thought you might feel that way." I pulled the Miter out of my satchel and unwrapped it, laying it on the table.

Abraham blinked, staring at the object on the table. "Holy Mother of God." He rubbed his hand across his chin. "Is that really…?"

I nodded.

"Why…How?" He looked at me, fear and excitement warring in his eyes.

Thinking quickly, I said, "We were commissioned to transport it for the Vatican, I cannot of course tell you its final destination. They thought it would be safer to take it in an unmarked ship."

He nodded soberly. "I understand now why this meeting is secret."

"If you reveal that I showed you this, it could mean the gallows for us both." I replied.

"Indeed. May I?" He gestured to the Miter, his hands trembling, and I nodded. He stared at it in awe for a moment, holding it as if it might bite him. Taking a deep breath he began a minute examination. After a quarter hour of I asked him, "What can you tell me about this object?"

"The Miter has been part of the Holy Roman church since its early days, immediately following the death of Christ. Tradition has it was commissioned by the original St. Peter in his quest to create symbolic garments that would help tie all the different factions of the church together. The garments have of course changed over the years, but priest's robes are basically similar now to what they have always been. There has only ever been one Miter, and it is passed from pontiff to pontiff."

He paused still staring in awe at the object on the table. "Now," he said, clearing his throat. "The Miter was not always as ornate as what we see before us. History tells us initially it was made of felted wool and linen, with a basic decorative border made from some sort of rope, supposedly representative of the cincture that Christ wore." He ran his fingers over this portion of the Miter, pointing to the rough hempen strands. "Over the years, the different pontiffs have added decoration and embellishments. The gold thread was added some centuries ago, and the pearls even more recently." He paused and ran his hands over the Miter once more as if spellbound by its presence.

"The reason this is all so fascinating is twofold. Firstly, it shows very little wear despite the fact that it is worn frequently and exposed to the elements on a regular basis. No one," he paused. "Well, no one outside the Vatican at any rate, knows how this has been accomplished. Secondly, as I mentioned earlier, it is said the original Miter contained the last scripture as presented to Peter by Christ. This scripture is supposedly so dangerous that if it is ever read aloud it will destroy the Church."

Something that could destroy the church was powerful indeed. "Because of what it says, or because of some mystical, unknown power?"

"Unknown. My assumption has always been because of content, but I cannot verify that without more information."

I picked up the Miter and carefully turned it inside out. "In studying the Miter earlier this evening, I found this." I showed him the script in the unknown language, and his eyes widened.

"Can you read it?" I inquired.

He studied it for a few minutes. "No. But given sufficient time and study I can translate it. It is written in ancient Aramaic, the language of Christ."

At this point he was sweating and pale. "It's good that you are transporting this for the Vatican, and that it's not stolen. I consider myself a rational man, but lore has it that if the Miter is stolen it releases fallen angels, followers of the Son of the Morning. Trapped in Hell, bound to protect it, they are tasked with returning the Miter to its proper owner. Even if that is merely a story put about by the Vatican, I imagine any thief they caught with this would wish for the tortures of Hell before the Vatican was done with them." He ran his fingers over the small stiches, pausing at the discoloration I had noted earlier.

I held my tongue. Dwelling on the possibility of torture was not advisable in my line of work. "I must go soon. If you copied the inscription, could you work out the translation? I could pay for that, but it must come to me first, before any publication."

He nodded. "Give me half an hour to make some sketches, and copy the inscription." He took out a pencil and notebook from his coat and began sketching. I pointed out the rust colored smear to him and he took down a note, but made no comment, his hands trembling slightly.

Moving out of his light, I watched from across the room, not wanting to interfere. The Miter took shape under his pencil, illustrations with dimensions, and a surprising amount of detail.

I sat taking in everything he said. The church was old, powerful, and from everything I had seen, corrupt. Perhaps not at the parish level, where priests cared for the poor and fed the hungry, trying to ease suffering where they could. At the higher levels, however, most leaders were interested in nothing but power.

"So what would you say the value of the Miter is? In the unlikely scenario that the Vatican was trying to sell it, for example?" I asked, as thoughts whirled through my head.

"Oh, given its age and historical relevance, for the right buyer, several hundred thousand gold I imagine. Though I don't know who would have that kind of money other than the Vatican or one of the royal houses. But would anyone dare purchase it and face the Church's wrath?"

"Merely a speculative question. Though, I imagine there are collectors out there who would love to get their hands on it."

"Of a surety. Including several museums who are less than scrupulous about how they acquire their antiquities," Abraham replied, sketching quickly. When he was done, some minutes later, he stood up.

"Thank you for this." He held up the notebook with the sketches. "How do I contact you when I have the translation?"

"Leave a message with the Airfield Master here and I will contact you."

"How long do you think it will take you to translate it?" I asked.

"I'm not completely versed in ancient Aramaic. That will depend entirely on whether I can find anyone who speaks it or if I will have to rely on research." Abraham stood and stretched, massaging his shoulder. "I imagine it will take a few months at the least. Unless I happen to get very lucky.

I wish you safe journey, Captain."

I wrapped the Miter quickly in its concealing cloth and put it back in my satchel, slipping out the door behind him.

Onboard *The Indiana* I felt myself starting to yawn. It had been a long night. I sat at my desk and took out a small sewing kit and began stitching the lining back into the Miter. My eyes felt heavy and I kept nodding off over the fine work. As I sat there, mind fogged with tiredness, it came to me that it would be useful to hide one of David's tracking devices in the lining. The trackers were hard to make and hard to power. I had one embedded in my elbow that allowed me to call *The Inara* to me if she was within range and allowed the crew to track my movements. It had proven very handy in the past. Unfortunately, I only knew of the one in my elbow that connected me with the ship and with my airhopper.

The sun was just peeking over the horizon. I stopped by the galley and poured two strong mugs of coffee before knocking on the door to Marie's quarters.

She answered the door, hair charmingly disheveled, coveralls half on, and only half awake. I handed her the cup of coffee. "You are up early, Captain."

"I haven't been to bed yet," I replied. "Have you worked out how to build trackers like those David has provided us in the past?"

"*Non.* Not yet," she said, yawning. "He brought us a new one he wanted to test. Longer range, but we don't know if it works yet."

"Okay. Can you show me?"

"Of course. But David will be here soon. He can explain how it works much better than I can." Without bothering to brush her hair, she led the way to her workshop, pulling up her coveralls as we walked.

This device was smaller than the one David created for

me. A lightweight, flat circular disk about the size of a doubloon. "It still has to be calibrated to the ship as well," Marie said. "We were planning on doing that today." I picked it up and marveled.

"Oh, hello David! We were just discussing your tracker."

"Good morning Marie! Jac darling, I hadn't expected to see you so early. Is everything okay?"

I explained my idea about putting his tracker in the Miter. Marie nodded in agreement. "*Oui*, that makes a good deal of sense. A little extra security."

"David, *mon chéri*, what do you think? Would you be willing for us to use your creation in such a fashion?"

He looked pensive, staring off into the distance. "You know I don't like this business you are about, and I certainly don't like helping you to do it." He paused for a moment longer, shaking his head. "But it would be safer—for you, especially—to have a tracking device on that thing, at least until it is delivered. Jac, the things you do sometimes…" He growled in annoyance. "This has longer range than the one you currently have, three miles instead of one. Assuming it works of course. I haven't tested it yet."

"Thank you for letting us use it at all," I replied, standing on tiptoe to kiss his cheek.

"I assume you will want to put it in as soon as possible, so I'd better calibrate it to *The Indiana*." He reached for the device, plucking it from my open palm. "I'll bring it to your cabin as soon as it's ready."

I kissed his cheek again. "Thank you. You are marvelous."

David left to go upstairs. When he was down the hall Marie commented, "You have a good one there, Captain. I hope you realize how lucky you are."

"You are quite right Marie, and he deserves so much better than me," I replied thinking about my late-night meeting with Abraham. Lying to David about involving Abraham in this venture was weighing heavily on me.

"I know that look, Jac. What's bothering you?" David came in to my cabin, carrying the tracking device.

"We're being watched. It would be best if we left today."

David wrapped his arms around me, holding the tracking device up in front of my nose. "For you, my dear. Fully calibrated." I turned around within the circle of David's arms and kissed him. "I'm still sifting through the history lesson your friend gave. Fallen Angels? Really?"

"It is an entertaining history to be sure. But you did ask, and he is well versed in Catholic theology and history." David bent his head down and kissed my forehead. "Just be safe, would you? I worry about you, you know."

I stroked the side of his face, smiling up into his eyes. "As safe as I can be, *mon chéri*."

We fell into each other's arms, his lips crushing against mine. Danger had its downsides, but it had its compensation as well. Just as I felt David's hands start to slide up under the edges of my shirt, Niccolò burst through my door.

"Captain! Captain!" He slid to a stop in front of the two of us. "Captain! That Guard Captain from before." Looking back and forth from David to myself he stopped, stammered, and blushed furiously. "Um. Perhaps now is not a good time." He started to back out of the room.

"Niccolò!" I said, more sharply than I intended. "If you thought it was important enough to come bursting in, then tell me what it is."

He stopped backing up and took a deep breath, still red to the ears. "Captain. I saw the guard captain from the Vatican. He's here." He took another deep breath. "I don't think he saw me. Or if he did, I don't think he recognized me, but he is headed this direction."

I grimaced and untangled myself from David. "Thank you for bringing this to me so quickly."

Niccolò stood up a little straighter, ignoring our disarranged clothing. "Yes, but it will take him a while to get here. The Airfield Master is walking with him."

"*Merde.* Do you know where Tyler is?" I combed my fingers through my hair to straighten it. Turning to David, I said, "I'm sorry, *mon chéri*, it may be nothing, but I have to look into this."

David smiled, hiding any annoyance. "We can pick this up again later."

I gave him a quick kiss and followed Niccolò up on deck, slipping the tracking device into my pocket.

JACQUELINE

Tyler was nowhere to be found, and Nina was out buying last minute supplies. I let Seamus know about the problem and kept an eye on Charles's progress with my spyglass. He did appear to be coming this way. The Airfield Master was waving his arms angrily and shouting at him.

The Indiana's hull and profile design were not unique. The base ship model had been very popular two decades ago when ships moved from floating on the sea to floating above it. Unfortunately, because it was an older model ship in excellent repair it stood out, and the modifications we had made over the years, the *grand poche* holding multiple smaller balloons instead of the standard large balloon, the carved railings, the cargo platform at the base, gave it a subtly unique appearance.

"Niccolò, help Seamus start preparing the ship for departure."

There was a speaking tube at the pilot's station that led directly to the engine room. "Marie, are you down there?"

"*Oui*, Captain." Marie's voice came floating out from the depths of the ship.

"We've spotted the Captain of the Guard that boarded us on the way here. Prep the engines for departure."

His progress was slow. As he got closer, I could see he was checking off notes against a sheet of paper, and handing papers over to the Airfield Master.

David came up on deck. "Who is this Charles? With as much attention as you are giving him I may have to be jealous," he said.

I chuckled, my stomach still in knots. "Here, have a look. See the man in gold and blue? That would be Charles, Captain of the Swiss Guard. He will recognize me if he sees me, something I would like to avoid, and it appears our ship is his intended destination." My palms grew sweaty at the thought, but a part of me thrilled to the danger.

My nerves jangled, and I paced the deck discarding one bad plan after another. We could leave without Nina and Tyler but I preferred not to if possible. Nina was a much better pilot that I or anyone else on board. When my pacing became too much for David's nerves he grabbed me. "Jac, stop it. Wearing a hole through the deck isn't going to solve anything."

I growled in frustration. "Unless he is blind he is sure to find us out."

David held my shoulders firmly. "What exactly do you think he can do while you are in Port? They cannot come on board without the French authorities' permission. And why would they even be looking for *The Indiana*, she was never in Rome."

I cocked my head to one side and looked at David like he'd grown two heads, then planted a kiss on his lips. "You're partially right at least. Rome has no reason to suspect me in this. That doesn't mean he won't recognize the ship, or the crew. Tyler knows where to meet if we get separated. I'm afraid you will have to come with us though."

"Seamus, Niccolò, Marie," I called into the ship-wide communication tube. "Prepare for departure." I strode to the pilot's stand and began the un-tethering sequence.

"David, please pull that lever on the clank to release the hull," I directed, pointing at a large lever twice the length of his arm.

The sounds of 'Aye Captain' came floating up through the tubes. I heard the rumble of the gas jets igniting as Marie pre-heated the balloons. "Henri, keep watch." I shouted down into the hold. He scrambled up the ladder and grabbed my spyglass, standing with his back to the pilot's station, within easy speaking range so he could keep me apprised of everything that passed.

Niccolò and David were casting off the tether lines when Henri saw Tyler and Nina at the main gate of the airfield.

"*Merde*. There is no way they'll make it in time," he muttered.

I watched from the pilot's deck at Charles's angry, open mouthed expression as the clank opened its mandibles. He started running across the airfield shouting. I could hear 'Stop!' floating up on the breeze.

I pulled the lever allowing helium to fill half the balloons. The ship rose, bumping on the edges of the docking clank. I winced and steadied the wheel. "He's coming captain!" Henri said, with the spyglass trained on Charles. Glancing over the railing I saw Charles sprinting up the stairway that connected the ship to the ground.

Niccolò and David untethered the remaining lines with a shout, and Marie gave me the all clear for full burn on the engine. I pulled the release allowing the flame jets to super heat the air in the remaining balloons. The ship rose straight up, and I turned the bow west, maneuvering over the tops of the docked airships. Henri relayed that Charles was sprinting back across the airfield for his own ship. I smiled. We would be gone before they could heat their engines.

Henri found Nina and Tyler again. "They're leaving, Captain. What's the rendezvous point?"

"Aubagne. Let's hope they can make it by tomorrow evening. It's twenty miles or more. Keep an eye for Charles's ship."

CHARLES

Furiously angry, Charles sprinted back across the airfield to the *Blue Raven*, shouting for his crew to prepare for takeoff. He had just received a writ from the mayor of Marseille allowing him to board *The Indiana*, and the dammed Airfield Master had delayed him just enough to let the ship slip through his fingers again.

To hell with bureaucracy, he thought, as he took the stairs up to the boarding platform two at a time. *Next time I'm just going to board* the *ship and let Rome deal with it later.*

By the time he arrived on deck, the crew had everything prepared. He gave the order to take off. *The Indiana* was already far ahead of them and heading out across the ocean.

JACQUELINE

I guided the ship west, out over the ocean, and then south until we rounded the peninsula. When nothing but trees and mountains were visible, I turned the ship east toward the valley where Aubagne sat, nestled among a ring of mountain peaks. We had a small head start, and I hoped we could lose the inevitable pursuit in the mountains. Navigating an airship through mountains took special skill. The higher peaks created their own weather that made airship travel dangerous and unpredictable. Updrafts buffeted the ship, causing the deck to sway and jump under foot, and the darkness of night came swiftly, hiding us from our pursuit. We reached the Aubagne valley well after dark and rather than attempt to dock at the small airfield, we set the air anchor, hovering over a small alpine lake above the town. We left the lanterns unlit, and blacked out all of the portholes to hide us through the night.

David was down in Marie's workshop flirting and discussing possible ship upgrades. Seamus and Niccolò were in the common room, huddled over a crate with a tiny lantern. Seamus was teaching Niccolò to play a card game that looked familiar. After checking over the ship, I relieved Henri and took the next watch. Most of the crew didn't like the late-night watch, but I found it an excellent time to think without distraction.

I didn't like leaving Tyler and Nina in Marseille, but I wasn't too concerned. The bookstore at Aubagne was one of our rendezvous points if we got separated. We had set locations in a variety of different regions. Aubagne was however the nearest small city to Marseille – even if we hadn't lost our pursuers in the mountains, it was likely that Charles or one of his Lieutenants would come this direction. I decided we would leave the ship anchored here, out of sight, and take the airhoppers into town in the morning.

"David, darling. Are you certain you don't want to simply stay here in Aubagne and make your way back to Paris from here? It's terribly dangerous for you to stay onboard with us…" I trailed off, watching his face.

"Jacqueline." He shook his head. "I'm not made of glass. I'll stay onboard and help Marie with a few things while you go find Tyler and Nina." He smiled. "I'm half afraid that if I went with you to town, you'd find a way to take off without me just to keep me safe. I was disreputable long before you knew me, and though I've mended my ways… mostly. I can still take care of myself."

"Fine then. I shall rely on your disreputable nature to keep you out of trouble," I replied, laughing. If David was not inclined to leave, then I wouldn't make him. One of the harder lessons I had learned when we met was that he was his own man and would do as he pleased.

Petri's bookstore was a few blocks from the airfield, but I didn't want to take any chances. I landed *The Inara* next to a hay manger on a farm just outside the city wall and paid the farmer a few coins to let me leave her there for the day.

The streets of Aubagne were charming, shopkeepers sweeping their stoop, the baker setting out fresh bread and pastries on his counter, a small market with vendors setting up stalls of ribbons, and pies, and hardware, a clock-smith taking advantage of the morning light, focused intently on repairing an open clock, an oculus held in one eye.

The dim interior of the bookshop was welcoming. I had a small library, but there wasn't much room to store books on the airship. It was one of the few things I missed about the estate. My father had loved books, and my sister and I had been encouraged to read and study despite our sex. We were educated much more in line with the way male heirs were treated, and I cherished my father's memory for that, as well as so many other things. I missed my father and sister – both dead in an untimely fashion. I couldn't prove that my sister's death had been foul play. My father had tried and had, himself, disappeared.

A bell jangled when I opened the door to the bookshop, and a petite, birdlike man popped his head up from behind the counter.

"Monsieur Petri, it is so good to see you again." I smiled, and a grin split his face.

"Jacqueline! It's been too long. Are you here on business or pleasure this visit?" he asked, holding up a book in each hand.

Monsieur Petri and I had known each other for a very long time. He only knew me as the Contessa and had always treated me as an adored grandchild. "A bit of both, though I came down mainly for the pleasure of your company," I replied lightly.

He smiled warmly. "You do know how to flatter an old man. I have some lovely new fiction that I think you will adore, and several biographies have recently come in as well."

Nothing at this bookstore ever seemed to change. My father had introduced me to Monsieur Petri when I was young, bringing me to the bookstore on a family holiday. I found out in later years that many of the books in the estate library had come from this shop, and that the two men had carried on a great deal of correspondence. Monsieur Petri was always finding new books and always had excellent recommendations. He handed over one of the two books he was holding. As I flipped through it, I said, "I need a book or two on the city of Rome and the Vatican. I'm interested in the architecture of the Vatican in particular, and a history of the city, and the church there."

"Oooh, now those are interesting topics. Yes, we have several books on Rome. The Vatican specifically, that's a bit harder to come by." He led me deeper into the shop, the smell of leather and books filing the air. I breathed in the soothing scent; it made the outside world feel muffled and distant. He pulled down several volumes and handed them back to me one by one. They had titles such as *The Architecture of the Masters, The Influences of the Vatican on Southern Italy*, and others equally dry. When I had a stack of four or five he turned to me. "I think that's about it for the moment. Shall I put them on the front counter while I show you what's new?"

I heard the bell tinkle at the front of the shop. "It sounds like you have another customer, Monsieur Petri. I will carry these up and let you deal with them."

He smiled his appreciation and turned, saying "Coming. I'll be right there." After he disappeared around one of the bookshelves towards the front of the shop, I took a slip of paper out of my pocket and scribbled a quick note letting Tyler and Nina know where we were anchored. Leaving it unsigned, I slid it in between two of the books on Rome and put them back on the bookshelf.

I made my way slowly through the narrow aisles of bookshelves with my treasure, barely hearing the low murmurs of conversation between Petri and the newcomer. Near the front I stopped to pull a title down from one of the shelves that caught my eye. *The French Way, an Inappropriate Romance.* Chuckling I put it atop my much heavier reading *The History of Relics and the Catholic Church*. Monsieur Petri came bustling back, passing me with a nod as he headed towards the back of the shop. I smiled as I added the new book to my pile and turned. Rounding the corner of the bookshelf, I ran headlong into a very solid chest and my pile of books went tumbling.

"*Je m'excuse.* I am so sorry, Madam. Here let me help you," he said in heavily accented French.

I stood rooted in place, mind whirling as the young man in blue and yellow picked up my books and handed them up to me. Handing up the last book, Charles stood and made a low bow. "I apologize for my extreme clumsiness."

His golden eyes looked me full in the face and he blinked, looking puzzled.

Oh mon dieu *what do I say, does he know who I am?* Thoughts ran through my head frantically. The last person he had seen me as was Contessa, so I took a deep breath to calm my nerves.

He shook his head. "We've... met..." He thought for a moment. "In Rome... Contessa?"

"Monsieur... Charles? From Rome, *oui*?" I pitched my voice higher, using my Contessa voice, and I worked my face into some semblance of surprise. "Are you here on holiday?"

His eyes opened wide. "You remember my name? I admit I am surprised. What are you doing here, Contessa? And why..." He gestured to my outfit, trousers and a vest, decidedly not appropriate for a Contessa.

I quickly put a finger over his lips. "*Shhh...* I am in disguise. Monsieur Petri is the best bookseller in the region. I like to come do my own shopping, which is terribly improper. He does not know who I really am, and I would like to keep it that way. Will you help me?"

Charles's lips quirked and his eyes narrowed. "Where is your page? It is not safe for a woman to be out alone shopping, even in the middle of the day."

I frowned. "Aubagne is safe enough. I do not bring my

page along on such expeditions either, as I should like to enjoy my book shopping in peace. Now, will you help me with my charade?"

Disapproval flit across Charles' face, but his lips were trying to quirk up in a smile. "*Sì, signora*. I will help you. If I may not address you as Contessa, what should I call you?"

"Jacqueline will do," I replied.

He looked slightly startled, but took my hand in his own, bowed over it charmingly then took my stack of books and placed them on the counter. Seeing the novel, he smiled knowingly, glancing quickly at the rest of the stack. "Heavy reading for one so tiny," he joked, looking at me out of the corner of his eye.

"One must exercise both the mind and the body to stay fit in this world. These will help me to do both. My recent trip to Rome piqued my interest in such things. What type of reading did you come in search of?"

Monsieur Petri chose that moment to pop up seemingly from nowhere, holding another book. I jumped, startled, having forgotten about him entirely. Monsieur Petri handed the book to Charles. "Your book Monsieur." It was a cheaply made, paper bound pamphlet titled *The Weekly Gossip*.

I raised an eyebrow. "I would not have suspected you read such questionable things."

He looked slightly embarrassed. "I am here on official business, unfortunately, not holiday. I am trying to track down someone who may have stolen an item from the Vatican. While these rags are more sensational than not, they do hold some nuggets of truth. I expect my quarry is somewhere in this area, but I don't know for certain yet, and I wanted to see if there were any unusual activities that had made it to the *Gossip*."

"Ah *oui*. Best of luck then," I replied. "I am sorry you are not on holiday. You should return here when you have a chance to see all of Aubagne's loveliness instead of working.

There are several delightful cheese shops, and the mountains trails make for excellent walking and riding."

"Having seen you, Jacqueline, means I have seen the loveliest of lovelies Aubagne can offer," he replied gallantly, bowing over my hand once more.

I giggled. "Oh, Charles, you flatter me. Perhaps when you have caught this notorious criminal you will come back and visit our fair city."

"If you wish it, it shall be so."

Trying not to blush, I retrieved my hand from his grasp.

"May I wrap these for you, Jacqueline?" the book keeper asked.

"Yes, thank you, Monsieur Petri. I will take them with me directly." I turned to the counter and paid. "Thank you for your assistance in finding them."

Charles paid for his purchase, and we stepped out of the shop together. "May I walk you to your residence? I do not feel comfortable letting you walk by yourself Cont... Jacqueline."

Oh dear. How do I get rid of him without leading him back to The Indiana. *There's a nice hotel up a few blocks I can pretend I'm staying there. Maybe that will work.*

"Very well, monsieur, since you insist. I am not staying far from here. Just up at the *Hotel du Frisee*." I nodded my head in the direction of the hotel, and hoped it was still there. I hadn't stayed there since the last time I travelled with my father, many years ago.

After a few steps Charles stopped, and shook his head. "You must think me an unimaginable boor, Jacqueline. Here, let me carry your parcels." He held out his arms to receive the packages, shaking his head. "I cannot imagine why you would travel without your page, it's not ... usual...You yourself are a most unusual woman," he muttered, more to himself than to me.

"Charles." I gave him a playfully stern look, maintaining my grip on my books. "You forget yourself. You asked to accompany me. I find you quite charming, but I will not tolerate having my actions questioned by someone I have met by chance in a shop. If you can't imagine me travelling without my page, you are welcome to imagine me walking without your company; I am quite capable of carrying my own parcels."

I could see I had wounded him, a little, but he merely replied with, "Hmph." And continued walking with me in the direction of the hotel.

"Tell me," I asked a few moments later. "How is your investigation going? Do you have any leads?"

He perked up at my question, but seemed guarded, watching me out of the corner of his eye as we walked. "We had good information the thief was in Marseille. In fact, I very nearly caught h… him, but they escaped at the last minute. I know what the ship looks like, but I need to have more solid proof. There are a couple of ships with similar profiles, and most are honest merchants. If necessary my men will board and search every one, but that would strain political relations in unnecessary ways. I went through the airfield in Marseille very carefully yesterday examining the airships in dock, and there was one that … well, it lifted off before I was able to board, and it did so in a hurry. I would surmise that's my quarry. Aubagne is the nearest airfield to Marseille, and close enough that I thought it worth checking."

"Oh?" I asked.

"Yes. I am certain I've seen that ship before, but under a different name." He continued to watch me out of the corner of his eye, and I held a bland, mildly interested expression on my face. He shook his head and stopped himself. "But this can't be of interest to you, my lady. Oh, and here is your hotel." He stopped and looked up at the grand hotel, with a small cafe out front.

"Thank you for your assistance, Charles," I said, turning to go into the hotel.

He stopped me. "Might I..." He looked around briefly, stammering. "Might I buy you a coffee?" His golden eyes stared at me longingly and with an unexpected intensity. "Please?"

Jac, you're playing a dangerous game here. Do not encourage him in this.

Despite the fact Charles was trying to lock me up (though he didn't know it), I did find him quite charming. Pushing thoughts of David to the side, I replied.

"One coffee, and then I must retire for the evening." I smiled up at him with wide eyes, inviting flirtation.

We sat and chatted in the cafe for an hour, sipping our coffee and nibbling on tiny shortbread biscuits. He tried to draw me out about my past, and I spun him tales about the estate, forgoing any mention of my mechanic's shop, or interest in airships, and drawing liberally from my sister's hobbies – reading, painting, riding, and other ladylike pursuits. He spoke freely of his time in the guard as a young guardsman, but any time I tried to draw him out about his investigation, he artfully dodged my questions. When the last dregs of espresso were drained, he stood and bowed over my hand. "I must go, for if I stay any longer I shall be inclined to ask you to dinner." He hoped, I could tell, that I would ask him to stay, but I smiled and bid him "*Adieu.*" He nodded and left, back straight, cutting a fine figure through the crowd.

I watched him go, lingering until I could no longer see him. He was headed up the street, away from the airfield, and I did not wish for him to see me leave. When he was out of sight I picked up my packages and rushed back to my airhopper, and the ship, hoping Tyler and Nina had found my note.

CHARLES

Streets of Aubagne

Charles walked away from the cafe, away from her, with an unsettled, unfamiliar feeling in the pit of his stomach. "Behave yourself. She is a noblewoman, far above your station. You have no right to even think such thoughts about her. The fact she allowed you to have coffee with her indicates only that she is gracious." Charles muttered this to himself as he walked up the street, ignoring the passersby. He received a few strange looks, which he also ignored.

"On top of that," he continued to himself, "you are here to do a job. The Holy Father has put his most sacred trust in you to find the Miter, post haste. Do not let the most charming Contessa distract you from that, or you may find yourself without employment, and possibly lacking in life."

But the Contessa's petite figure haunted him still. He couldn't banish the strong desire to wrap his hands around her tiny waist and pull her close. He could practically feel her lithe form in his arms. The brief moment when he carried her at the Vatican came clearly back to him, her smell, the way she weighed practically nothing in his arms.

She had a way of wrinkling her nose when she was amused that he found entirely endearing. The fact she would consider stepping out without a proper escort bothered him greatly. It wasn't safe, it wasn't ladylike, and it left her open to all sorts of dangers a woman of her stature couldn't afford. Why, her reputation could so easily be besmirched, even by going to coffee with someone like himself!

His mind, refusing to stay on the topic of finding the Miter, jumped back to the color of Jacqueline's eyes, and her lustrous hair. He wondered if the faint scent, caught when she bumped into him, was her own womanly scent, or that of a subtle perfume.

In this state of mind, he found himself in front of a small chapel dedicated to an unnamed saint. He pushed open the door, crossed himself and approached the altar. He had never felt inner turmoil over a woman before – his life was dedicated to the Pope and the Vatican, his every ounce of being focused on serving God and the Church. And yet, this woman, with her polite courtesy and witticisms, had plucked a string within him, that sounded, beckoning him off the path that had been laid before him. Pouring out his confusion and the inner turmoil the day's encounter brought him felt right, and he laid it at the feet of his heavenly father, asking for guidance.

In the silence, after his plea, he heard a soft, sympathetic chuckle. He whirled around to find a brother, tonsured, with his cowl around his shoulders and a soft rope belt securing his robes standing behind him with a friendly, sympathetic smile.

"My son, it is always a woman isn't it?"

Charles stood, anger and embarrassment flaming across his face. "My pardon, brother. I thought I was alone in my prayer. I did not intend for anyone to hear it but Our Lord."

The brother bowed his head, eyes twinkling, but still sympathetic. "And perhaps Our Lord heard you, and sent me to answer?"

Charles opened his mouth to reply glibly and stopped. He had come seeking guidance, perhaps the brother could help. He gestured, inviting the cowled figure to sit beside him.

"Tell me then, what it is I need to know. Though how a celibate brother could know about women is beyond me." Charles faced the brother, embarrassment still bubbling within.

"My son, this is France. My order is a small one – we believe that men and women, to be happy and follow the Lord's teachings must understand one another. And to understand one another is to love one another. You have found your way to the chapel of lovers – so dedicated by the Count of l'Ouray a half century ago. He sought the advice of my order, against the wishes of many, when it came to who he was to marry. He was so in love with his mate, that he had this chapel built, for others to find similar guidance on matters of the heart. Coincidence, I think not. But, as for your plea to our Lord – the best advice I can give you is this. You must see her for who she is. If you insist on seeing her as something she is not, only you will be to blame for your broken dreams."

Charles raised his hand to protest, stopped and thought about what the brother had said. "See her for who she truly is..." he murmured. "Thank you for your wisdom, brother. I will think on what you have said. God be with you." Charles bowed and started to walk back towards the entrance.

The brother smiled and made the sign of the cross in the air. "And with you, my son. May you find what you seek."

With great force of will he turned his mind back to the problem of the ship. *The Indiana* was supposedly the ship of the infamous Captain Jac.

His mind stopped on that for a moment, as the priest's words echoed in his head. Jac – Jacqueline. When he laid out everything around his encounters with the Contessa her odd behavior, her appearance and style of dress, her reading materials from the bookshop, and the timeline of their encounters, he didn't like the picture it painted.

His mind jumped back to *The Indiana*. It had been sitting right there in port. And he hadn't been quick enough to board it, and as a result, they had gotten away. He was angry with himself about that. Airfield Master and protocol be dammed, he should have just boarded the ship.

He re-played the encounter in his head. The ship had looked quite a bit like *The Bessie Quinn* – not surprising, as that make of ship was common, but even the coloring had been the same.

He wracked his brain, comparing the two ships – he'd seen a great deal of the interior of the *Bessie Quinn*, and had studied it from a distance as they pursued it. Were the hull ports in the same locations? The *grand poche* was of the same design, of that much he was certain. He wanted the Contessa to be an innocent, slightly frivolous noblewoman with beautiful eyes and a flirtatious smile. He was afraid she was nothing of the sort.

"See her for who she truly is…" he resolved. "And if I am correct in my suspicions, I will be seeing her again very soon."

JACQUELINE

Tyler and Nina made it back to this ship just after I did. Seamus and Niccolò saw to the take-off checklist as I stashed the books in my cabin. David watched our proceedings with the fascination of a small child. This was a different world for him. The trip from Aubagne to Sicily would take about a week if everything went smoothly. When the last of the minor details were taken care of, we took to the sky.

The first three days we had smooth sailing, clear skies and nothing on the horizon. David and Marie spent hours closeted down in her workshop while I read through the books I picked up in Monsieur Petri's shop. There wasn't much of use, but I did find mention of ancient tunnels beneath the city predating Rome and the Vatican. The author, Mestockle, postulated that the tunnels sheltered the early Christians from the wrath of Pontius Pilate immediately following the crucifixion. He also suggested that they were older by far than even that ancient date, housing the secrets of early humans back to the inception of Lilith and the fall of Adam and Eve.

On the fourth day, David brought me down to Marie's workshop to show me what they had been working on. Parts and components were scattered across the tables – it looked like a small whirlwind had come through the room. This was far from Marie's normally neat and tidy style, but her eyes glowed with accomplishment as she presented their project. Or projects, rather.

Marie handed me the small cylindrical tube I had taken from one of Charles's men. "That, Captain, is a beautiful little device. As you yourself saw, it is capable of projecting a beam of light. Very handy. It worked on a system of mirrors inside the tube to project the light, and chemical combinations providing the light source. Henri and I worked out which chemicals they were using and have been able to duplicate the effect." She handed me a metal cube about the size of my palm. One of the faces was made of clear glass, and there was a small lever on one side, flush with the metal. "Unfortunately, we don't have the materials onboard to make the smaller cylindrical versions, but go ahead, give it a try."

I pressed down the lever and a dim, clear light came out of the glass face of the cube. "On the up-side, you won't have to worry about this rolling away under one of the shelves," Marie said.

"I can see a number of fantastic applications for this." I pressed the lever again, and the light shut off.

Marie continued, "It has a limited number of uses – it should give off light for about an hour before it will need to be refreshed."

Listening while she told me about the chemistry involved, I turned the cube over in my hand examining it. "How susceptible is it to damage? If it's dropped for instance, or the glass breaks?"

"Ah, yes. That would be important. The metal is fairly durable, but if the glass is broken and the lever is engaged at the same time, it will emit quite a nasty smoke. It smells awful." She grimaced.

"Now this." David held up a flat object that looked very much like the tracking device we had sewn into the Miter. "This is a duplicate of the tracking device I showed you earlier. Luckily Marie had the materials I needed on hand to finish a second. My thought was to install these in the airhoppers. They're two-way Jac, much like the one in your arm. It can be used to track the airhopper, or call it back to the ship, once we upgrade Nina's navigation console." He flipped it over in his fingers. "The primary difference is range. This is up to ten kilometers, whereas the one in your arm is only one."

"So, once you get the console upgraded we'll be able to track both the hat and the airhoppers within ten kilometers?" I looked at the small device with new respect. The implant in my arm had saved me many times.

"I have one last item I'd like to show you, Captain." Marie went to a table against the wall and picked up a small wooden device with two metal prongs on the end. The entire thing was slightly larger than my two hands put together. She brought it over to demonstrate. I looked at it curiously. It was like nothing I had ever seen before.

"This uses a friction generator to produce an electrical discharge. Quite nasty if you press it against human flesh, though generally not deadly." She popped off the end of the box and pulled the cord several times, until the metal tip glowed and arced, giving off small sparks.

"It's a nonlethal weapon, Captain. It will totally incapacitate a target without leaving more than a small burn." Marie showed a burned patch on her forearm, and David pulled down the shoulder of his shirt showing a similar mark on his shoulder.

"We've both been the victim at least twice testing out this little baby. The effects have been the same each time. It is dreadfully unpleasant, but unless you charge it too high, I don't think it will kill you," David said, pulling up the shoulder of his shirt.

"That is quite impressive. Perhaps next time let Henri know before you test weapons on each other so he can be standing by? I'd hate to lose either of you to accidental experiment failure!"

Marie chuckled. "No fear there, Captain. I value my life, and Henri would kill me if I died due to stupidity! I intend to build several of them and place them at key locations around the ship."

"How many can you build with the supplies on hand?" I asked.

"I think probably three more with what we have here on the ship. With David's help it shouldn't take very long to get them built, perhaps a day."

Shaking my head, I handed the small device back to her. "You really are quite brilliant. I'm glad you're on our side."

Marie beamed with pleasure.

JACQUELINE

I asked Henri to check out both David and Marie to make sure neither would suffer long term effects of testing the weapon on each other. Henri pronounced them both fine but recommended a few hours rest. I tucked David into my bunk and gave him a book to read. Within a few minutes I heard him snoring gently, and I smiled to myself.

Back on deck Nina was at the helm, staring serenely into the distance. "Afternoon, Captain."

"How does it look?" I stared out over the sky full of puffy white cotton clouds.

"Storm's brewing. I can feel it, but we've got at least an hour." Nina pointed off toward the south. "See where the clouds change?"

On the horizon ahead of us, barely visible, was a solid grey line. I pulled the spyglass off my belt and studied the storm line. "It will be quite a blow when it hits."

Following the horizon around I saw a tiny dot that didn't belong. I adjusted my spyglass for a better look. "Nina, we've got a ship flying Vatican colors off the stern."

Nina cursed in Bantu, her native language, and then switched back to French. "What do you want to do, Captain?"

"Are we near any of our usual safe havens?" I looked from the Vatican airship to the storm ahead.

"*Non.* We've nothing but sea beneath us for miles."

The blue hull of the *Blue Raven's* gondola and white *grand poche* were designed to make it difficult to see in clear weather. I had almost missed it in the distance.

"*Merde.*" I pressed the large lever next to Nina's console. "All hands, on-deck. All hands!" I yelled into the copper tubing. The sounds of running feet filtered up through the communication system moments before the crew appeared on deck.

"We have a situation. The *Blue Raven* is behind us, a massive storm front ahead of us, and no safe haven between here and there. They are closing fast—they'll be within range in an hour, no more."

They had seen us. The shift in their airspeed and trajectory was subtle but produced results. Within twenty minutes I could see them clearly behind us.

The boom of a cannon and the whistle as the ball fell just short of our starboard side made all of us duck. I looked over my shoulder in awe. "Mother of God, that was close. What are they using to get that kind of range?" Marie and Tyler both grabbed the railing and hoisted themselves up for a better look.

"Nina, run for the storm," I directed. "To your stations!"

"Captain, what do you want me to do?" Niccolò asked, his eyes wide with fear.

"Help Marie in the engine room," I said, clapping my hand on his shoulder. "She'll put you to work."

Marie looked at me and nodded, eyes grave as she grabbed Niccolò by the arm and raced below decks.

Our propellers and auxiliary fan started whirring at high speed just as a gust of wind from the storm front hit the ship. The ship's carriage swayed against the cables attaching the *grand poche*. I grabbed for the steering deck railing as I felt the pit of my stomach drop.

Nina shouted over the wind. "Captain. It's coming on quicker than expected!"

Another boom filled the air as a cannonball sailed much too close to the prow of the ship. "They're getting their distance on us Nina."

"Aye! I expect you're right, Captain!" she shouted above the noise of the propellers.

"Storm's coming in fast, tie down anything loose and double check the airhoppers!" I shouted down, hearing my voice echo throughout the ship.

Nina braced herself against the gusting wind and pulled down on a stiff, seldom used lever next to the steering column. Two panels opened in the deck and sturdy seats rose from within. Each chair had shoulder and waist straps designed to keep a person in their seat. Nina's was close enough to the steering wheel that she could sit strapped in and guide the ship without worrying about being thrown overboard. She took a moment to grab her goggles off the back of the chair, position them over her eyes, and strap herself in.

"Better see to yourself, Captain!" she shouted, her words stolen by the rising wind.

I strapped myself into the second chair. Mine, unlike Nina's, could swivel three-hundred-sixty degrees allowing me to keep an eye out for threats. The tracking station was behind my chair, allowing us to sit back to back. It would allow the crew to track either me, or *The Inara* with the original tracking devices David had created.

Nina, ever fearless, flew us directly into the heart of the storm. The *Blue Raven* followed, and their cannon boomed again. I heard the splintering of wood as a shudder went through the ship.

"Nina, hide us in the heart of the lightning. Four degrees to port. Marie, give us everything you can!" I pointed, shouting into the comm tube. *The Indiana* wasn't equipped with cannons or other firepower. We too often posed as a passenger or plain cargo ship, and cannons would make us too much of a target. Today however, I wished we had them.

The rain started, soaking us as I called out course adjustments, trying to avoid cannonade fire. The wind drove the pellets of water into sleeting, blinding sheets. We rose higher and higher, buffeted by gusts that threatened to tear the ship apart. The rain, gentle on the ground, pierced and clawed its way through clothing at this altitude and ran icy fingers down backs and faces, making everyone on deck miserable. Tyler and Seamus were checking the rigging on the lower deck, barely visible from my seat. We were approaching the center of the storm, and the Vatican ship was still right behind us.

Lightning arced from cloud to cloud, dispersed by the rods attached to the hull and fine wires around the envelop. With every crackle, sparks danced across the grid, surrounding the *grand poche* in a shower of Chinese fireworks. The ship bucked and rocked against its cables, rising and then pitching down as hard as any ship fighting the ocean.

Though we had weathered many such storms, it was never any less thrilling to make it to the top. We burst from the clouds above the storm, once again out of sight of the Vatican ship and were sailing with blue skies above and pouring rain below. Dark clouds roiled and sparked beneath us. Every so often a finger of lightning would reach up before being neutralized by the lightning rods and coils. The wind continued to gust strongly, but at least we could see. The storm stretched for miles in all directions. Patches of cloud were, in some areas, lit frequently from within, while other sections saw no lights at all.

Moments passed as I peered through the driving sleet trying to locate the *Blue Raven*. A faint crackle of unnatural lightning below us was my only warning. "Nina! Hard to starboard," I yelled.

The Vatican ship burst through the clouds rising rapidly, its *grand poche* scraping the side of *The Indiana* as it rose. I heard the wood groan as we made contact with their hull, and a harsh shudder ran through the gondola. I could hear the shouts of men from the other ship, as they tried to disengage. The *Blue Raven* veered off, still crackling with dispersed lightning, their gondola swinging wildly. Several of their cables had snapped, fore and aft.

Quicker than I thought possible they sighted their cannons on us. "Nina, emergency dive! Now!" I shouted. I heard the rush of escaping air as Nina blew open the heated balloons and we lurched into free fall. For a moment everything, including my stomach, seemed to float, and then the ship slammed down below the cloud level. My head slammed into the back of my chair, and I saw stars.

"Captain we must head to the true heart of the storm!" Nina shouted above the gale. She pointed to a black maelstrom in the distance. Lightning crackled around its center creating a fearsome sight.

"We'll never survive!" I shouted back.

"We will with me piloting!" she shouted, a mad light in her eyes. "This is going to be a wild ride." Nina laughed as she steered us directly towards the pulsating heart of Hell.

They followed. I will give them this, their pilot had nerves of steel. *The Indiana* threatened to tear herself apart. Cables snapped, whipping about like tormented snakes. Where they hit the ship, huge gouges appeared. I had no fear of cannon fire from the *Blue Raven* at this point, *The Indiana* was ripping herself apart.

Right before we entered the heart, amidst the deafening gale Nina shouted out, "For Merida!" and deployed the updraft sails. I didn't have time to puzzle that out.

The ship shuddered. I heard wood crack, and metal screech as the ship strained upwards. We rose with such haste that the cables went slack, and the body of the ship met with the *grand poche*. The fabric enveloped us, pressing suffocatingly close. For a brief moment, we were held up only by the wind. Time seemed to slow as the storm raged. Nina persevered, holding the course and we popped like a jack in the box above the clouds.

We sailed up and over the eye of the storm, the awesome power swirling below us. Rain pelted us, and rims of frost formed around the edges of my goggles.

We cleared the storm. *The Indiana* was in bad shape, cables swinging free. I felt bruised from the belts holding me in my seat. Only half of the cables attaching the *grand poche* remained, and the ship listed to one side badly. There was no sign of the *Blue Raven*. A twinge of worry flashed through me. Despite our current situation, I hoped Charles had made it to safety.

The island was extremely small, composed of nothing but sand and a few, very sparse trees. Nina brought us down as close to the water as possible. We couldn't float because of several large holes in the hull, but the cables had to be fixed before we could go any further. In the wake of the storm the sea was cloudy, the waters disturbed and roiling. Strange fish rose to the surface in search of food.

Tyler, Marie and Seamus came on deck with Niccolò trailing behind them, eyes wide with shock. I clapped him on the shoulder. "Congratulations my young friend – you're real airship crew now. You've survived one of the big ones."

He nodded, shivering. "Does it often do that?"

I considered him for a moment. "Storms are a part of life, to be met with bravery, intelligence and courage." Smiling at him I said, "But no, it doesn't often blow that hard."

Marie exclaimed in horror when she saw the damage to

the cables and the hull. She had been protected from the worst of it in the engine room. Tyler shook his head. "Jac, we can fix these cables temporarily, but they're going to have to be replaced. Any patchwork we do here isn't going to hold for very long."

I nodded in agreement, surveying the damage. "It's not ideal, but let's see what we can do so we make it to port. We must make it back to *The Flaming Mug* in time for the rendezvous with Franco."

"We have a more pressing problem Captain," Seamus said grimly. "We're out of splice cable."

Nina swore. "The extra was in the supplies I was picking up when we had to scurry out of Marseille."

I swore under my breath. No splice cable meant we'd have to pick and choose which cables to sacrifice, leaving us in a precarious position if we had to run, fight, or weather another storm.

"Captain. I think the land anchor cable would be long enough to handle the worst of the splicing – if we fix the hull first then we can raise the anchor and strip it." Seamus suggested.

I nodded. "*Oui*. That's a good suggestion. Let's get started!"

Niccolò, Henri, Marie, and David worked to patch the holes in the hull while the rest of us inspected cables and provided support. David was sporting a bruise across half his face from where he had slammed into the edge of the bunk. He had tried to get up to find out what was going on just as we crested the storm. Marie and Henri were both moaning about broken items in their workshops.

As we worked, I pondered why Charles had opted to attack us at this point. It didn't make sense. He had opportunities before this and didn't take them. Why now? What had changed? I had more questions than answers, and I didn't want to voice what we were all thinking as we worked on repairs. Would our beloved *Indiana* fly again? And was it all worth it for a hat?

JACQUELINE

The airfield at Palermo was empty. No intelligent airship captain stayed in port during a storm. The Airfield Master was a short, portly man who had worry lines permanently etched around the corners of his eyes. He looked over our ship as we limped into a berth at mid-morning. "Why is it every time I see you, your ship looks like it's about to fall apart?" He swung nimbly over the railing of the ship and onto the deck, a surprising feat given his appearance. "That was a rough blow, Captain, was it not?"

"*Oui*. It was a hard ride. She's not fallen apart on us yet though. As you can see, we'll be needing some repairs. Hopefully we won't run into one like that again. This is only a brief stop for us, is there any chance you can have them done in two days? Any other ships come back yet?"

"Oh, one or two. Yours appears to be the worst hit. That must have been exciting from up in the air." He grinned, looking about expectantly.

"I'm not sure exciting is the word I would use. Do you have a repair crew available?"

"Oh aye. It shouldn't be too much of a problem. You arrived before the rush. We'll get the clanks over and get started. Given the level of damage, we should probably move you into the construction hangar for repairs. It's more than twice as high and will give the men plenty of room to work" He gestured one of his men over and began giving instructions. I could see the hangar in the distance. The open doors were wide enough to allow two airships entry side by side, and tall enough that there were two traffic lanes, top and bottom as well. The young man went running off to summon the repair crew.

I nodded with resignation. The Airfield Master knew we wouldn't make it to the next port, and he knew I knew it, too. We had barely made it off the island, and that was only due to Seamus's solution to the broken cables. The haggling over price was merely for form sake. In the end, the price was more than I liked, but not as much as it could have been. He signaled, and the giant repair clanks started towards us. The repair crew began swarming over the exterior of the ship.

"Tyler, you supervise here. Nina and I are going to *The Flaming Mug* to see what surprises might be waiting for us."

The Flaming Mug wasn't there. It should have been easy to find. It wasn't far from the airfield from what I remembered. Nina and I looked for at least an hour. The building was there, but instead of a pub, there was a leather goods shop, showing shoes and flying gear and other odds and sundry.

"Nina, have I gone crazy?" I looked around at the block we encircled for the third time.

"Captain, if you've gone crazy, so have I."

My hackles rose and my fingers twitched against the knife at my belt, but I kept my tone light and conversational. "Are we going to have to go back to the ship and tell the boys we can't find the pub?"

"Aye, Captain. I believe we will." Nina said. "And we'll never live this down." She shook her head for effect. In a barely audible whisper she said, "We're being followed. The man in the doorway to our right is watching us."

"Shall we go in and meet the new management?" I proposed, opening the door to the leather shop. In a quiet voice I said, "There's another up there on the left too."

"Aye, Captain. I think that sounds like a fine plan." Nina pulled open the door and gave a mock bow, gesturing me through it.

The layout of the shop was similar to *The Flaming Mug*. The bar was now the counter where the shoemaker laid out models available. The walls were a light stucco, and sparsely decorated. The wood of the bar was covered with sections of leather, sewing implements, and leather punches. The shoe-maker stood behind the counter, his face screwed up with concentration as he carefully stitched a sole onto a shoe. I approached him, peering over the counter. "Excuse me. Has this establishments changed hands recently?"

The older man looked at me as if I might be touched in the head. "No. I've owned this shop for many years. Finest shoemaker in Palermo – ask anyone!" He said proudly. "Why do you ask?"

"Have you ever heard of a pub in these parts called *The Flaming Mug*?" I leaned my elbow on the counter and gave my most charming smile.

He pulled the leather punch out of his mouth, where he'd been holding it, thinking. "Doesn't sound familiar. If you two ladies are looking for a decent meal though, there's a nice little cafe two blocks up. Not terribly original in its naming, *Palermo Café*, but the food is good."

"So you've never heard of *The Flaming Mug*?" Nina reiterated.

"No. Can't say as I have. Odd name for a pub though. I wonder if they light their drinks on fire." His manner was easygoing and open, and I didn't see any of the telltale signs of lying – shifting eyes, nervous behaviors – he either thought he was telling the truth, or he was a very good liar.

"It was right here, in this very building, just about a month ago," I pressed.

He shook his head, his shaggy grey hair flipping into his eyes. He brushed it back with his free hand. "I'm afraid not madam. I've owned this shop for fifteen years, and my father owned it before me. It's always been a shoe shop."

I looked to Nina and back to the shoemaker. "Nina, lock the door."

He did react to that. "Hey, you can't do that. This is my business." Nina ignored him, shooting the bolt closed and leaning against the door jamb, watching the street.

"What's going on?" he was a small, older man, and fear sprang up in his eyes.

"That is what we would like to know. A month ago, we came here, and this was a pub. Now it's a shoe shop, and you claim it's always been a shoe shop. Clearly one of us is lying, and it's not me." I took my knife out of my boot, six inches of very functional steel, and set it menacingly on the counter.

The shoemaker gulped. "I swear to you madam, this has always been a shoe shop."

"And where were you a month ago, shoemaker?" Nina asked, from her lookout post by the door.

His eyes flickered over to Nina and then back to me, assessing our attire and attitude.

"Are you," he gaped, still fearful but with a tinge of something else. "Are you pirates?"

"Where were you a month ago shoemaker?" I repeated.

"Pirates in my shop! Well I never. This is exciting!" He looked back to me, and the knife I was holding, and turned pale. "Ah. Pirates. What was the question again?"

"Where were you a month ago, shoemaker?" I repeated a second time.

"A month ago." I watched him think, counting back the weeks on his fingers. "Oh! My wife and I went on our yearly trip to Italia to visit her mother. It was a short trip this year, only a week, thank goodness. Her mother is a handful, but we go every year to visit on her birthday." He beamed at the two of us, almost pleased to answer.

"Imagine – pirates in my shop. This is the most exciting thing that's ever happened here. I can't wait to tell my wife." He was practically giddy. I raised an eyebrow. Not the reaction most people had when confronted with a 'pirate'.

"Do people around here know you leave to visit your mother in law every year on her birthday?" I asked.

"Oh yes. We've been doing it for years," he confirmed. "Usually we're gone for a month."

I paused, thinking on this. "Does anyone mind the shop when you're gone?"

"No. I had a son, and he used to mind it for me, but he died two years ago when sickness came to the city." He rubbed a hand across his eyes briefly. "Since his death, I've not taken an apprentice, and we've done well enough over the years that I can close for a week now and again without too much hardship."

"So, someone could have planned to come in here while you were gone, re-decorated, and then put it back before you returned, with a fair certainty that you would be gone for at least a week." I mused. "Unconventional, but not impossible."

"Wait. You think someone turned my shop into a pub while I was gone? No. That couldn't happen. Things like that don't happen. That's something out of a fairy tale." He looked at Nina and I as if we had sprouted extra heads.

"Do you mind if we take a look around shoemaker?" Nina asked, still looking out the window.

"No, please do. I can't imagine you'll find anything unusual though." He watched with interest as Nina and I moved pictures, shifted bolts of leather and examined the walls. After a few minutes, a realization hit me. "Nina, the diamond. See if it's still there."

"Aye you're right." Nina rushed to the back corner where our party had been sitting the night we took the job.

Bolts of cloth were stacked neatly on shelves where the table had been. "Help me shift this Captain."

The two of us strained to move the heavy shelf, but finally it slid out a few feet from the wall. Dropping down to her hands and knees she peered at the floorboards. Carefully she slid the tip of her knife underneath a small object embedded in the floorboards. "Here it is, the little beauty." She held up a small diamond for my inspection. I took it from her.

"Shoemaker – I dropped this diamond the night I was here. Circumstances prevented me from retrieving it. Is this the kind of thing you keep in the floorboards of your shop?" I showed him the small, perfectly cut diamond, and his eyes widened.

"I… I am at a loss. I have never dropped something so valuable. I have never possessed something so valuable. And no customer of mine would be in that area. That my little shop could be so transformed without my knowledge. This…" he looked troubled and faint, reaching for the chair behind him. "This is incredible. The most exciting thing that has ever happened, and also the most troubling. Pirates in my shop! Someone stealing in here and turning it into a pub!" His emotions ran across his face, clear as water. Excitement, fear, incredulity. "I can't wait to tell my wife!" He wiped his brow with a spare bit of cloth, eyes wide with excitement.

"You cannot tell anyone about this – you know that, right? It would put you and your wife in considerable danger if the men who did this thought you knew about it." I leaned on the counter, staring at him. His face fell immediately.

"But… this is the most exciting thing ever, and I can't tell anyone?"

"Not if you value your life and the life of your loved ones. Nina, we need to go." I walked to the door and lifted one corner of the shade carefully, looking out to the street. Franco's man, still in the doorway, was looking down the street at something.

"We need to go. Now. This was a setup from the beginning. Shoemaker, do you have a backdoor?"

He waved us through a door behind him. "This lets out onto an alleyway, but there is a door directly across that goes into the bakery – I bet this man you said was outside isn't watching the bakery! You can escape that way!" Excitement tinged his voice and he almost looked as if he wanted to come with us.

"Thank you, shoemaker, you've been very helpful. Keep this diamond as a token for your assistance. Now remember – we were never here." I handed him the small diamond and slipped into the alleyway with Nina close behind. We dashed across the narrow alley and pushed on the door. Locked. I heard the sound of booted feet, marching in step coming up the main street. Taking a quick glance around the alleyway corner I saw guards wearing the Vatican colors of blue and gold. *Merde. Setup indeed.* I thought.

Gesturing in the opposite direction, Nina and I slipped down the alley away from the main thoroughfare. The further we went, the more noxious the air became. Trash and unpleasant things that squished underfoot littered the narrow, darkening streets. I heard a shot behind us and Nina ducked as a bullet hit the stone wall just above her head. Glancing back, I saw Franco's stooge at the end of the alley.

"Quick, around the corner, Cat and Mouse!" I said. She dashed around me. She would take the lead as the 'mouse', encouraging our pursuer to follow her, while I would endeavor to get behind him, and turn the tables. Once around the corner, I looked for open doorways, or something to hide behind. The walls were unbroken by doorways here, so we kept running. Two more turnings and we found an alley that would work for our purposes. I ducked into a shadowed doorway and pulled a sleeping dart off my belt. Nina kept running. Franco's man turned the corner, just as Nina made it to the next corner. He sprinted past me, and I threw the dart at his back. It hit him between the shoulder blades and I saw him flinch, but he continued running. This alley was long and narrow, with few doorways. I saw the man take aim at Nina's back – the sleeping dose had not yet taken effect. I slammed into him, knocking him off balance. The shot echoed loudly in the confined, narrow street and his bullet went wide, hitting the stone well above Nina's head. He pitched sideways into the side of a building as the drug took effect, his pistol waving wildly as he slid down into a heap.

Retrieving my dart, I returned it to the sheath on my belt and rifled through the man's pockets. I recognized him from the night we made the deal. He was one of Franco's guards. A front pocket revealed a small coin purse and a pair of dice, but nothing of note. I dragged his inert body over to the same doorway I had hidden in, and propped him up. I would have liked to question him but knew from experience the sleeping dart would take at least half an hour to wear off, and he was too heavy for Nina and me to carry very far.

I don't like killing. I do it only at great need. I bound his hands behind him with his belt. Taking a pencil made from wax and ground ashes from my vest, I wrote the word SNITCH on his forehead in large, clear letters. It would wash off, but if any of the underworld of Palermo found him first, they would be wary.

Leaving him, Nina and I continued through the back streets of Palermo, until we found our way back to the airfield.

JACQUELINE

"Captain, I'm afraid we have another problem." Tyler greeted us with that dire pronouncement as soon as Nina and I returned to the ship, now ensconced in the enormous repair hangar. "While you were gone, the *Blue Raven* came into port. They seem to have weathered the storm well. I could see very little damage from here." He pointed out the cruiser, flying flags of blue and yellow bisected by a cross.

A small thrill of joy plucked my heart. Charles had made it through the storm. Nina blistered our ears, cursing unintelligibly, shaking her fist at the apparently undamaged war cruiser. I promised myself I would examine my feelings later, but at the moment Nina was right. This was not good.

"Okay, we need a new plan." I looked around at the repairmen crawling all over the ship. Gesturing towards the common room I quietly filled Tyler in on what Nina and I had found, and the presence of the Swiss Guard already in town. "There is no doubt now that this was a setup. It will be the Swiss Guard waiting for us at the drop tomorrow, not Franco or his buyer. We don't know who Franco is working for, and the ship needs repairs. She won't make it to another port in the state she's in."

I ran my fingers through my hair. "We have, as I see it, two, maybe three options. Steal a ship and vanish, get rid of the Miter, or wait here another day while the ship is repaired, but run a very high risk of discovery."

"We can't fence the Miter on such short notice. It's too high profile of an item, and it's too hot right now. I don't think any of our usual people would take it." Tyler replied.

I nodded. "You are right on that – but we could send it to someone as a way to get rid of it temporarily until we could arrange for a buyer."

"There is another option, Captain." Nina said, frowning. "We've already been paid well for this. What if we just… gave it back? This is the Catholic Church. If they know who stole it, they will keep coming after us until they have it."

Mentally, I rebelled at the thought of giving back something so valuable, even with the monies we'd already collected. Chastising myself for being greedy, I examined Nina's suggestion from all angles and felt the blood drain from my face as a horrifying thought occurred to me. If the Holy Father knew my familial connections, the entire crew was in danger, whether we returned the Miter or not. Unbeknownst to my crew, if our theft became public knowledge my uncle, the King of France, would have no qualms about killing me and every one of them. The King and I had an agreement – I stayed low profile and occasionally performed jobs for the crown, and he tolerated my alternative lifestyle. If I became an embarrassment or a liability, our agreement would be at an end. I worked hard to maintain my cover and keep my true lineage hidden; some secrets had to be kept. Taking a deep breath I said, "Let's keep that as the very last option. Tyler, what other ships are there in port?" I asked.

"Not many, Captain. The Vatican cruiser, a junk that limped in worse off than we are, and a couple of slow-moving freight transport airships."

I chuckled softly with the irony. "So we either steal the Vatican ship, get rid of the Miter, or both. Even if we send the Miter away, this was a setup, and they probably have Franco stashed away somewhere willing to testify that we took the job. *Merde*. What does Franco have to gain in all of this?" That was a question to ponder later. "I doubt they're going to allow us the luxury of finishing the repairs on *The Indiana* before they come for us. We might have until tomorrow."

A frown creased Nina's forehead. "Captain. I have been running through a list of our contacts in Europe – there's no one here we can send the Miter to without significant risk. Not that I can think of. The Vatican has too much influence and too many people fear the wrath of the church.

I nodded. "Tyler, let's figure out how to steal that ship." Tyler laughed, thinking I was joking and Nina looked at me incredulously. I stared back at them. "Gather the crew. Tell them the plan. Nina, I think you're right, but see if anyone has any other contacts that they can propose that might be closer, but still safe."

Tyler choked. "You're serious."

"Unless you have a better idea," I replied.

Movement caught my eye as David strode across the deck. *Merde*. I had forgotten him in the excitement. "I need to have a conversation with David."

Mindful of the workmen still clearing rigging and making repairs I caught up with David and said in a light, teasing tone, "*Mon chéri,* I needs must show you something in my cabin."

"Now?" he replied, gesturing at all of the repair work going on around us.

"*Oui!*" I said enthusiastically, grabbing his hand and pulling him towards my quarters. He laughed and followed, ignoring the crude comments that followed us. Closing the door I turned to him, and without preamble said "*Mon chéri,* we have been set up. Nina and Tyler are gathering the crew to work out our escape. I will join them shortly. I need you to choose." I took his hands in mine. Looking into his eyes I said, "You can get off the ship and find your way back to Paris with plausible deniability, and not be drawn further into this mess. If we get caught, no one will mention your name. I should not have brought you along when the job wasn't done, it was selfish of me and has put you in danger."

"And the second choice?" His deep voice made my heart contract with aching.

"We're going to steal a ship and make our escape. High possibility of being caught. Very little chance of pardon if you're caught with us." I kissed him then, thinking it might be the last time for a long while. "I love you. I cannot make the choice for you, and I will not push you one way or the other in this. I must go and work out the details with the crew. If you decide to stay, come help us plan. If you decide to go, I *will* see you again. You must decide before midnight."

CHARLES

Charles stood on deck holding the missive from the Vatican, re-reading it for the hundredth time.

We are not interested in the buyer at this time. Do whatever it takes to retrieve the Miter and capture those who took it. Your lack of results thus far has been highly disappointing.

He understood the value of the Miter and the desire to have it returned to its proper place, but this lack of concern over the buyer seemed shortsighted, and the reprimand stung his pride. Charles reminded himself that he was new to his position and needed this mission to be successful but found that he had crumpled the paper in his fist angrily anyway. He found he was searching for *The Indiana*, hoping it —or more specifically her captain— had made it in to port safely, regardless of what was to come. The airfield at Palermo was nearly empty, with only a few slow-moving cargo vessels immediately apparent.

In the distance, on the far side of the airfield, clanks moved in and out of massive repair hangars. They would be busy in the coming weeks, repairing all of the storm-damaged ships.

He flagged down the first mate. "Have the men spread out and search the hangars and the surrounding area. *The Indiana* should be nearby if they made it through the storm."

"Aye, Captain. If they're here, we'll find them," he saluted and made his way aft, gathering the crew.

Turning his thoughts to the storm he and the crew had just weathered, Charles shook his head in amazement. The fact that the *Blue Raven* hadn't been reduced to matchsticks, and had in fact sustained very little damage, was due entirely to the pilot. The man who hadn't been able to bring them into a proper berth in Marseille had done an incredible job riding the storm. Clearly the man, surly and unpleasant as he was, had more skills than Charles had first imagined.

JACQUELINE

Staring at the map of the known world tacked to the wall in the common room I asked, "Who can we ship this thing to?"

"I'm afraid all of my family are good Catholics, so no help for us there," Seamus replied.

"I don't have much in the way of family, and my friends are either here, or in the English Air Corps, and I can't imaging sending it to someone in the Air Corps would be a good idea if we ever want to recover it for ourselves," Tyler said apologetically.

I nodded agreement.

"There is my Mother, in Africa," Nina said.

"Africa." From the silence behind me I knew they were all staring with incredulity. Marie laughed, a note of hysteria tinging her voice. "You want to send the Miter to Africa?"

"I'm fairly certain they wouldn't expect it." I replied.

"It's not the craziest thing we've ever done," Nina said. "It would be harder for us to recover, but we could send the Miter to my mother. Her village is remote, and my mother is not Catholic. And it is doubtful that anyone in the village, even if they found out about the Miter, would even know how to contact the church."

Tyler raised an eyebrow. "I didn't know it was even possible to send items to Africa."

"There are some complications, and items must be carefully packaged. It is not a quick transit time, but I send things from time to time." Nina replied.

I was intrigued with this possibility. Nina was notoriously closemouthed about where she came from. "Where is she located?"

"She is based in Jebel Kumra in the heart of Africa. My people maintain a tribal communication network. It will take months for it to arrive, and must be packaged very specifically, but it will get there barring normal hazards of sending packages."

"Will she keep it for you?" Seamus asked.

"I believe so. She would not have reason to send it anywhere else."

Looking around the table I saw agreement in everyone's faces. "Very well, we shall send it to your mother. How does it need to be packaged so that it remains safe?"

She thought for a moment. "I'll need a sturdy wooden box twice the size of the Miter, fabric to wrap the hat in, waterproofing paper, a bolt of muslin, three spools of copper wire, a packet of steel needles and a spool of thread, two small bags of multicolored glass beads, and a slightly worn pair of men's shoes, sized narrow."

"Men's shoes? Glass beads?" Marie said with puzzlement.

"Aye. Essentially payment for postage along the route. It will only go via the postal system so far, and then we must rely on African methods." Nina shrugged. "It is unconventional by European standards, but it works quite well."

I was fascinated and curious to see how she would put the parcel together. We had never traveled to Africa, and there was much speculation about what could be found down there.

Henri, Marie, Niccolò and Nina left to find the supplies while Seamus built a box matching Nina's specification. Some hours later the four of them returned. Nina and Niccolò left to package up the Miter.

"Henri! Come join us. Tyler and I have worked out a plan to take the Vatican ship. Tell us where we're likely to get our asses shot off." My heart spared a moment to think of David, but he had to make his own decision in this.

<hr />

Nina and Niccolò dropped off the crate. I hadn't seen it, but they told me that the Miter lay wrapped in waterproof cloth under a false bottom with the other goods on top, David's tracker secured in the lining. The repair crew was gone for the evening – they made significant progress during the day, re-stringing cables and patching the balloon. The roof to the cavernous hangar was lost in the distance above us.

The biggest problem was now the engine. It would run, but the catalyst pin –a heavy, heat resistant, metal bar that helped regulate the heat going to the balloons– was bent. Either we'd rise too fast, or not at all until it was fixed.

The plan, in the end, was simple enough. Under cover of darkness we would board the Vatican ship, subdue any sentries, round up the rest of the Vatican crew and take them prisoner. Marie had a couple of the sleep grenades prepared, I had one and Tyler had one, and the rest of the crew would carry the electroshock devices in addition to their normal weapons.

We should have been more prepared. We were prepared to board their ship; we were not prepared for what happened.

David's shout alerted us to their presence moments before they swarmed the deck of *The Indiana*. Blue and gold clad soldiers dropped in from above, some sliding silently down ropes with practiced precision, others gliding in wearing specially designed suits with wing webbing under the arms for maneuverability in the air.

"Marie! Emergency launch, now!" I shouted into one of the speaking tubes going down to the engine room.

"Nina, Tyler, get up here!" I shouted into the next tube over.

There were five soldiers on deck already, and I could see more coming. Two more were tangled in *The Indiana*'s cabling, hacking at their own rappelling lines trying to release themselves. David had one of Marie's electroshock devices in one hand and was trying to get close enough to one of the soldiers to use it. Another soldier landed on deck. I lowered my shoulder and ran, using my full body weight to knock him over the side before he could get out of his rig. He was meaty, and heavier than I expected. The impact jarred my shoulder down to my fingertips, but he tumbled over the railing. One of the other soldiers made a grab for me and I ducked, taking out my dagger.

From the corner of my eye I saw Nina sprinting for the pilot's chair with Tyler right behind her. He ran for the emergency release lever at the prow of the ship as Seamus ran for the one at the stern. I knew that when they had line of sight with each other they would depress the linked levers.

I heard their shout and the ship shuddered and jerked as the mooring cables were cut. Two of the soldiers lost their footing. We began to rise in the air, much too fast. A terrible scraping noise filled the air with the sound of rending wood and iron. The repair clanks were still below us, and we hadn't cleared the cradle.

Looking over the side of the ship I could see the release lever some twenty feet below us. Without stopping to think, I grabbed a thick cable, and jumped over the side of *The Indiana*. Wind whistled past my ears as I swung over to the giant clank and released the cradle lever. As the giant arms came down, the ship rose to the upper regions of the massive hangar, leaving me dangling precariously in midair.

Hand over hand, I climbed the cable, my left arm still numb from my earlier encounter. The hangar floor danced crazily below me. The wind from our ascent spun me around in circles; the repair crew's safety net a mere suggestion of gauze as the loose cable swung free.

I struggled over the railing, my fingertips grasping at the smooth wood. There were three soldiers surrounding David and Seamus on deck, none of them looking my direction. I grabbed a belay pin and clubbed the nearest one in the back of the head. He fell like a stone, a surprised expression on his face. My momentary distraction was all that Seamus needed to finish off the soldier in front of him. I could see more soldiers gliding through the air trying to angle their rigs to land on the deck. The soldier attacking David pressed his attack.

With the airship rising quickly, Nina steered us expertly out of the hangar before we hit the roof. I could see the airhoppers the Swiss Guard had used scattered in the air below us.

David stumbled and grabbed the doorframe as the ship rocked. Suddenly looking green he raced for the railing, barely making it before losing the contents of his stomach. We were gaining altitude quickly and my ears popped several times in succession.

"Nina, head for Crete. I don't think we've irritated anyone there yet." The airfield and Palermo fell away, spinning below us into an indiscernible morass of speckled lamplight.

Nina swung the ship, already high in the atmosphere, around without a word.

"Can you keep us hidden from the Palermo airfield? Charles is sure to follow." I rubbed my arms. We had risen quickly and this high up the air was cold and would only get colder.

"I'll keep us high for as long as I can. Too much though and we'll either freeze or suffocate. Can you grab my coat and gloves from below?" Nina asked.

I put on my coat and brought up Nina's coat and gloves as well. Her teeth were chattering by the time I got back. I took over the wheel for a moment while she dressed and warmed her fingers. The rest of the crew was below. "Nina, if they capture us, turn me over right away, and then the rest of you scatter and lay low for a while. There's no reason for the rest of you to suffer my mistakes."

"You know I'm not going to do that, Captain."

"Nina, you will. I don't want to hear any arguments. I will tell them I was acting on my own and you all were just following orders."

"You know the rest of 'em aren't going to go along with that either, right?" She took the wheel back after pulling on her gloves and turning up the fur lining of her hood.

"We're not going to leave you behind to save ourselves. Now if you don't mind, I have a ship to fly."

JACQUELINE

We stayed in the upper atmosphere until we were all so cold, and dizzy from lack of air that we were seeing things that weren't there. As a bet once, Nina had taken us up this high before. It's beautiful up there, and quiet. Even during the brightest point of day you can see the starfield. I had no time to admire the view. We were still rising too fast, and Marie was working to bypass the catalyst pin.

The air was scarce and thin and it was hard to breathe. We all moved slowly and deliberately. I had to hold on to the railings to keep from falling as my head reeled.

Using my spyglass to see if we were being followed, I caught a glimpse of the Vatican ship. They were at a considerably lower altitude, and nearly directly below us. They seemed to be searching for us on the same plane of their flight path.

"Captain, I'm taking us down a thousand feet. Any longer up here and we'll do permanent damage to ourselves. I'll keep us directly above them and out of sight for as long as I can." Nina's lips were blue, and a dusting of frost had formed on her eyebrows and lips.

I nodded, short of breath. "We're going to have to opt for speed. Normally I'd say keep us in their blind spot in the sun, but we can't stay at this altitude. When we hit the warm airstream below us, give us as much speed as you can get. We won't be able to control our altitude reliably until Marie fixes that pin."

As *The Indiana* descended Nina's lips lost the blue tinge, and I could feel my blood start to flow again.

I went below. The rest of the crew, except Marie, was here, gathering what warmth they could. "Niccolò, switch our colors over to the *Bessie Quinn*. We're making for Crete. Tyler and Seamus we need lookouts above – we're opting for speed instead of stealth. Keep an eye on our own blind spot, we don't need any surprises." I took a sip of coffee, wrapping my fingers gratefully around the warm cup and looked at the rest of the crew. "The Vatican ship is below us...

I was cut short by a loud crashing noise and found myself flying across the room. I hit the wall and felt the breath woosh out of my lungs. My head was ringing. The rest of the crew lay in a jumble of moving arms and legs, trying to untangle themselves. I staggered upright and ran up on deck. Nina was slumped over her console, blood dripping from a cut on her cheek.

A motley crew of men swarmed the deck. Their ship, a hulking, weatherworn silhouette in the darkness, lay close against the starboard side of *The Indiana*. They had slammed into us, using grappling hooks on the railing to tie the two ships together. Rovers – pirates, flying the skull and crossbones in black and white.

One of the men leaned over Nina, a belay pin in one hand. Bending, I drew out my boot knife and threw it as hard as I could. It appeared in the middle of his back, and he fell across Nina's body, pushing the steering wheel and causing the ship to lurch.

I shouted: "We're under attack! Rovers!" Pulling out my other dagger, I ran at the nearest pirate, slamming into him with my shoulder. He fell and slid across the deck. My momentum carried me halfway to the railing with him. We were still tilting at an odd angle and I fought my way up to the steering deck and Nina. Tyler, Seamus and the rest of the crew poured out of the hold brandishing what weapons they could find. Niccolò I noticed from the corner of my eye, had armed himself with a kitchen knife and heavy skillet.

On the steering deck, a man with long greasy locks and threadbare clothes was trying to pull his fallen companion off the steering column. The man's belay pin had fallen and rolled towards the stairs of the main deck. I scooped it up and cracked him across the back of the head with it. He stood for a moment, stunned, and then toppled forward. I rolled him out of the way and retrieved my dagger before shoving the dead man off Nina.

The steering wheel, suddenly free of his weight, righted itself, causing the ship to lurch the other way, throwing friend and foe alike to the ground. I hit the communication lever and shouted down to Marie. "Fire the turbines!"

A hulking brute of a man slammed a sword down, cutting the communication tube in half. He chuckled cruelly as I backed away, my two knives crossed in front of me suddenly seeming inadequate.

"You must be the infamous Captain Jac. When I saw your little boat sailing around up here all by itself, I thought to myself, well now, wouldn't that make a pretty little prize. And you with no lookouts posted." He laughed evilly. "It was the easiest thing in the world to come in out of the sun and take you by surprise. And then of course, I get to say I'm the one that took you out. That'll be a nice feather in my cap for sure. Captain Gillian, the Rover who bested Jac. You're a lot smaller than I thought you'd be, to be honest."

I stood up straight and looked at him, eyes full of disdain as my anger bubbled to the surface. "Seriously? That's why you attacked us? I'm in the middle of a high-profile job, I do not have time for this. Get off my ship."

He laughed again. "Or what? You'll kill me? Seems unlikely. I, however, will enjoy killing you quite a bit." He pulled a pistol out of his belt. Lunging, I caught him off guard as he fired his weapon wildly. I didn't manage to do more than slice his belt. His fetid breath made me wrinkle my nose in disgust.

Ugh. Rovers. The scum of the airways. I maneuvered so the railing was at my back. He rushed me, the barrel of his pistol gripped in one hand, swinging it like a club. I kicked him in the stomach, then grabbed his arms and, with foot still planted in his belly, rolled backwards and tossed him over me. He went sailing over the railing, a startled look on his face.

Tyler and Seamus both bravely fended off attackers. Niccolò dodged between the clusters of fighters, hitting people in the kneecaps with his skillet. I could hear Henri shouting, but couldn't see him. Suddenly, a piercing whistle came from the doorway to the hold. Everyone looked up as two silver spheres came rolling out on deck. Seamus and Niccolò dove to the deck and covered their heads with their arms. Tyler ducked behind an overturned barrel. Our attackers looked on bewildered, with the smarter ones taking cues from the crew and ducking. The spheres began spinning, shooting needles out in all directions.

One of the pirates plucked a needle out of his arm, holding it up and chuckling. "You thought to stop us with these tiny splinters?" He laughed. Then, looking surprised he slowly fell forward on his face. I winced to see it; he did not fall lightly.

One by one the other pirates fell, landing heavily on the deck. Only two had avoided the fate of their companions and quickly surrendered. Tyler and Seamus tied both their hands.

I pointed my dagger at one of the conscious men. "You. What's your name?"

"D..d... Daron," the man stuttered out.

I pointed to the hulking shape off our starboard side, the *grand poche* looming above ours, casting shade across the entire deck. The paint on the side said *Dreadnought*. Its *grand poche* was mottled in hues of dark blue, dirty white and various shades of grey, and the scarring on the hull showed it had survived many engagements.

"How many men still aboard your ship?"

"Only two others. The ship's boy and the pilot."

I nodded, putting the point of my dagger under his chin. "Who do you work for? How did you know about us?"

Daron's face turned pale, "I… I don't know. The Captain – he knows those things, not me."

I pressed the dagger more firmly, the point drawing a slow trickle of blood. "Who. Do. You. Work. For."

"I swear lady – I swear I don't know. We… the crew I mean, we didn't want to attack. The Captain insisted."

"We're going over there. You're coming with us. If you're lying, you'll be the first to die. I will personally see to that."

He paled slightly but nodded. I continued, "I'm not looking to kill anyone else, nor do I have any desire to take your ship. We're going to disable it so you don't take it into your head to follow us. If you and your two crew members over there cooperate, then that's how it will go. If you don't cooperate, then we'll kill you all and scuttle the ship. Understand?"

His eyes widened in panic. "I'll make sure they cooperate, ma'am."

"Good. Tyler, Seamus, come with me." I saw David standing in the doorway leading down to the hold, looking lost. "David, help Henri with Nina if you would." I freed Daron's hands. "We're going to swing over."

Marie began deploying the extendable gangplank, cranking the large lever. I backed over to where our prisoner was standing and took hold of the rope. "You first." I nodded in the direction of the *Dreadnought*.

He took a deep breath, grabbed the rope and swung across the dizzying space. I landed moments after he did. "Luma, Marco? Where are you?" Daron called out. I heard the click of a pistol behind me.

"Luma, don't!" Daron shouted. This woman he called Luma was a pale woman with filthy black hair and a well-worn pistol. Tyler and Seamus swung over, landing behind her, pistols out.

"If you want your crew members back alive, stay out of our way, and we will be gone in short order." She spat in my face. I sighed and shrugged wiping spittle from my cheek. "Tyler, if you please."

Tyler reversed his grip on his pistol and hit her in the back of the head. I caught her as she slumped forward and eased her down onto the deck, taking the pistol away. I was surprised to see that it wasn't loaded. Marie had extended the gangplank and joined us. "Marie, you and I will disable the ship. Maybe you can find that catalyst pin you need. Tyler, you and Seamus work with Daron to get the crew back over here." I looked over at Daron.

"Help them move the bodies over." Daron, still pale and sweating, nodded fervently.

"Which way to the engine room?" I asked before releasing him into Tyler's custody.

He pointed below decks and stammered. "Down below... All the way to the stern."

Marie and I set off below decks. Most airships had at least a few similarities, and the location of the engine room was one of those. They tended to be at the back of the ship so that smoke didn't blow across the deck.

Once in the hold, I pointed out several devices that looked like they should be deployed through the hull. "Are those what I think they are?"

"Lightning cannons!" Marie said excitedly. She ran her hands over one of them, fingering the delicate levers, and copper wiring.

"Captain, do you think we could take just one." A strange lust filled Marie's eyes.

"Marie, we're in a hurry. The *Raven* isn't far behind us."

"Yes, but Captain, a lightning cannon."

"Fine. Let's disable the engine, then take one of these." I gestured down the hallway to the engine room.

"This is a beautiful machine," Marie said, marveling at the great set of chrome and bronze pistons and cogs before her. A giant central shaft spun slowly, powering multiple smaller shafts within the structure. "It seems a shame to have to damage it." Marie took a wrench off her belt and began unscrewing bolts from several long pieces of pipe. She then pulled a lever and jammed it into place, breaking the handle off at its base. Reaching between two large gears she freed a long metal pin with square spokes at different intervals.

"That should about do it, Captain. They'll have a very hard time steering without a steering column. They'll do nothing but go in circles for a long while. And once they figured that out, someone has to replace all of the bolts." She had a smug look on her face. "And we now have our catalyst pin.

I clapped her on the back. "Good. And now let's get that lightning cannon."

The cannon was heavy and bolted to the floor on a rail that allowed it to slide out the gun port. But with a spanner and some determination, we managed to drag it inelegantly up to the deck, where Tyler, Seamus, and Daron had just finished bringing the *Dreadnought*'s crew back over.

I nodded to Daron. "They should all wake up in a few hours. I don't ever want to see your ugly face again." From the fear in his eyes I could tell this was a warning he would heed.

We dragged the lightning cannon back across the gangplank and disengaged from the *Dreadnought*. Henri was tending to Nina when we got back. She had a large bruise covering half her face. "How long until she wakes?"

Henri shook his head. "I'm not sure."

"Let me know as soon as she is up. In the meantime, I'll be at the wheel."

Our course and heading were still laid in. I called down to Marie. "Fire her up, let's get underway."

Slowly we pulled away from the derelict Rover's vessel and headed to Crete.

An hour later Tyler joined me on the steering deck. "Do you think the *Dreadnought* will follow us, Captain?" He leaned on the railing while he stared out at the vast ocean below us.

"Not if they're smart." I was more worried for Nina and concerned that Charles might locate us. I was kicking myself for not having posted a watch earlier – the *Dreadnought* used the same tactics we had, flying in out of the sun in our blind spot, and I *knew* better. There had been no sign of the *Blue Raven* but he was out there. The *Dreadnought*, barring Nina's injury, was an inconvenience, no more.

CHARLES

Damn the woman, Charles though. She kept slipping through his fingers. First the storm, then evading the guards at *The Flaming Mug*, then throwing off their attack at the airfield. Assuming he was correct about her identity he was seeing that her reputation was deserved. She was not some flutter headed noble. He also had no idea where she might head next and cursed the guards that let her get away.

Pulling out a map, Charles studied the available options. *The Indiana* had seen significant damage during the storm, he had noted as much when they boarded her. She wouldn't be going far, and that limited the options dramatically. Three small islands on the map seemed likely, but they were in opposite directions. Two of the islands were within a day's sailing distance, and the third, nearly a two-day journey. He slammed his fist onto the table next to the map, gritting his teeth in frustration. "Where are you going, Jac?" he muttered staring at the map. He didn't want to face the men above without a plan so he paced his quarters, coming back to stare at the three small islands. But which one? He didn't have enough men with him to search all three, and every moment he hesitated *The Indiana* got further away.

"Captain!" Charles recognized the first mate's voice as the man pounded on the door to his quarters. "Captain, you need to come out and see this." Charles emerged from his quarters and joined Yusef on deck.

Two guards had a dirty, scruffy looking man restrained between them. "Sir, please. Can you help us?"

Yusef handed Charles a spyglass and pointed to the southwest. "I've been watching that ship for the past half an hour Captain, and it does nothing but go in circles. This man tried to board us using a nearly derelict airhopper."

Charles studied the ship. *Dreadnought*. The ship was in poor shape and at a glance probably belonged to that class of pirate called Rovers – men and women without a code that preyed on the upper airways and ships that ventured outside of established routes. The deck was deserted, and the ship circled aimlessly. The man must be in dire straits to try and board the *Blue Raven*.

"Is that your ship, man?" Charles asked.

"Aye, sir. Well – the Captain's dead. The rest of the crew have been drugged, and the ship's been disabled. We need help sir, please." The scruffy man looked frightened. Unusual. Rovers were known to be cutthroat and merciless.

"How did this happen?" Charles asked, facing the man.

"We. Ah."

Charles could see that the man was trying to come up with a lie and hadn't thought this through in advance.

"Speak up, man. We are on a mission from Rome and cannot afford much delay. Let me help you – you were clearly defeated in battle. Who were you fighting?"

The man slumped. "*The Indiana* disabled us. The crew – our crew – didn't want to fight them, but our Captain insisted. He's dead now."

"Today is your lucky day then sir. I am not going to arrest you for piracy, if you tell us which direction they went." Charles said. "Though I suggest you reconsider your life choices."

The scruffy looking Rover pointed out a heading. Charles smiled in satisfaction. God was on his side and had provided a direction. He knew which way Jac had gone.

"Thank you. Yusef, please put this man back on his airhopper with some food and basic medical supplies. I'm afraid they'll have to figure out their mechanical problems themselves."

Summoning the crew Charles said, "Men! We have thus far failed to capture this notorious felon, despite circumstances being in our favor on several occasions. I think some extra incentive is in order." Charles paced the deck in front of the assembled men.

"I believe they are headed to Crete. Given the extensive damage that their ship has taken, they cannot have flown further than that. Divide up into three Squadrons to cover more of the island. The crew that finds *The Indiana*, or its captain will be rewarded well. The crew that captures *The Indiana* or its captain will understand what the full generosity of Rome means."

Pausing he said, "Squad leaders prepare your men and your ships, then meet in my quarters. Dismissed."

JACQUELINE

Early the next morning we could see the coastline of Crete, with massive cliffs along a rocky shore. Small towns dotted the coastline, shining white in the shimmering heat, tucked back into the cliffs, sheltered by white sand beaches. We sailed high, looking for a secluded cove to put in at, preferably one with a small creek or river for water.

Marie caught me right after breakfast. "Maybe it would be okay if we took a few days away from the ship?" Marie asked a hint of longing in her voice.

"Maybe," I replied, focused on the coastline. "Let's see what we find when we get there."

She nodded and sighed, turning her gaze to the shore.

I could see that the crew needed to rest. We had been running thin for too long, and they were exhausted. They were starting to make small mistakes, letting things slip that shouldn't.

We landed near the city of Xaviá and found a quiet cove not far from the city. The fine sandy beach surrounded by the deep blue waters of the Mediterranean was peaceful.

"Marie, deploy the canopy balloons. Let's see if we can change our profile from a distance" The balloons were the best I could think of. They held up a large netting that covered the entire ship, making it hard to distinguish our features. The balloons and netting were inconvenient and required the entire crew to deploy. Once the netting was in place we set up a small camp with a fire pit and spent the afternoon sunning and swimming.

David sat next to me on the sand, not saying much, just twirling a lock of my hair in his fingers. I twitched, restless. I felt like a sitting duck, waiting for Charles to find us. "Jac, I can see as well as you that the crew needs time to rest." David had the knack of reading my thoughts on occasion.

"I know. And we have to repair the ship, and this is as secluded a spot as I could find that would allow us to do so. I still feel like we have a giant target painted on us, and it makes me twitch."

David rubbed my shoulders and neck, kneading out the knots that formed there. "You've taken all the precautions you can."

For the next three days we worked on the ship and didn't see anyone except a couple of local fishermen out on their small boats hunting for crabs.

Once the repairs were completed, I told Marie she could take the few days leave she had requested. She took the second airhopper and left for the city, a smile on her face. To my surprise, she did not ask Henri to accompany her.

Propping my cabin door open to catch a breeze, I pulled down *A History of Angels,* a book on Church legend and lore and started reading. The author had a talent for making even the most interesting subject matter dry, and my mind kept wandering away from the pages. I found I had to drag my attention back, and after the fourth time I found myself staring off into space, I put the book down with disgust. I did not enjoy being earthbound.

I caught sight of Nina walking out on deck, and with sudden resolution I called out, "Nina! How would you feel about going a few rounds? I haven't sparred in far too long." Her face was turning motley colors from the bruise, but she seemed to be feeling better.

Nina stuck her head in the cabin door. "It's been a while," she replied. "On deck, five minutes?"

Nodding I took off my jacket and set it aside neatly, going out to join her. Nina stood and stretched, then with no warning came at me with a flying roundhouse kick. This was not my first time sparring with Nina, so I ducked and caught her leg midair. "You shouldn't lead with that every time."

She laughed and wrapped her other leg around me as she was falling, taking me to the deck with her. "You talk too much, Captain."

We sparred for the better part of an hour, until we were both dripping in sweat and exhausted. Niccolò came to watch, as did David, and Seamus. After letting us wear ourselves out, Seamus began instructing and correcting our form. When I could barely lift my arms for another round Seamus called a halt.

"I wish I could get you two to practice like this several times a week, but your form is still looking pretty good. You two go wash up, Niccolò and I will get dinner."

I laughed and turned to Nina. "Do you think it will be safe to eat?"

She chuckled as we made our way to the bathing room. There was a small hole in the floor to let water escape, but that same hole also created an unpleasant draft when it was chilly out. I dipped the clean cloth in the barrel and sponged myself off quickly, then rubbed myself dry with another towel, feeling refreshed after our exertions.

Stumbling with weariness I wrapped the towel around me, gathered up my sweaty clothes and made my way back to my cabin.

"Jac, I need to go into town and purchase some parts for some new modifications I'm designing. Would you like to join me?" David asked over breakfast on the beach the following morning.

"Oh good. I need to get some parts for the ship as well. I would love to join you. I'm hoping we have all of the repairs done by tomorrow." I had a few things on my mind. There were so many unanswered threads to this tangle we found ourselves in. Whether it was pacing or walking, I always thought better on my feet, and though I didn't want to say this to the crew, the fact that the Vatican ship hadn't located us was bothering me. Crete was remote, but we were not that well-hidden.

"Fantastic." David sat up leaning on one elbow from his place in the sand, his bare chest gleaming in the sun.

"Town isn't far." I stretched and drew my hair above my neck, letting the breeze play with the small curls that escaped.

"Give me a moment to fetch a clean shirt."

I watched him walk across the sand towards the ship, admiring his tall form. He was getting a tan from being underway with us, and it suited him.

We strolled along the road leading to town hand-in-hand, occasionally passing locals carrying their shopping or taking their goods to the market. For a time we walked in silence, enjoying the scenery and the quiet company. Occasionally David would watch me from the corner of his eye, thinking I didn't notice.

Finally I said, "I wonder if the lore surrounding the Miter is true, and it is something powerful enough to destroy the church. If it is, that presents the question of what to do with the knowledge." I ran my free hand through my hair, pondering the possibilities.

"It will be a hard decision to make. The church is corrupt and full of deceit within its ranks, but in the parishes many of the priests still do good works, and that cannot be wholly discounted." David stared off into the distance, thinking.

"So is it better to save the church for the good it does, or destroy the church for the evil within it? Or alternately give the power to someone else to use as leverage." I took a deep breath, a strange tightness in my chest. "Beyond the theoretical, we have the more pressing problem of what to do about the Vatican pursuit. Charles, their commander, is not stupid, and he is tenacious. I anticipate he will find us."

"Yes, that seems likely," David agreed, keeping pace with me.

"If we continue to run, he will just keep following us. That becomes our life – always running – until eventually no port in Europe or the Americas is open to us. I do not relish that thought."

We reached the outskirts of town. Xaviá was a mid-sized town with several shop-lined streets. All of the roads met in the center, forming the town square, where a daily market held vendor stalls full of dates and olives, and a variety of other fruits and vegetables. Today they were having a small festival. There was a cheese maker, places to buy ribbons and bolts of fabric, and many other things from the useful and mundane to the fancy and impractical.

"Perfect!" David said, as he saw the market. "I was hoping to lure you away from the ship. You force your crew to rest, but never take any time yourself." I looked up at him, startled, and he chuckled.

"Do you think I didn't notice why we've been here so long. They are loyal to you, and you take care of them, even when they won't take care of themselves. Someone must do the same for you, my dear."

I flushed. "But I don't need–" I trailed off. I had also been making mistakes. Underestimating Charles, the encounter with the Rovers, a multitude of other small things. David was right. He raised an eyebrow and I lifted my hands in surrender. "Okay, you are right."

He smiled. "Very well then. You will allow me to buy you lunch, and perhaps some ribbons for your hair, and we will enjoy the morning in the market. Then we will get the supplies and head back."

I bowed my head in mock acquiescence. "You win this round, *mon chéri*."

David and I continued our discussion of the church as we walked, examining the booths and stalls. "Do you think the information could be used simply to remove those in the church who crave power and wealth rather than the good of the people?" he asked, returning to the earlier conversation.

I pondered this question for a few minutes. "I'm afraid without knowing the nature of the message, it is impossible to determine." I picked up a blue ribbon from a ribbon seller and held it up for David's inspection. "What think you? Will it go with my hat?"

"I think it's lovely." David held out a few coins for the vendor. I chuckled and smiled and kissed him on the cheek.

"Thank you, *mon chéri*."

Suddenly someone grabbed me from behind. My elbows were pinned together by strong hands. I was whirled around and wrestled up against the wall, my face pressed against the rough stone surface. Reacting on instinct I stamped down with the hard heel of my boot on the instep of my assailant. I felt a satisfying crunch and the man cursed and loosened his grip. I hooked my right foot behind his knee and threw my entire bodyweight backwards, overbalancing him and landing on his sternum with my elbow. I punched him in the crotch before rolling off and coming up in a low crouch. The man was wearing blue and gold, curled up in a fetal position, gasping for breath. Three men had grabbed David. I slid my boot dagger out of its sheath as one hit David across the back of the head with a small club. Before I could see more, rough hands wrestled me back and someone pulled a sack down over my head and cinched it closed. I reversed my dagger and stabbed backwards and up and was rewarded by a yelp of pain. "She's a wildcat this one! A little help over here," a male voice behind me shouted.

I still had hold of my dagger but couldn't see with the sack on my head. It smelled strongly of onions, and blocked out the light. Trying to claw it free with one hand, I waved the dagger in front of me. Someone kicked me in the back of the knee and I went down, rolling on my shoulder. I felt my dagger connect, but not hard enough to do any real damage. "Grab her arm, get that fucking knife away from her."

I felt a booted foot step on my forearm and someone grabbed my arm on the other side, holding it extended so that I couldn't move. A sharp blow to my wrist made my hand go numb and I felt my fingers loosening on the dagger. "Tie her up. Make sure she's secure."

I screamed when I felt myself picked up and thrown roughly over someone's shoulder, anything to draw attention. "Help!" I shouted.

My assailant, this one at least, was wearing body armor, and his shoulder digging into my diaphragm knocked the wind out of me. I kicked and struggled, mostly bruising my knees and elbows. I heard someone in the marketplace scream. And a loud voice ordering people out of the way. "We're here on Rome's business, and this is a wanted criminal. She is quite dangerous. Do not interfere."

Closer to my ear, I heard, "Oy, you settle down you, or I'll have to be rough with you."

"You put me down, or I'll see to it you die." I gasped as his armored shoulder drove into my stomach again.

The man laughed. "That's not very likely. Now you just be still until we get where we're going. I've got someone who very much wants to talk to you." He patted my backside, holding me securely, chuckling at my attempts to escape. Fury coursed through me, and my face flamed with heat.

It wasn't long before we left the noises of the marketplace behind. I continued to struggle, forcing him to move me from shoulder to shoulder while I tried to wrench my arms free so that I could reach the dagger at his waist when someone hit me in the back of the head, and everything went dark.

JACQUELINE

I woke up feeling sick, head throbbing. I was lying on my side on a hard, wooden surface. My hands were bound together, burlap pressed close around my face.

Light filtered dimly through the loosely woven sack, but I couldn't tell much about my surroundings. The faint, solitary light source suggested a vast space in the resultant darkness.

The bindings around my wrists were thin and strong. Picking at them, there didn't seem to be anything to unravel. Flexing my arms and wrists I tried to break the thin line but only forced the bindings to cut into my wrists.

Sounds were muffled by the sack, but I didn't hear anyone nearby. I rose to my feet, feeling woozy and off-balance. The world spun, but I planted my feet solidly and willed it to stop. That only seemed to make things spin faster and my feet collapsed under me.

"*Merde.*" I swore softly. "David? Are you here?" There was no answer. My voice echoed eerily in the space, and with each passing moment my fury grew. I replayed the scene in the marketplace, but I hadn't gotten a good look at the men who grabbed us, just the impression of blue and gold. I had no idea if they had killed David, taken him as well, or left him unconscious in the middle of the market.

Anger coiled in my stomach and stayed there. I tried standing again and was rewarded with a strong desire to throw up. My head continued to pound, and my mouth felt fuzzy and dry. I inched one foot in front of the other, sweating with the effort of remaining standing as the room spun. Ever so slowly I drew a map of the cell in my head. It was approximately six feet wide by eight feet long, and there were no walls. Just bars. Hence the feeling of space. There was a slight sway, a familiar back and forth. I was in a cage in the hold of an airship.

I sat down in the center of the cell and closed my eyes, gathering my strength and formulating a plan for whatever came next.

Hours later I heard footsteps and tensed. My hands had gone numb from lack of circulation and at some point, I had dozed off. I inched myself back to the back of the cell, whimpering and cringing, pretending to be more hurt than I was. The guard chuckled. "Not so tough now, are you," he said as I heard the cell door open. When I felt his breath on my face, I bashed my head forward, feeling the satisfying crunch of his nose. Cursing, he backed up.

I felt hands grab me through the bars and an arm snaked around my neck tightly cutting off air. Gasping for air, blackness filled my vision.

"She's a feisty one," a deep male voice said as I heard him enter the cell.

"Well what would you expect from someone with her reputation?" another male voice, higher this time, replied. "Here, this will quiet her down."

That was all the warning I got before one of them drove his fist into my stomach. It was unexpected, and I gasped in pain. The arm choking me let go and I slid down the bars. Tears leaked from my eyes as I tried not to throw up, gasping and choking. A booted foot kicked me, and I cried out.

"Here now. Enough. She still has to be able to speak when we take her up," the first voice said, cautioning the other man.

He grunted and grabbed the back of my shirt, standing me on my feet. I started to collapse again, and he caught me by the back of the shirt. "On your feet! I'm not going to carry you."

They stood me up between the two of them and marched me out of the cell. I still couldn't see, and tripped and stumbled. "Stairs," one of them said as I banged my shin and pitched forward onto the staircase.

He sighed and grabbed me by the back of the shirt, pulling me up. "Come on. Up."

It wasn't a very long staircase. At the top I could feel a strong wind on my face, and through the fine mesh of the bag I could see a small patch of blue sky. Based on the sounds, the wind, and the sound of machinery I guessed my earlier assessment was correct. We were on an airship, and we were underway.

They turned and marched me through a doorway. We walked a few feet in, and one of the guards put a hand on my shoulder and pushed me roughly down into a chair.

"Sir. You were right, they were holed up on one of the islands. The *Dreadnought* pointed us truly, and your plan went near perfectly. While in town we managed to apprehend the notorious Captain of the airship *Indiana*, Captain Jac."

"Nearly perfectly?" I heard the note of inquiry in an all too familiar voice. The guards relayed our encounter in brief, noting that I had injured one of their men, and that they had left the man accompanying me unconscious and bleeding in the marketplace. Relief and anger both suffused me. David had been alive when they left him but leaving the *Dreadnought* in one piece had given us away.

"Ah, very well, thank you. You have done well. I'll see to your reward. You are dismissed."

"Sir, are you certain you want us to leave? She just broke Jonathan's nose, and Sergei had to forcibly restrain her just to get her out of the cell."

"Thank you for letting me know. I will take precautions. You may go," Charles said.

"Thank you, sir!" Their response was crisp and formal, and I imagined them clicking their heels together and saluting behind me before turning to go. I heard the click of the latch on the door, and the onion sack was suddenly removed. Taking a deep breath, I found myself blinking and staring into the angry golden eyes of Charles, Captain of the Pope's personal guard. "You disappoint me, Contessa."

Merde. He knows who I am.

"Captain Jac." He stared at me for a long moment. "Also known as Contessa Jacqueline de Valois, whom I have met on several occasions." He sighed and looked less pleased than I expected, given that he'd been trying to capture me for nearly a month.

"I had hoped it wasn't true, but I see fate wishes me to suffer for my hubris."

His last remark made no sense to me, so I chose to ignore it. As the Contessa, Charles and I had spent time pleasantly, so I chose to approach from that direction, fluttering my eyelashes at him appealingly and raising my voice to a slightly higher, more feminine pitch. "Charles, it is so nice to see you again, though the circumstances are not what I would prefer. Perhaps you might loosen these ties? They do cut cruelly tight."

I kept my tone even and leaned forward, indicating my bound hands. They were swollen and bloody, my fingers discolored from lack of circulation. Charles blanched and gasped in horror. I felt a knife slide between my hands and the bindings. The bonds snapped and I slumped forward, coughing. I still couldn't feel my hands. Everything below the wrist felt numb and wooden. Charles strode to the door and opened it, speaking to someone outside.

"Get the surgeon in here immediately," he snapped. A murmured reply was all I could hear.

"You are a prisoner, but I will treat you as the noblewoman you pretend to be. For the moment. What other damage have you suffered?" It pained him to ask, I could see that. He wasn't sure then, if I was a noblewoman or a privateer, and he wanted to cover all contingencies. I could use that.

"Bruises, a cracked rib, an awful headache and..." I held my hands out for display.

Charles winced to see them. "Notorious Captain or not, they should not treat a woman in custody this way. Where is that surgeon?" he muttered fervently.

The man in question appeared shortly thereafter. "You called for me, sir?"

"Please treat the Contessa and examine her thoroughly. Her hands in particular need attention, also she has taken a blow to the temple and perhaps more. She is a prisoner, but to be treated as one of noble birth."

"Aye, sir." The surgeon nodded. He stood there, waiting and Charles looked at him askance.

"What are you waiting for?"

"Sir. The lady will want some privacy for this examination," the surgeon said.

Charles looked pained. "I think not. She has already proven that she can dispatch trained guards, Simon. I'm afraid it would not be safe for you, noblewoman or not."

"Charles," I said, looking up at him through lowered lashes. "I'm on your airship, surrounded by your men. Where could I go?"

He ignored me. "Two guards. Examine her. Report to me when you are done."

Charles stepped out of the room and sent two men in. I heard the click of the lock as a key was turned. From the rigid correctness and squared shoulders of his back I could tell he was angry.

Simon worked efficiently, ignoring the two guards. He cleaned the wounds on my wrists and examining my fingers. Circulation was starting to return, and it felt like a thousand tiny pins were pricking my skin. Looking at my ribs he declared them bruised but not broken and wrapped them tightly.

"Your fingers will be fine, but they're going to hurt quite a bit as the circulation returns. Give it a day or so, and you should have full mobility back." He poured something in s small glass and handed it to me.

"Here, drink this. It will help with the discomfort."

I looked at the glass askance, holding it lightly in my tingling hand. Bringing it to my nose I smelled nothing but fine brandy.

"Drink it, or don't. It makes very little difference to me," Simon said with some impatience.

I nodded and drank it down. "Thank you, *Monsieur,* for your kindness."

"I do you no kindness, merely what my oath demands," he replied. I felt neither animosity nor liking in his reply, only a statement of fact as he saw it.

JACQUELINE

Jacqueline,

Despite these unfortunate circumstances, it is my hope you will consider joining me for dinner this evening in my cabin. I wish to hear your story. One of the crew will come to collect you at seven o'clock.

Charles

I took the time to try and make myself more presentable. I let down my hair and brushed it out with a brush I found in the small bureau. In the scuffle, I had lost a number of my jeweled hairpins, but found that I had three remaining. And one of them held a dose of Henri's sleeping serum.

Beyond straightening my clothes and redoing my hair there wasn't much I could do about my appearance. Examining myself in the mirror I winced at the dark, purpling bruise on my temple.

Simon, the surgeon, tapped politely on my door before entering. Two guards accompanied us to Charles's cabin. His room, much like mine on *The Indiana*, was built both for function and for the entertainment of guests. He had a small dining table set up with two place settings, and was standing behind one chair, ready to pull it out for me.

"Jacqueline, I'm so glad you could join me. Please, have a seat." There was no sarcasm or mocking in his voice, just controlled courtesy. Charles gestured to the chair and pulled it out slightly. I could see his anger under the surface, held tightly in check.

A roast chicken sat in the center of the table, with a bottle of wine and a small plate of seasoned vegetables. The smell of fresh bread wafted over everything. I ignored the proffered seat, standing in the center of the room until Simon had withdrawn.

"Where are you taking me?" I asked, in my Contessa voice, higher pitched and younger sounding than I was wont to use in most circumstances. I was certain I knew the answer already.

"Should I call you Captain Jac, or Contessa Jacqueline?" he countered, and I could see the hurt in his eyes. He strode across the few feet that separated us, standing just within arm's reach he stroked my cheek with a gentle finger. "I so wanted to believe that you were just the little Contessa who liked books, that I had the pleasure of helping." He hardened his voice and his eyes changed in the light from yellow to a deep golden and back again. "Truth, however slow I may be in discovering it, will out."

I dropped my voice back down to its normal tone. "Would my claiming one or the other change how you feel about me?" I replied.

His eyes hardened, and he leaned in close, gripping my shoulders. "Which is it? Which do you claim as truth?"

"The truth, just for you my dear Charles, is that they are both true, and sometimes even I don't know where one starts and the other ends. You had surmised as much. I am the Contessa Jacqueline de Valois. I am also the Captain of *The Indiana*. I'm not sure where the notorious criminal reputation came from, we are an honest crew, but there you have it."

He pushed me away and made a frustrated noise in the back of his throat. "Sit. Eat." He gestured to the seat he had been holding when I came in.

I took the proffered seat, allowing him to guide it back under the table. "I am not as you expected. I will not apologize for that." I looked over the small feast set out before us. "To what do I owe the pleasure of tonight's invitation?"

"Jacqueline," he paused. "Or should I call you Jac?"

"Either is fine. It isn't as if it matters." The words came out more callously than intended, and I flinched, hearing my own harshness.

He looked at me sadly. "Although I must hold you prisoner until we reach Rome, I see no need to treat you below your status." Charles took the seat across from me and held up a bottle of wine, offering to pour. "I would also like hearing your story. We have enough evidence that you will stand trial for theft of the Pope's Miter, but I cannot imagine how a noblewoman ended up here."

"I should like to see this evidence that you say you have, since I haven't the faintest idea what you're talking about. Theft of what?"

"There are too many coincidences surrounding you and your crew and the theft. But let us not talk of that now," he replied. "I wish to know your story."

He was right of course, insofar as he knew. And my story was not the usual one for a noblewoman. I hadn't tried the coded sequence on my arm to summon *The Inara* yet. I needed to walk on deck, preferably without supervision for that. Feeding his curiosity seemed like the best option.

I held my glass up for him and watched the crimson liquid fill the goblet slowly as he poured. "How long will it take us to get to Rome?" I asked setting my glass down gently.

"I expect about two weeks. We shall have plenty of time to get to know one another." He bowed his head briefly, uttering a simple thanks for our meal before carving slices of chicken and passing the serving tray over. He carefully kept the carving knife at his end of the table. "I'm afraid we don't have any dresses on board, or other appropriate women's clothing."

"Since what I am wearing is my normal attire, then it will do just fine, thank you very much," I replied, giving him an exasperated look. I served myself a small portion from the dishes as they came around.

We sat for a moment in silence. He did not take the bait for an argument that I was long familiar with.

"Tell me Charles," I asked finally, "how did you get to be the Captain of the Guard at the Vatican? The Captain of the Pope's personal guard no less? You seem very young for a position of such responsibility." I needed to know more about this man. I had underestimated him once and was careless. Anything I could learn would be of use.

He looked at me suspiciously, scowling. "The better question is how a woman of noble birth becomes an airship Captain and notorious pirate. You puzzle me, Jacqueline. Why would you leave behind money and comfort to live a life of crime and hardship, never having a place to call home?"

I chuckled. "Spoken like someone who was never forced to do needlework and equally useless tasks because it looks good for prospective husbands." I took a bite of the chicken. It was savory, and his cook had done an excellent job. The meat melted in my mouth, and I sighed in appreciation.

"While noblemen have many options open to them, noble women are expected to marry, bear children, and see to the oversight of the perfect home." There was bitterness in my words. But not so much now as there had been right after my father died.

Charles looked up, startled at my tone. "But that's what all women want, is it not? Is it so bad, children, a home?"

"If that is what you want in life then of course not. Children and family can be very fulfilling for some women.

But if you want something different, something more, only to be told constantly that you may not have it because it is not ladylike, or not appropriate leads to sheer misery." I took a sip of my wine. "But that's not actually my story. It could've been, but I took a different route to get here."

Charles looked intrigued at this. I sat back in my chair toying with my glass of wine, watching as he studied me. "Now tell me something about you. How did you get here?"

He smiled, shaking his head. "It's a simple enough story. Born in Italy to a merchant family. My parents were very religious and insistent upon a good education, when all I wanted was to go out for the guard. The more they pushed me to books, the more I ran for the training grounds. When I was of age, I ran away and joined a mercenary company and discovered I had a true talent for both pistol and swordwork. We were on campaign for some noble or another when I came across the Swiss Guard. When my contract with the mercenary company was up, they recruited me. I moved up quickly through their ranks." He paused to take a bite of chicken.

"I'm sure my parents would be most amused to discover that the Swiss Guard values education as much as they did. Many of the members are themselves priests or lay brothers of some of the more militant orders within the church."

I raised an eyebrow, tucking the tidbit of information away. "And you? Are you a priest, doomed to celibacy, or have you taken a more secular route?"

He looked up, amused, surprised at the forwardness of my question. "I have taken no vow of celibacy. I choose to serve our Lord through the strength of my arm rather than locked away in a cloister. Though, as you say, there is no shame in either. Now, I have been most open with my history. Please, share your own."

I took a moment, pausing to compose my thoughts before answering. "You know bits and pieces of it already. I am the second daughter of the Count de Valois. My sister died under somewhat mysterious circumstances. The family believed it to be murder, but we were not able to determine who orchestrated her supposed accident. My father was killed on his way to Paris to entreat the king to open an investigation. As the remaining heir, the title fell to me. I was much more interested in my mechanic's shop and flying than I was in finding a husband or running an estate, so after two years of trying to do both I appointed a steward and ran away to join the English Air Corps."

Charles snorted with disgust. "The English?"

"The English, with their history of strong queens, take a much more liberal view of what women are capable of." Taking a sip of wine, I stared into the glass, remembering.

"When my time there was done, I put together a crew and bought a ship. And that's about all there is to it." I did not share how close a relation I was to the king. If Charles knew the French monarchy at all, he would know, and if he did not, then there was no need for me to tell him.

THE CREW

"We need to go in now and get her," Nina shouted, thumping her fist on the table.

"And just how do you propose we do that? It's a suicide mission," Seamus shouted back. "She's surrounded by an entire squadron of Swiss Guard, in the middle of a flotilla for all we know!"

"She'd come get any one of us." Nina glared across at Seamus.

Seamus pounded his fist against the table. "She wouldn't be stupid about it though. And I've a mind to live, thank you very much. An all-out assault is not the answer."

Tyler watched the crew, sitting back in his chair, listening and thinking.

"She's definitely not within range of the tracker the moment," Marie said, in a much calmer tone. "If we can at least get within a mile of her she can call *The Inara*. But it's not like that's a stealthy option. They'd hear the engine coming and be ready."

"We also don't know if she's injured. She's bound to be under heavy guard. Even if she can get on deck, she's probably not in a position where she could call *The Inara*. And Marie's right. The noise of the engine would alert them before she could get away," Henri said.

Marie looked startled, having not expected help from that quarter.

David was propped up against a cushion in the corner of the room, face and arms covered in bruises and cuts. "What if we sneak *The Inara* to a point near the *Blue Raven* and signal her. Or send in just one or two people to get her out," David offered, worry written large on his face.

"I'm telling you it's a suicide mission to go after her. We go in guns blazing and we'll get mowed down, we go in stealthy and we'll get caught," Seamus said again.

"I'm not leaving her in their hands." Nina shot Seamus an angry look. "They'll take her straight to the gallows as soon as they arrive in Rome."

"No." Niccolò was pale and scared, but he stood up. "No. They will only take her to the gallows if she lives that long. Prisoners die in transport all the time. We must rescue her before they arrive in Rome or we have no hope."

Tyler took a deep breath. Leadership did not come easy to him, but he had learned from watching Jac. He had to keep the crew together, and he had to keep them pointed in the right direction. Standing up he said, "I have an idea. Let's use all of your suggestions."

Five pairs of eyes turned to look at Tyler with incredulity. "All of them?" Nina asked.

Tyler nodded. "Listen and tell me what you think. It's crazy, but so are we. I think we can pull this off."

Grabbing a handful of tokens used for planning heists, Tyler laid out his plan. If there was cloud cover in late in the afternoon *The Indiana* would hide behind the clouds and Marie would spark the steel cables protecting ship from lightning in a sequence, hopefully alerting Jac to their presence. Marie, Henri, Tyler and David would man *The Indiana* for a frontal assault, while Seaums and Niccolò worked to tether *The Inara* to the bottom of the *Blue Raven*. Nina would sneak onboard to release the Captain. If she was successful, they would re-call *The Inara* to the ship without issue. If she was not, they would signal the Captain that *The*

Inara was nearby and hope that the Captain could formulate a plan for her own escape.

Seamus nodded. "Seems workable, but folks attacking from *The Indiana* need to bail quickly. It wouldn't do to get the ship captured."

Nina looked down at the strategy board impressed. "Not bad, Tyler. I didn't know you had it in you."

He nodded in acknowledgement. "Let's go get the Captain."

JACQUELINE

Charles would try and surprise me with questions about the Miter, trying to get me to confess, or tell him something that I shouldn't know. I in turn, questioned him, trying to discover where his loyalties lay – with the Pope, or with the Church. And did he equate the one with the other.

After the thousandth question about why I had stolen the Miter I said, "Charles. I did not steal the Miter, but supposing I had, how would you suggest I make amends and still retain my freedom and that of my crew? Hypothetically speaking, of course."

He looked nonplused. "What do you mean?"

"It seems unlikely that if I had, as you have suggested, stolen this object, that I could simply return it and walk away without punishment. So given that, what would you suggest?" I found that it bothered me, this lie rolling off my tongue to Charles, and this surprised and discomfited me.

To cover my confusion I looked at him and raised an eyebrow. "Well?"

"Ah, yes, you raise an interesting point. Someone must be punished. This is not a treacle tart filched from the market." Charles looked troubled by this. "It is possible that penance could be assigned, and a show of contrition. Likely it would be public penance, and harsh, but that would be for His Holiness to decide." He had set his hand down on the table beside his wineglass. Gently I touched the back with one finger, tracing a pattern along the vein.

"And if it were returned anonymously – it seems unlikely that you will stop looking for the thief and simply improve your security. If it were me who had stolen it, how would you suggest I correct the error of my ways?"

He flushed and snatched his hand away, changing the subject. A tale for a tale, I would tell him stories of my time with the English, or from my childhood on the estate. When the subject of *The Indiana* came up, I would tell him of our perfectly honest jobs, doing my best to avoid naming the crew.

Through my walks on the ship I had determined that there were at least twenty crew members, with Charles in command. I did not see any way that I by myself could take over the airship. There were too many of them. My crew would be coming for me – they could track the same beacon that *The Inara* followed, but they had to be in range.

Through my dinners with Charles I was coming to have a great deal of respect for what he had accomplished in so short a time. He had served in his original mercenary company and risen to the rank of Sergeant there during the conflicts between Venice and Florence. During combat he had saved his squad when their commander had fallen, by keeping them together and outflanking the enemy. When he joined the Swiss Guard, he was allowed to compete to join a cohort assigned to special missions for the Vatican.

Though he would not speak of those missions, I gathered he had gained the attention of His Holiness through them and been assigned to the Pope's personal guard. I was surprised to learn that his promotion to Captain had been a recent one. I found him to be charming and witty when the mood struck. I did my best to keep our conversations lighthearted and flirtatious; not showing how worried I was about what I might find in Rome.

JACQUELINE

On the eighth day, Charles and I were walking on deck, a guard trailing behind. Off in the distance a flicker of light behind some clouds caught my eye. I turned to watch it for a moment. Charles noted it also. "Sheet lightning. We may see some rain tonight."

It did look like sheet lightning, if one didn't know what to look for. I watched the series of flashes again. Marie was charging the wire structure around the *grande poche* in a coded series. I would be ready. Turning to Charles I said, "Indeed, it may rain. Perhaps we should go below."

There was a tap on my door at around midnight, then I heard the bolts click. I threw off the bed clothes and slid out of bed fully clothed dropping into a crouch next to the bed.

Nina was holding one of Marie's new light sources. It glowed dimly in the darkness. I ran to the door and slipped out between her and the doorframe. She followed me up the stairs and pointed to the right where *The Thorin* was tied off to the Vatican ship.

I heard shouting behind us and a bullet whizzed past my head. Ducking back into the doorway I heard Nina ask, "How many of them are there Captain?"

"Too many. There are at least twenty on board ship." I stuck my head out the doorway once again to get a look at the situation. There was a cluster of five men on the steering deck. I felt certain the men on watch were at the other end of the deck, behind us.

"I'm pleased to see they didn't hurt you. We weren't sure what we would find," Nina said quietly. "I have one of Marie's grenades with me, and the electroshock device. And your spare knife."

I nodded, taking the knife and sliding it into the top of my boot. Nina handed the electroshock device to me as well and pulled out her pistol. The men on the steering deck were firing out towards where I assumed *The Indiana* was. I could see some of the crew in hand-to-hand combat on the main deck.

From the hold I heard boots, many of them running our way. Nina heard them too. She held up the grenade and gestured down the hallway. I nodded and primed the electroshock device. We flattened ourselves against the wall. An unfamiliar silhouette in the doorway would surely alert the men coming up from below. Nina pressed the button on Marie's grenade and rolled down the hallway. She grabbed my arm and we ran.

Tyler came up behind us, also running. I heard the barking of pistols from the doorway and felt something scream past my left ear. Looking back, I saw Tyler flail and fall to the deck. The crew of the *Blue Raven* wasn't far behind us. I ran back to help Tyler to his feet. He was bleeding profusely from his left shoulder. I threw his uninjured arm over my shoulder and helped him to the railing. Nina, ahead of us, reeled *The Thorin* in closer to the ship. We threw Tyler inelegantly and ungently into the webbing. I heard him groan in pain. Nina jumped after him to make sure he was secure. "Come on, Captain!" she called back to me.

I was standing on the railing preparing to jump when hands grabbed the back of my shirt and pulled, toppling me backwards onto the deck. I heard the ominous click of a revolver and felt the cold metal pressed to my temple. "Don't move." Charles's matter of fact tone did more to convince me than anything else would have.

"Get out of here!" I shouted. Charles slapped me angrily. Nina cut their tether ropes and pushed off. I could vaguely make out Tyler clinging to the webbing on *The Thorin*. She looked back at me and shouted, "Petunias!"

That was certainly not what I was expecting to hear as a battle cry, and it gave me pause.

Charles was furious and came storming into my quarters. I let him shout for a few minutes. This was the reaction of someone thinking with his heart, not someone using his judgement. When he was finished I looked him in the eye. "If our situations were reversed, and for some reason I held you captive, taken from the marketplace for no valid reason, would your crew come for you?"

Charles looked at me, mouth hanging open, poised to respond. He shut his mouth. "It's not the same."

"Really? You kidnapped me, held me against my will, and are taking me to Rome on false charges. And you expect them to not try and rescue me?"

"I have a perfectly valid reason." He glared at me, anger simmering beneath the surface of his gaze.

"You think you do, but my crew doesn't know that. Though, to be fair, I imagine they would try to rescue me anyway. We take care of each other." I stood watching Charles as he paced back and forth like a caged tiger.

"I must take more extensive security measures from now on. I have let my feelings for you cloud my judgement on this. That will not happen again." He squared his shoulders, but I could see the conflict within him.

"You will do what you feel you have to do. What you should be doing is letting me go, since you have no proof."

He scowled. "I have been told that there is proof in Rome"

Looking at him levelly I replied, "For your sake you'd better hope so."

At that Charles's stormed out, slamming my door. I thought he had forgotten to lock it, then I heard the 'snick' of the deadbolt. I slumped in my chair feeling defeated. It was the middle of the night, but after all the excitement I couldn't sleep. Looking down I noticed the blood on my hands and clothes. Tyler's blood. If he died it would be on me for taking this job. A captain is responsible for the lives of her crew. Pouring water from the pitcher into the basin on the bureau, I did my best to wash the blood stains from my hands and shirt, scrubbing them angrily.

Why would Nina yell Petunias of all things?

JACQUELINE

An outright assault didn't work, I mused. Perhaps I should try seduction.

I was still trying to puzzle out Nina's cryptic flowers. Clearly it was a message. It was a callback to when I had been thrown off *The Indiana* over Paris; naked and drugged. Later, the crew had laughed when I told them that the first thought I'd had while falling was 'petunias'. But what did Nina mean? That I should jump off the ship? Over Paris *The Inara* had been close enough for me to call. It had caught me from below. Was *The Inara* somehow below me? I hadn't seen it in the fight.

Charles had once again invited me to dinner. Seduction wasn't really my strong point, but I had nothing to lose. I took my time getting ready, twirling my hair up and pinning it with my jeweled hairpins and tucking the shirt in as best I might. Pinching my cheeks to bring some color to them, I examined myself in the mirror.

The bruise on my temple had faded to a green, unhealthy tinge, and I pulled a lock of hair out to cover it. I was tired, and it showed. I did my best to compose my features into a pleasant mask. My vest was still damp. I debated putting it on anyway, but decided that the loose shirt was more provocative, so left it off, wearing just the shirt and flying pants.

Charles greeted me courteously enough at dinner, but I noticed that his pistol was never far from his hand. He noted my changed apparel but made no comment. "Tell me Jacqueline, what is this device?" His finger hovered over the trigger button on Marie's silver needle grenade, its bulk filling his hand. I flinched, then remembered that it had been discharged the night before.

"It is an impressive device. You saw what it can do," I said lightly.

Charles scowled. "I had ten men that we had to pull needles out of. All of them slept like the dead well past midday."

I smiled and nodded. "I will point this out to you. They only slept. This could have just as easily been loaded with something lethal, but that isn't how my crew works. We don't kill people without cause."

"A pirate crew with ethics," he said sarcastically. "I will keep that in mind when I go up against them again." He shook his head in frustration. "Miter or no, you are a notorious pirate – reputations like yours are not built on fantasy."

Deciding that silence was the better part of wisdom in this case, I took a sip of wine and watched as his desire to follow orders, warred with his desire for me.

"I cannot let you escape. I must fulfill my duty to His Holiness. I must treat you as the prisoner that you are. You will be confined to your quarters with meals brought to you there until we reach Rome."

Staring out the porthole he said, "Jacqueline, why? Why couldn't you be that pretty little empty headed noble that I met in the palace?"

"Look at me, Charles." The tone was gentle, and I held his gaze when he turned to me. "Is that really who you would want me to be? Frivolous, vain, and well above your station? Someone who would never even look at you twice, who you could idealize, but not approach? Or worse, who would toy with you, then discard you without a second thought? My life would be considerably easier though substantially more boring if I had married, stayed on my estate and been the good little Contessa that the world wanted me to be."

I leaned forward, my shirt hanging open slightly, showing the curve of one breast. I saw his gaze travel down my neckline and pause. Marie was better at seduction than I, but I had watched her, and I learned. "Don't you see, if I was like everyone else then we would never have met. But we have met, and we have time to spend together. Let us make the most of the time while we have it." I tried to put as much earnestness into my voice as I could, but after the events of the night before it was difficult, and my voice cracked.

He squeezed my hand gently and brought it to his lips for a kiss. "Jacqueline, as charming as I find you to be, as much as I would wish it otherwise, the reality is we cannot be together."

I ground my teeth in frustration. "'Cannot' sounds to me only like you do not wish to try. I have overcome more 'cannots' in my life than most people."

Charles had an infuriatingly amused look on his face. "And do you see some way around the fact that I am charged with arresting you and returning you to Rome."

I waved my fingers in the air dismissively. "Details. Mere details. As there is no evidence I have committed this crime, one could say you kidnapped me so we may spend time together. I do not know where your Miter is, I do not have it in my possession, and for the time we are onboard this ship, it is immaterial." I kept my tone light, raising my wine glass in toast. "But surely a man such as yourself does not lack for desirable female company."

He chuckled and looked away. "Yes, I suppose my desire to spend time with you is as good an explanation as any."

"Now you understand, because you have kidnapped me it is requisite I attempt to escape as often as possible. Not, mind you, that any of these attempts will succeed. But I must give you reason to chase me." I said this in a teasing tone as I winked at him over my glass with a cheerful look, though in reality I very much wanted to strangle him.

"And should these escape attempts occur and fail, you would be well within your rights to demand recompense in the form of a kiss." I smiled slowly, pretending to ponder the thought of kissing Charles. I could see now that his shoulders had loosened and that he was at least playing along with my inappropriate teasing, if not taking me too seriously.

"Now that hardly seems fair. If it turns out I am a good kisser, then you shall forever be trying to escape, and I shall have to forever chase you. But if I am a bad kisser, then you shall stop trying to escape, and I shan't have the pleasure of kissing you." He took a sip of his own wine.

I tried not to remember Tyler's blood on my hands as Charles and I bantered back and forth. "That is indeed a conundrum. And I myself must not be too good at escaping, lest I not have the chance to receive kisses. And yet I must not be bad at escaping, or I am doomed to stand trial in Rome. It is indeed a fine line to walk."

I took another sip of my wine. "I have already tried to escape once and failed. Do you demand your recompense?"

"I will take only what is freely given. But should you so choose, I could hardly stop you."

Noting that he did not let go my hand, I ran my thumb across his knuckles, and stroked his palm with my fingers. It seemed to me he was uncertain how to proceed, so I tried to show him the way. With a second glass of wine he seemed more amenable to my advances. I subtly and not so subtly encouraged him.

When we finished dinner he insisted on walking me back to my cabin. Standing outside the door he smiled tentatively and bent his head down for a kiss. I smiled and turned so his lips brushed my cheek and bid him good night. I would play this out a bit longer before I appeared to surrender to his charms. Charles, I could see, relished the chase more than the catching.

Once in my cabin I pondered my poison hairpin. It would only make Charles sleep. I would only have one shot. If, as I surmised, *The Inara* was somehow below me, then I would need to slip over the railing and climb down the outside of the hull without being detected. No mean feat.

Charles wouldn't be merciful a second time, no matter how much we joked. I wasn't yet sure if he was serious about confining me to quarters or not. The next night would be soon enough to implement my plan.

He had come to my quarters instead of summoning me to his, sending the food in ahead of him. At dinner Charles looked troubled. "Did I misread you, Jacqueline? I felt certain you would allow me a kiss."

"I would welcome a kiss, but I prefer men who are bold in their actions. I have no interest in a man who, on being told that a kiss would be welcome, then hesitates for fear of offending."

Charles nodded, considering my words. "I shall keep that in mind for future. We are nearing Rome. We only have a few days left with one another." A flicker of sadness crossed his face. "Despite some challenges, I have very much enjoyed our time together."

"You could prolong our time together by not delivering me to Rome." I looked entreatingly at Charles.

Dinner dragged on and my stomach clenched as I thought about what I would have to do to escape. After dinner and a few rounds of cards, Charles stood to go. At the door, he paused and looked back at me. "Stay a bit longer? It's been a lovely evening; I hate for it to end," I said entreatingly.

He looked surprised. "Certainly, Jacqueline."

I smiled and took his hand, kissing his knuckles and drawing him to me. Drawing his arms around my waist I slid my hands behind his neck, pulling him down for a kiss. Pressed as I was against him, I felt him stirring and smiled. I pulled the pin from my hair, releasing it to tumble over my shoulders. He smiled appreciatively and ran his fingers through it. When he leaned down again, I twisted the hairpin so the needle extended, and jabbed it into his neck.

Charles hissed in pain and grabbed at the needle. I pulled it out and stepped away from him. "What did you do?" he asked, staggering around, trying to catch his balance.

"Don't worry, my dear. You will make a full recovery. You will want to lie down, though." I nodded at the bed. He gave me an angry stare and lunged towards me.

"I'm going to..." But his words trailed off as the sleeping dose took effect and he toppled to the floor.

"Yes, I'm sure you will." I turned him so he was on his back and covered him with a blanket from the bunk. "Sleep well. You are a delightful kisser," I whispered to him, then tiptoed to the door and opened it quietly. The hallway was clear. Sneaking up on deck I kept to the shadows as much as possible, making my way to the airship's stern. Coils of rope were stacked neatly, stored for convenient use. I tied one end of a rope around a heavy barrel, using the other end to create a sling for myself. I tucked in behind the barrels and tapped the coded sequence on my arm. It flashed green briefly and I heard a thumping from below. I had deciphered Nina's message correctly.

Feeding the rope over the side of the ship I waited until I couldn't see any of the watchmen. Taking a firm hold, I slid over the edge, leaning my weight backwards against the rope, my feet planted firmly on the hull.

I was still in the shirt the crew-member had given me, and I didn't have my flying leathers, so the air felt cold and damp. Footsteps and voices were coming towards me. The tone and cadence sounded casual, so I kept walking down the hull, willing them not to look this way. They passed by, still chatting and didn't see me.

Once I had passed the swell of the side of the hull I could see *The Inara*. She was tethered, trying to break free. My arms were burning and I could feel my grip on the rope slipping. Taking a deep breath, I pushed off the hull with my legs, allowing more of the rope to slip through my fingers. The sling caught me, and when the rope hit the side of the hull, I was propelled upwards towards *The Inara*.

I missed. My fingers grasping at air, inches from her webbing. I swung back out past the side of the hull and glanced upwards just in time to see one of the crew coming peering over the edge. He spotted me and opened his mouth to raise the alarm. I put my finger to my lips and he looked at me quizzically right before I swung back under the hull.

I was able to pull myself onto the airhopper this time and quickly removed the rope tying me to the ship and untethered *The Inara*. I could hear shouting from the airship above, as I turned *The Inara*. Unfortunately I didn't have as much speed or maneuverability as I would have liked because of the balloon, and no easy way to stow it while in the air. For the moment I was still hidden beneath the ship, but that wouldn't last long. An awful thought occurred to me as I pulled my harness tight. *I can't go back to* The Indiana, *they'll just follow me and take the ship.*

I turned *The Inara* northeast. I wasn't exactly sure where I was but picking a direction and staying the course seemed like the best idea.

They had their airhoppers deployed and in the air faster than I thought possible. Pushing the throttle on *The Inara* as far as I could, I felt the vibration of her engine as she roared into the darkness of the night.

A beam of light from one of the Vatican airhoppers pierced the darkness beside me, a more powerful version of the lamp they had used when searching *The Indiana*. A second light appeared on the other side. The lights moved in a search pattern, rotating back and forth until one of them highlighted me. I dropped altitude, but a beam found me again. Changing direction, I doubled back to get behind them. The search lights and airhoppers were behind me but I was now headed directly back towards their ship. I turned *The Inara* east, perpendicular to my original course. The air currents were changing, and I could feel the updraft that signaled land nearby.

Shots rang out from behind me and I ducked reflexively. They weren't aiming at me however, but the balloon on *The Inara*. Bullets tore through the *petite poche*; the balloon collapsed and *The Inara* plummeted. I very nearly cheered. The shoulder straps on my harness bit deep into my shoulders, holding me onto the seat. *The Inara* was specifically designed to fly without a balloon, but it would take a moment for her stabilizers to kick in. Grabbing the stabilization lever I waited. It was hard to judge in the dark, but if I pulled up right before I hit the water I might be able to lose some of my pursuit. After a count of thirty I pulled it towards me. With a bone-jarring jerk *The Inara* stopped free-falling and leveled out. I barely saw the top of the tree before I felt the impact. I hadn't been over water at all. I spun crazily, tree branches crashing around me. I felt a blow to my head, a sharp pain in my side, and then I knew nothing for some time.

CHARLES

Charles woke, head pounding, furious with himself, furious with her. He had let himself be played and once again, she had escaped. It was still dark outside, and he shook his head, trying to throw off the effects of the sleeping dose. It must have been less than she'd used on the crew members in the last attack. Stumbling out of the cabin, he made his way up to the main deck and judged that he'd been unconscious for less than an hour. Crewmen were launching airhoppers and already in pursuit.

"Captain! Are you alright?" One of the crewmen paused, looking at him. Shaking his head Charles said, "Drugs – she drugged me. Do you have her in sight?"

"We're deploying a search pattern – one of the crewmembers saw her jump over the side. She had a hopper waiting for her."

Charles cursed, still trying to throw off the effects of the drugs and stumbled. "Continue with the search. Find that woman, alive or dead. Send the ship's surgeon to my quarters and have my second in command report to me as soon as there is news." The man saluted and ran towards the search party. Charles pushed the door to his cabin open, eyes scanning the room. Closing the door, he unleashed his temper, pummeling his fist into the back of the door until the wood groaned and his knuckles were bloody.

That bloody woman. Never had he felt so irritatingly incompetent. He knew, *knew*, he was capable of this job, he'd tackled any number of much more complicated assignments before, and yet she kept slipping through his fingers. And he let her. That was perhaps the most infuriating part of all. There was no point in lying to himself. She'd been in his custody and he'd let her escape, allowing her to get too close, falling into her trap.

He punched the wooden door one more time and turned to pace through his quarters. She was a con-woman, and a good one. She had that knack of relating to people and winning their trust. People liked her.

He'd seen it before – the street urchins in the market used the same sorts of tactics. Get close, make people trust you, take everything they give and then some, and make them feel good about it. She was just much, much better at it. He reminded himself of all of these things, over and over again, trying to drown out that quieter voice in his head. What if she wasn't like that? What if she was genuine? What if he -could- trust her, and she was just in a bad situation? He wanted to strangle that voice in his head – part of him had clearly bought into her, despite the evidence.

Good people do not steal. Good people especially do not steal from the Church.

Sunrise did not improve his temper, and the arrival of a messenger from the Vatican only confirmed his suspicions that the crew neither trusted him, nor were loyal to him. The messenger presented himself to Charles with a click of his heels, holding forth a sealed envelope with the Pope's seal.

Captain,

You are recalled to the Vatican immediately. You have failed in this endeavor too many times. Do not delay. You will present yourself no later than two days hence.

By my hand,
His Holiness, Pope Clément

Charles winced and nodded to the messenger. "We will be returning to the Vatican post haste. You are welcome to ship with us or return on your own transportation. I expect the timeframe will be about the same."

"Is there a return message, sir?" the messenger asked, not looking at Charles directly.

"I will deliver it in person it seems. Thank you." Charles replied, crumpling the note in his fist. Striding out the door of his quarters he called to Yusef. "Bring in the search parties – we leave for the Vatican immediately. Full power all the way. Mark these coordinates so we may return and begin our search from here again if needed."

Charles's belly clenched at the thought of his upcoming audience. Pope Clément was not a forgiving man. And then he looked around at the crew. Someone here was reporting their movements back without his knowledge.

Their arrival in Rome, and the intervening days, had brought Charles no closer to discovering who was reporting back on his movements. As soon as they docked at the airfield, he presented himself at the palace. The guards standing outside His Holiness's private receiving chamber announced him.

Striding into the room in what he hoped was a confident manner, Charles went to one knee in front of Clément. Looking up, Charles noted Father Michael, who had been speaking with the Holy Father. Charles had not yet determined where Father Michael stood in the hierarchy of intrigues at the Vatican.

"Ah. Charles. It seems that my confidence in you was somewhat misplaced. You have had Captain Jac in your custody twice now, and she has escaped, not to mention numerous times when you could have taken her ship and you have not. I am most displeased." Clément looked down at him frowning.

"Your Grace," Charles started, lowering his eyes and Clément cut him off abruptly.

"I did not ask you to speak. I will give you one more chance to capture this pirate and retrieve our relic. Father Michael will accompany you. He is one of my trusted advisors. You will listen to him in all things." Clément gave him a hard stare. "Do not fail me a third time.

Charles looked up, his pride stinging, and a creeping sense of fear coiling in his belly. The last thing he wanted was a priest staring over his shoulder questioning his every move. "As Your Grace commands," was all he could get out through clenched teeth.

"You may go. Father Michael will join you at the airfield directly." Clément waved a hand dismissing him.

Charles chose to walk back to the airfield to give himself time to regain his composure before facing his men. Being shackled to a priest hurt his pride. He reminded himself over and over that pride was a sin, and that he must do whatever was necessary to complete this assignment, but it didn't help much. He wanted to punch something. Anything to help alleviate the roiling mass of anger in his belly. He had only met Father Michael a few times, and while the man seemed innocuous enough, Charles had never heard anyone speak very highly of him. The man would be a hindrance; underfoot constantly, and undoubtably reporting every perceived wrong decision back to the Holy Father.

Arriving at the *Blue Raven* in no better frame of mind, he was shocked to find that Father Michael had somehow managed to arrive before him. Yusef informed him that Father Michael was waiting in his quarters.

"Prepare the ship for departure. Father Michael is joining us." Charles strode to his quarters, composing his expression to deal with the man.

Father Michael was waiting for him, sitting at the dining table in Charles's quarters. When Charles entered, he rose. "Captain Durstain. I hope you do not mind that I asked your cabin boy to bring us a pitcher of wine to drink while we discuss our current circumstances."

Charles waved his hand in what he hoped was a casual manner, as he seethed inside at the presumption. Bad enough to be saddled with a priest who was likely a spy, now the man was ordering about the crew from Charles's own quarters.

"I feel that perhaps we have gotten off on the wrong foot, Captain. I am only here to help and to council if needed. Clément is most disturbed by this theft, and it is more a reflection of his temperament that I am here, than any commentary on your skill." The man looked sincere; Charles would give him that.

Nodding Charles poured himself a cup of wine from the ewer. "Father Michael, being recalled to Rome, whether it be for censure or to add you to my crew has ensured that I have lost several days in the pursuit of Captain Jac. We must make up that time quickly if there is any hope in catching her. There is already a spy among my crew. If you are truly here to help, then I will accept your assistance gratefully. If you are here to spy, then kindly stay out of the way so I can do my job."

Father Michael smiled into his cup. "Perhaps I can be of some assistance in the matter of the spy among your crew. Put about that you don't trust me, and you dislike the interference of my presence – both of which I assume are probably true anyway – and I will ferret out who among your crew is the spy. It will keep me out of your way, give me something to do, and perhaps ingratiate you with the rest of the crew more thoroughly."

Charles gave the priest a sidelong glance. "Why would you volunteer to help me? That is most certainly not why the Holy Father sent you."

"The Vatican is full of intrigue, my son, and building alliances is sometimes all that keeps one alive. We could be powerful allies in protecting the church. Or perhaps I want to see what you are capable of, so I can report back. Or both. At the moment, my reasons are my own." Father Michael took another sip of wine, and his gaze never wavered from Charles's own.

"Very well." Charles said, not feeling that he had much choice. "Find the spy, and I will find Captain Jac, and we will see where this all takes us."

JACQUELINE

Pain can be a great motivator. I hurt. All of me hurt. I opened my eyes to find the world tilted at a crazy angle. My brain centered itself on the greatest regions of my pain: my arm, my side, my head. My eyes refused to focus; everything seemed blurry and distant. I touched my forehead with my good hand, and it came away sticky with blood. Moving my other arm I nearly passed out with pain. I took a few deep breaths trying calm myself.

I was upside down, still in *The Inara*'s harness. The straps bit into my shoulders but kept me from falling to the ground ten or so feet below. One arm felt broken, I couldn't tell how badly. When I reached to touch the area of pain on my side, I felt a slow seeping of blood. Wrapping my good arm through one of the straps I braced my feet and pulled the emergency release for the harness. I felt the harness release, and as carefully as I could, righted myself. I dangled briefly before letting go and falling to the ground. I landed hard and blacked out.

I woke with the sun noticeably higher than before—a shaft of light had briefly blinded me. Blinking and groaning I rolled over. I staggered to my feet with the help of the tree. The effort left me sweating and nauseous.

I appeared to be in the middle of a forest. There wasn't a path as far as I could see, and *The Inara* was at least ten feet up in the tree, hanging pitifully upside down, one of the wings broken at a crazy angle. A few items from her saddle bags had fallen to the ground. I spotted my towel a few feet away, and one of my knives beside it, along with a few other odds and ends.

Working one handed with the knife I cut the towel into several long strips. One of these I wound around my midsection, trying to put pressure on the wound in my side. I could do no more than tuck the ends in. I took the second strip and wound it around my broken arm, trying not to look at the jagged fragments of bone sticking out from the skin. Creating a sling without assistance was beyond me, so I draped the other strip of towel around my neck and tried to stand again. The blackness at the edges of my vision threatened to overwhelm me, and I closed my eyes, willing the world to stop spinning.

Staggering from one tree to the next, I tried to stay on my feet going in a vaguely east direction. I hadn't made much progress when I heard voices. Stumbling, I slid to the ground, my back against the tree.

"Hey Belkin, any luck with the mushrooms?" a cheerful voice cried out.

"No, something's got Daisy spooked today. Can't get her to focus at all," a male voice replied.

They were close by, so I pulled myself into a small hollow nearby to remain unseen. They sounded like farmers, but I was loath to reveal myself. The choice was taken from me; a small pig came to the edge of the hollow and began squealing.

"Sounds like Daisy's found something!" one of the men shouted.

"Let's go see what she's got. I thought she'd be done for the day what with that commotion around dawn."

I saw two shadows moving at the top of the rim, coming to find Daisy. The pig, seeing me, or perhaps smelling blood, came to investigate. I felt a nose rooting around in my side and tried to push her away.

"What have we here?" One of the shadows blocked the light, and I opened my eyes to see a beard covered face staring down at me.

"Help?" I asked weakly before fainting.

I woke sometime later in a rough bed. Daisy the pig was asleep in a pen across the room, and there was a woman standing in the doorway regarding me with disapproval.

"I have set your arm and bandaged it. It's probably for the best that you slept through it. The wound in your side needs stitches, though."

I nodded, wincing. I had a splitting headache and tried to sit up. She pressed me firmly down against the bed. "Stay here. Let me look at the other wound."

One-handed, I raised my shirt, carefully looking at the ceiling, or anything other than the wound in my side. I couldn't tell, but it felt fairly serious. Looking it over, she nodded and *tsk*ed. "Yes, I must take care of this as well."

She handed me a smooth piece of bone about six inches long. "Bite down. This will hurt." She washed it first in salt water, and I screamed. The salt burned and stung down to my very core. Then she sluiced it with fresh water. I could see the blood running freely, staining the water red, as well as the cloth she used to stanch the bleeding. She took out a needle and thread and eyed me briefly.

"Do I need to have them hold you down, or tie you to the bed?" She held up the needle glinting in the light.

The pain from the salt got worse, and I felt sure I was going to black out again. "You will not need to hold me down. I've been stitched before."

"I can see," she grudgingly replied, "but please hold on to the bed board at least. I don't want your hands to get in my way."

It hurt. The gash on my side turned out to be both longer and deeper than I expected. As she stitched me up, between gasps of pain I asked about where we were.

"Currently you are in that idiot's cabin." She nodded her head in the direction of a closed door. "That idiot of course is my husband, Belkin. He claims our pig found you in the woods." I started to nod in agreement and thought better of the idea. She didn't seem at all pleased at my being here.

"And where is here?" I asked, counting beams in the ceiling to take my mind off the stitching.

She looked at me strangely. "You don't know?"

"My airhopper crashed not far from where your husband found me. I have no idea where I am."

She patted my cheek. "Oh, you poor dear. You are on the Isla de Ponza. And from the look of it, likely to stay here for a while. That arm has a nasty break, and the bump on your head is quite large. Not to mention," she gestured down at the gash in my side. "It is a good thing my Belkin found you. I expect you would have bled to death if he had not happened upon you."

"What was he doing in the forest?" I asked, trying to distract myself from the pain.

"He was looking for mushrooms. Our Daisy has a nose for them. It's the wrong season, but once in a while she'll find a late bloom of them. They are quite tasty in fish soup."

She stopped talking for a bit, concentrating on her stitching. The needle felt like a fiery hot poker every time she took a stitch, and I was missing Henri's painkillers by the time she was done, but the stitches were small and neat and held the flesh together.

"You rest. My Belkin will go see what he can salvage from your air carrier and be back before dark."

"What... what is your name?" I managed to ask through the haze of pain.

"Oh, I am Donna Maria. Now you sleep. We will talk more later." She held an evil smelling concoction to my lips until I sipped it and fell back into restless dreams. I had vague memories of waking thusly several times, but everything was hazy and unreal, and every time her vile concoction was at my lips. Monsters chased me through my dreams wearing Charles's face. I heard voices speaking a dire language I didn't recognize, and then I was dropped into a clear and terrifying dream. I stood in a temple of pale stone. A great seal covered the floor, etched in the sandstone, with the markings highlighted in gold. There was a horrific cracking sound and the great seal was rent down the middle. Dust and fire swirled around me, and through it all I could see the head of a great beast rise, first one, then two, continuing until six foul creatures stood upon the stone. My heart thudded in my chest, and I fled the sight, but no matter which way I turned, six beasts with glowing, fiery eyes followed me.

I wrenched myself out of the dream, breathing heavily. My eyelids felt heavy as lead. I could make out the hazy shapes of Donna Maria and Belkin arguing. Donna Maria was gesturing angrily towards me, and Belkin was wringing his hat in his hands. I closed my eyes again, willing the pounding in my head to stop. I fell back into troubling dreams where a foreboding Charles held me in chains with Donna Maria forcing foul smelling drinks down my throat.

I woke up. My head felt clearer than it had in days, though my arm was still excruciating, and my side still throbbed. Moving my broken arm hurt, but I slid it over until I could feel the inside of my good elbow. My tracker was still intact, David had programed it so *The Indiana* could track me, if they were close enough. With light examination using my good hand, I could tell the bump on my head was somewhat smaller, and while still nauseous, I was hungry. There didn't seem to be anyone in the cabin with me at the moment, so I tried to sit up slowly and look around. Daisy's pen was empty, and I could see the cabin wasn't quite so small as I first thought. It was a small room, with a stove in one corner beside an open hearth, and a hand pump with a spigot directed inside for water. I was lying on a box-bed, the only other piece of furniture in the room was a small table with two chairs. There appeared to be a door leading deeper into the house, and then the door leading out to the yard that I had seen when I first awoke. Looking down, I could see daylight between the floorboards, which were none too close together. There was a crawl space beneath the house, probably for the pig during the hotter months.

I heard voices outside arguing. Standing slowly, I inched my way over to the window beside the door. David and Henri were standing in the yard arguing with Donna Maria. Relief made my knees go weak at the sight of them.

Moving slowly, I unlatched the door and opened it, staggering into the yard.

David spotted me in the doorway first, pushing past Donna Maria. "Jac! Oh my God! You're hurt! What happened? This woman swore you weren't here and wouldn't let us in."

"Captain. Let me have a look at you, then we'll get back to the ship. She clearly didn't want to tell us you were here, but I have no idea why." Henri gestured to Donna Maria who was glowering from the yard.

"Señora, these men – they are ruffians! You must not go with them. They appeared out of nowhere and they do not look trustworthy." Donna Maria scowled at the two men.

"Donna Maria, I assure you they are quite trustworthy. They are members of my crew, and I am very happy to see them. Now that they are here, can we pay you in some way for your trouble? You and your husband have been very generous."

She perked up a bit. "You have used up all of my medicines and my resources. Belkin has had to go seek work elsewhere because we had not enough to eat with you in the house."

I coughed into my fist. I didn't think I had been there that long, nor had I eaten anything but that vile potion, but I was hardly going to argue. She had saved my life. "I am sure we can adequately recompense you for your troubles,

Donna Maria. Shall we bring back food and medicines from our ship?"

She got a crafty look in her eyes I didn't like. "Perhaps you could take me to your ship and I could pick out what we best need?"

"We will go and return with plenty of supplies to feed you and your husband," I replied.

She harrumphed. "You will leave, and not return and we will starve."

Still dizzy with pain and sweating with the effort I coughed again. "That seems unlikely. Henri, how far is the airhopper?"

"Too far for you to walk, Captain. David and I put her down in a clearing not far from the wreckage of *The Inara*. Given that you can barely stand, I don't think you could navigate the path through the forest," Henri replied, eyeing me critically.

"David, can you get *The Thorin* and bring her here, so that the Captain can get safely aboard?" A part of me was surprised at the normally quiet Henri taking charge with authoritative efficiency.

Henri did not wait for David's reply before turning to me. "I must look at your wounds. I'm sure Donna Maria, has done a most excellent job, but as your physician I need to look at them immediately."

I coughed again, sending a stabbing pain through my side as phlegm rattled in my chest. Donna Maria *hmphed*. "You will leave and then you will not pay."

"We will stay long enough for the airhopper to return, and you will get your payment," Henri said with patience. "And in the meantime, I must examine the Captain."

David looked pained. "Jac, I don't want to leave you."

"I will be right here when you return, and Henri will have had time to look me over and see what else needs to be patched up. Please David?" Another coughing fit took me, and the world started to swim. I braced myself against the doorway, willing my legs to hold me upright. The thought of staying here longer was nearly unbearable, but I wasn't sure I could walk across the small yard in front of the house. Making it through the forest to *The Thorin* was out of the question.

He nodded reluctantly. "Donna Maria, I will be back within the hour. I hope you will allow us to impose on your hospitality for a small bit longer."

She nodded graciously as any queen in a palace, only her eyes showing her avaricious nature. "Yes of course. I will make sure they are here when you return."

David kissed me on the forehead, then turned and left.

Henri put an arm under my good shoulder and helped me back into the hut. "Donna Maria, can you please boil some water?"

"The pan is on the stove, and the water beside it. Boil your own," was her surly reply.

Henri looked at the squalid conditions within the hut, noting the pig pen and shook his head. "She's charming," was his only comment.

"Well, she did clean and dress my wounds, and set my arm. At least I hope she set my arm. But she does lack your charming bedside manner. She's been feeding me some foul potion for several days, but I have no idea what was in it." I eased down onto one of the sturdy chairs as Henri put the water on to boil, beads of sweat standing out on my forehead and the feeling of lightheadedness coming over me again. "How is Tyler? Is he?" I feared what Henri might say.

"Recovering. Though he lost a lot of blood. Everyone else is fine."

While the water heated, he came to inspect my wounds, unwinding the dressing on my side. It stuck, clotted with blood, and he used a pair of shears to cut away as much of it as he could. "I'll have to soak the rest of it off, Captain. It doesn't look good." He waited impatiently for the water to boil, then dipped a cloth from his bag into the boiling water, holding it up to cool briefly. He pressed it against the matted bandage, and I hissed in pain, but held my tongue. When the bandage finally peeled away it revealed a wound some six inches long with a putrid smell coming off it.

Henri cursed, using some language I was sure he had picked up from Marie. Looking down I could see red lines trailing away from the wound, and a pus filled, festering mass where it was centered. "This is going to hurt. A lot."

He took a scalpel and dipped it in the boiling water then pressed it against the infected flesh. A line of puss and blood ran out, following the trail of his scalpel. I was sweating and weak, on the verge of passing out by the time he handed me another hot cloth. "Hold this against the wound for a moment. No, don't look at it again," he instructed as I started to glance down. "I promise, you don't want to see it."

"I'm going to look at your arm next. You focus on holding this cloth against your side, okay?" I nodded, my eyes glazed with pain.

He unwrapped the bandage and splint around my arm, cradling it gently, pressing the tips of my fingers to see if there was blood flow. The arm looked nasty, a mass of swelling and black and red marks across it. He set it gently on the table. "Don't move, Captain, I want to get a hot cloth for this as well." Returning with a steaming rag he placed it gently over the arm.

"The arm is not so bad as it looks. I will need to put a proper cast on it when we get back to the ship, but for the time being I will re-splint it. The swelling and marking is normal for what it's been through. The one in your side however is quite nasty."

He let the cloth sit on my arm for a few moments then removed it, sprinkling a foul-smelling powder over the cuts and the places where the bone had pierced the skin. "Ugh, what is that?" I asked, turning my head away.

"Sulfa powder. I wish I had something stronger." He felt along the arm gently, nodding. "It was well set, now we just have to worry about keeping it free of infection."

Dazed as I was by pain, I didn't even bother to curse as he began re-wrapping it. When he was done, he dried the wound in my side and looked at me. "I need to wash this out with alcohol. It's going to hurt."

"It already hurts, just get on with it," I replied through gritted teeth. He opened a bottle and handed it to me. "Here, drink first."

I took a swig and tasted fine scotch. "You're using that to clean wounds?" I asked, nearly shocked.

"No, that's for going inside you, this is for the cleaning." He held up another bottle and doused the hole in my side with it. I screamed in pain and fought the darkness around the edges of my vision. When I came to, he was sprinkling more of the sulfa powder on the wound in my side. "Sorry. There's really no way to prepare someone for that."

He handed me the scotch and I took another long pull from the bottle as he finished dressing the wound. "We found *The Inara* upside-down in a tree. What happened?"

I started to recount the story and Henri raised his finger to silence me, listening. "I hear voices outside."

Henri looked out the window and paused. "It looks like a priest talking to Donna Maria. Maybe she wasn't sure of your recovery and asked the local parish priest to give you a blessing?"

"Given what I've experienced of her temperament, that seems unlikely. Let me have a look." I stood shakily and leaned against the window frame to look out. Peering at the priest he seemed somehow familiar.

A flash of memory. The Vatican, a priest mouthing the word *run*. I swore softly. "Henri, you need to hide. Or leave. I've met this priest before. This is the man who helped me escape the Vatican."

"If he helped you before, perhaps we can trust him?" Henri twitched the curtain aside slightly to examine the man.

I was sweating with the effort of standing, and tendrils of fear and hope both coiled in my belly. "I cannot fathom why he would be here in the middle of nowhere, and I do not trust that it is mere happenstance. He may be trustworthy; he may be working towards his own ends. Either way I do not want him to know more of the crew."

Henri nodded and asked, "Is there a backdoor to this place? Better if we both go."

"I haven't had a chance to look." I replied, hands beginning to shake. "But the floorboards are loose, and there's a crawl space."

Henri ran to the other door and opened it, gesturing me to follow. He grabbed his medical bag and put his arm under my good shoulder, helping me stay upright.

"Henri," I heard myself saying, "I'm never going to make it on a run. You must reach David and warn the crew. Quick, you must go out under the floorboards."

"Captain. I can't leave you here. David would kill me. Not to mention the rest of the crew."

"You must. I hear them coming. If he's here to help, then no harm done. If he's not, better you warn the crew." I was trying to pry one of the floorboards up with my good arm.

"It's only a priest and Donna Maria. I can overpower them, and we can both escape." Henri said, in an unusual show of bravado and determination.

Pausing and gasping for breath, holding the wound in my side I looked up at him, raising an eyebrow. "Henri, I am ordering you to leave. The priest must not see you here."

Cursing, Henri pried the floorboard up and slipped through the opening. "Damn you for always being right Captain," he said as I let the board drop back into place. I felt a pang of regret as the floorboard fell into place. I was alone again.

The door to the cottage opened quietly, and Father Michael entered. I was instantly wary, though he appeared unarmed and his mild demeanor gave no cause for alarm.

"My child, I am so glad I found you before the guard did. You are grievously wounded from what Donna Maria tells me. You must come with me quickly before they arrive."

I looked at him suspiciously. "Why are you helping me? Why did you help me before?"

Father Michael twitched the curtain aside looking back across the yard. "I cannot tell you that yet. Not here. You must come away quickly. They aren't far behind me. Trust no-one from the Vatican."

"How did you come to be here?" I was sweating profusely, and the pain from the wound in my side was making me nauseous.

He looked at me, lines of worry creasing his face. "Jacqueline, you must come away now."

I was torn, trusting him against my better judgement, sick and dizzy with pain. I had to leave one way or another. "I. Very well."

He nodded. "Come. Out the back. I do not want Donna Maria to see us go. She is an evil woman from what I can see." He gave me a shoulder to lean on and helped me hobble out the back. Once outside he peered around the corner of the house, checking to see that the way was clear. I held my good hand to my side, gasping. "How far to your transportation, Father?" I asked quietly, trying to save my strength.

He pointed to the north. "Not far. Just over the top of the hill there. Let us go while Donna Maria is distracted."

Judging the distance, I nodded. I think I can make it that far.

"Come. Lean on me, I will support you." With his shoulder under my good arm we started up the hill. As we struggled up the crest of the hill he asked, "Do you still have the item you took, that day at the Vatican?"

A cold chill washed over me. "No Father, I do not."

"Good. Better that it not be returned to the Vatican," he replied.

At that moment we crested the hill, and I saw a squadron of blue and gold. Shock washed over me. "You! Why?" I tried to wrap my good arm around Father Michael's throat, to take him hostage, but I was too weak. Stumbling, he shook me off and I collapsed to my knees. "Guards, take her," I heard him say. Anger and confusion warred within me as my head swam with pain.

Turning to me he frowned. "I told you not to trust anyone from the Vatican, my child."

I felt sick, and my head swam. One of the guards picked me up and carried me to one of several airhoppers that had set down in the field. Forcing me on board the other guards rode two to a machine. Father Michael, looking grim, had his own hopper. At the edge of the forest saw Henri's stricken face, staring angrily up as they took off.

JACQUELINE

"Jacqueline, I'm disappointed in you. You should not have tried to escape. Now I must treat you as any other prisoner." Charles stood in the shadows behind a lit lantern watching me. I sat, looking at him through the bars.

"Charles. Unless you have something relevant to say, leave. Your men kidnapped me out of a marketplace. Did you really think I wouldn't try to escape? I even told you I would." I leaned back against the bars, closing my eyes.

"I treated you leniently before." His previously warm gaze had turned cold and foreboding. "Do not anger me again, Jacqueline."

"What? You will beat an unarmed, injured woman trapped in a cell? You will put me to the question? Will that prove you are a man?" I threw back at him. "You will call your dog, Father Michael, on me?"

"How dare you drug me, after the decent treatment and liberties you were allowed," he growled.

"Ah yes, decent treatment from the man who kidnaps me. Forgive me for being ungrateful and plotting my escape." My head was pounding, and nausea threatened to overwhelm me.

"And I hope you enjoy your time down here in the cell. We will reach Rome tomorrow, and you will no longer be my problem."

"I suppose water and a blanket are too much for you to provide prisoners." I coughed wetly, shuddering at the sound.

Charles turned on his heel and left, taking the light with him, but a blanket arrived with the evening meal.

Even with the blanket it was a cold night, and I felt my fever returning. I alternately burned and shivered, regretting some of my hasty words to Charles. By morning I was fading in and out of consciousness, the shadows on the walls becoming the monsters in my nightmares. I lost track of time. At some point Charles's guards came and retrieved me and I remember stumbling first in darkness, then light then darkness again. The scenery changed around me, and I was no longer on the airship, but I had no notion of where I was. At one point I thought the earth was shaking, and I could barely keep my footing.

When I next knew myself, I was in a stone cell. This one had a blanket and a bucket of clean water, as well as a bucket that, from the smell, was intended for me to relieve myself in. There was a tiny window, well out of reach, that let in a modicum of light and air.

Parched from fever I gulped down the water. Twenty minutes later, I threw it up again, further soiling my shirt and the cell floor. I hurt all over. Groaning I curled up in a ball trying to stop the shivering chills wracking my body.

I lost track of time again. A guard showed up with a thin gruel and a heel of hard bread. I thought maybe I had seen him before, but I couldn't be sure. He set it down and wrapped the fingers of my uninjured hand around the hunk of bread. "You have to eat. You won't get better without food."

I put the bread up to my mouth and sucked on one corner until it was soft enough to break a chunk off. Chewing more slowly I ate a few bites and tentatively washed it down with a sip of water from the bucket. I managed to keep the first few bites down, so ate a few more, continuing slowly until the bread was gone. I couldn't face the thought of the cold, gelatinous gruel and left the plate untouched. The fever came and went. A physician visited me and told the guard I would either live or die, he wasn't sure which, but that they would know in a matter of days. Slowly the fever abated and the wound in my side started to heal.

I was very weak, and I took to watching the small patch of light travel across the cell walls and then disappear. I let my mind wander back to *The Indiana*, wondering how the crew was doing. What the crew was doing. Did they think me dead? Had they been hunted down because of my folly? Had Henri reached David in time? As best I could tell from the small window in my cell, the season was beginning to wane. The days were getting shorter.

After an infinite number of days, or so it seemed, there was a change in the routine. The guard came in, followed by a servant carrying pails of water, and another carrying a half barrel. Two more followed with more pails of water. The servant pulled out a cake of soap from a pocket and set it on the ground. She emptied the water into the barrel, followed by the others. The guard looked at me. "You have an audience with His Holiness this evening, and you will not appear before him filthy. Bathe. Clothing will be provided for you, as is appropriate for your station."

"And if I will not?" My voice was rusty with long disuse.

He frowned. "Then you will be bathed by the guards, and they will not be gentle. And the water will be cold."

This guard, though he hadn't spoken to me much, had never mistreated me, and had never shown me aught but courtesy in this dreary place. I nodded, blushing at the petulance in my question. "Thank you for the water and the soap."

"It is standard for those in your position. I will return in half an hour. Be done by then."

I nodded again, suddenly feeling the accumulation of weeks of dirt in the areas I hadn't been able to wash. My hair felt filthy, and my scalp crawled. When he shut the door I struggled out of my clothing and stepped into the half barrel. The water was lukewarm. The tub wasn't large enough to submerge myself, but I could kneel and wash adequately.

The soap was a harsh lye, but I used it anyway, scrubbing as best as I was able. My broken arm still throbbed, and I had no way of knowing if it had healed cleanly, or at all, or even how long such a thing would take, beyond Henri's offhand comment. I did my best to leave the splint on and undisturbed. When I had scrubbed as much of me as I could, I stepped out of the barrel and dunked my head, trying to wash my hair awkwardly, one-handed. By the time I was done, the water in the barrel was a filthy color, but my hair and body were considerably cleaner. My shirt and pants were filthy as well, and I hated to put them back on. The guard had provided a light blanket and I wrapped it around myself.

He returned bearing a plain but serviceable dress, followed by one of the female servants. Ignoring my unusual attire, he handed it to me and said, "I will come to fetch you in an hour and take you to His Holiness. Mary will stay and help you with the lacing." With that he turned and left.

Mary proved to be competent and helped me into the dress, lacing it tight enough to appear modest without pressing too much on the still healing wound. She *tsk*ed at the filthy bandages holding the splint on my arm. "That must come off. It smells something terrible and it's filthy."

She left and returned shortly with a pair of scissors. Before I could say anything she had cut the bandages and let the splints fall to the floor. My arm was discolored and sore and looked skinny and wasted compared to the other one.

Mary noted my horrified stare. "Oh aye, that's how my cousin's arm looked too when it came out of the cast. It'll be fine." She took a cleanish looking rag out of her pocket, dipped it in the remaining bathwater and bathed the arm carefully, so as to not get water on the dress. "Now, Carlin is making his report to Charles. He'll be back shortly. You keep your chin up."

I was touched by her attempt to reassure me but was also certain she had no idea what I had been accused of. "Thank you for your help Mary." My voice was rusty and weak with disuse. "One last thing. Can you help me do something with my hair?"

She smiled. "Yes of course. There isn't much time, but I can put it in a neat braid down your back if that suits."

"Thank you." I had no idea what I would be facing with the Holy Father and feeling like a bag of rags wasn't going to help matters.

Mary had my hair braided and secured within a few minutes, tucking in strands that kept trying to escape. "There. All set."

I nodded my thanks as Carlin, the guard, came in to fetch me. "It is time. Will you come easily?"

"I will come quietly," I replied.

He nodded, "Good. This way please," was all he said, gesturing for me to precede him out the door.

JACQUELINE

By the time we reached the second flight of stairs I was winded and desperate to rest. The long confinement had left me weak, and I tired easily. Carlin merely looked at me, pausing for a moment to let me catch my breath. The walk left me time to ponder my potential fates. Hanged? Burned? Branded? Or merely imprisoned for the rest of my life? All of them filled me with dread. I wondered if they had any proof, but as part of the nobility I knew that proof was immaterial when accused by a ruler. I was, despite the abjuration of my familial duties, still the Contessa de Valois and niece to the king of France. Beheading then. I shuddered at the thought and rubbed my neck.

In the upper hallways sunlight flooded through stained-glass windows, causing rainbows of color to dance across the tile floors. It was a busy hallway, and I found that we received many strange looks from the Cardinals and the Monsignors who were hurrying about their business. Carlin stopped in front of a large set of ornate double doors guarded by Swiss Guardsmen. They looked at him, they looked at me, and pushed open one of the doors.

The antechamber held a few seats against the walls, and a small table for flowers but nothing else. Carlin strode across the room with not so much as a glance, heading for a smaller door on the far wall. He knocked briefly and a man in cardinal's robes opened it.

"Ah yes, please come in." My mind registered surprise, shock, and anger as I came face to face with Father Michael, the man who had helped me escape with the Miter, and then subsequently handed me over to the Swiss Guard. He opened the door further and gestured me through, his eyes warning me to silence. "Carlin, thank you for your service. I will take her from here." Carlin gave a short bow and strode off without a backwards glance. I wanted to spit in his face. Taking a deep breath, I stilled my hands and stiffened my spine. Whispering I said, "Why? Why help me once and then betray me later? What game are you playing Father?"

Father Michael did not reply, merely gesturing that I follow him through two thick double doors.

An older man in snowy white robes sat in a high-backed chair on a small dais in the middle of the room. Wigs styled in the courtly fashion were on display against one wall as if they were items of great value. Other walls held paintings of scenes from the bible. 'Judgement Day', 'The Rapture' and others. Charles stood at Clément's right hand looking splendid in his pressed uniform. Father Michael walked up to within comfortable speaking distance and said quietly, "The Contessa is here to make her confession."

"Very well. Thank you, Michael. You may leave us." The Holy Father gestured with one hand dismissing him. The click of the door latch was loud in the silence, but we all held our poses until we heard it.

Turning to Charles he said, "Captain Durstain, is this the woman you brought in under arrest for the theft of Vatican relics?"

Charles glanced at me briefly. "Yes, Your Grace."

"And was she in possession of the Miter when you apprehended her?" the Holy Father asked formally.

Charles paused. "No, Your Grace, she was not." He stared straight ahead at the back wall.

"And did she confess her crime to you before she was apprehended or while she was in your custody?"

"No, Your Grace, she did not."

I wondered what the point of this was, but stood patiently, listening.

"Did you wonder if you were doing the right thing, arresting her without the proof of your own eyes? Going merely on faith that the information I gave you was correct?"

I did not know Clément, but he was up to something. I wasn't sure if this display was for me, or for Charles.

"Yes, Your Grace. I found my faith sorely tested in this regard but overcame my doubts to bring her to you. Father Michael, as you know, assisted me to accomplish this." His eyes flickered to the doorway in an unreadable expression. He didn't seem to know where this was going either.

"Thank you, Captain, for fulfilling your duties so admirably." He rang a small bell sitting on the arm of his throne. A side door opened and Franco the double-crossing bastard who had begun my journey into this hell, stepped through. I clenched my hands at my sides, as fury seethed through me.

"Jac, so nice to see you again. I hope you're having a pleasant stay." Franco oozed with false sincerity.

Clément studied Franco as a hawk might study its prey. "Your confession states you were paid a handsome sum to hire the crew of *The Indiana* to steal the Holy Miter. Is this the woman you hired?" Clément asked from his throne.

Franco turned and bowed low, smirking as if this were merely a theatrical production. "Yes, Your Grace. She accepted payment and promised to deliver the relic some days hence."

"And did she in fact deliver the relic to you?" Clément pressed.

Franco hesitated. "No, Your Grace. She did not show up at the agreed-upon rendezvous in Palermo."

"And having made the initial bargain with her, your fee paid, and the contract in place, you are now betraying her trust, providing witness against her."

Franco hesitated again. "Yes, Your Grace."

Clément shook his head. "I believe the traditional rate is thirty pieces of silver. Captain, you will find a pouch on my desk. Please give it to this gentleman and have the guards escort him to the cells below. We will determine his punishment later."

Franco looked confused. "But...we agreed upon..."

"Now." Clément said sternly.

Charles looked unsettled but gave a crisp bow.

"Charles, as this woman is a noble, she has the right to a private confession. I would ask that once you escort Franco out and hand him to the guards that, you wait in the antechamber."

Charles rested his eyes on me briefly. "Holy Father, that is not wise. She is clever and can be dangerous."

"Nevertheless, you will leave us." A hint of steel crept into the old man's voice.

Charles, with a moment's hesitation gave a salute, his spine stiff. "I will be close by, should you need me Holy Father. Signor Franco, this way please."

As he walked past, he paused, and looked at me with steely eyes. I could feel the heat of his regard. Returning his gaze coolly I nodded.

I remained impassive, looking up at the man on the throne. When I heard the door click behind me, I said, "You have gone to some lengths to bring me here... for a reason that does not actually involve my confession." My good arm cradled my still healing forearm.

"Very perceptive of you, my dear. But as there are no witnesses, none shall be the wiser that you did not actually confess. Though since we both know you did it, your confession hardly matters." He smiled a cruel smile from his throne.

"So, what happens now? You tell the world I confessed, though I haven't, and won't. You let Madame Guillotine have my head, and move on knowing you have rid the world of one more supposed pirate?" I paced deliberately, coming to rest in front of one of the magnificent pieces of artwork on the walls, hugging my arms to my body to still their trembling.

"Or perhaps you wish to make a deal. You want your property back, or you need something stolen, and you would like one of the best thieves in the world to do the job for you. After all, according to you, I have successfully managed to rob the Vatican. Purportedly one of the most well-guarded, secure palaces in Europe." I looked back at the Pope over my shoulder to see if that had hit the mark.

It did make him chuckle. "You are so young, and such an easy pawn. Entertaining, too. I suppose it is true that after our meeting I might say you had confessed and give you to Madame Guillotine. Easy enough to have one of my scribes write your confession and then forge your signature." He seemed genuinely amused by this scenario and continued to chuckle unnervingly. "But that would still leave me without my property. And I do want it back. I expect, by the end of this meeting you will have a strong desire to return it."

I raised an eyebrow. "Do you plan on torturing me yourself?"

"Don't be foolish. Violence is lazy and lacks imagination. I have no need to torture you. You will be dead soon anyway, and it is short-sighted to have blood on one's hands, when there are other alternatives. You see, Contessa, when you have lived as long as I you find there is more than one way to hang a sinner."

I pondered this while I looked around the room, still puzzled about the wigs. The audience chamber walls were filled with paintings by famous Masters. There was a large mahogany desk off to one side that appeared well used. On the desk were a variety of small carvings, paperweights and ornate boxes.

"So, if you have no plans of killing me, then why do you claim I'll be dead soon?" He enjoyed my confusion, and it made me angry.

With a rictus of a grin he said, "Obviously you had to be offered bait of a sufficiently rich nature to entice you to take such a high-profile job, and it needed to sound sufficiently difficult to pique your interest. What thief wouldn't take thirty thousand gold to rob the Vatican?" He shook his head condescendingly.

This confirmed my growing suspicion of who our mysterious employer was.

"A sensible one," I muttered under my breath chastising myself. "So, you're the mysterious buyer. Why would you set me up? I am nothing to you." I looked up, genuinely curious.

He ignored my question and continued. "Of course, I must congratulate you on stealing the real Miter and bypassing the copy left on the altar for you. That was unexpected and somewhat problematic. The fact that you have kept it hidden for as long as you have is decidedly impressive. But that brings us to the current circumstances which are most assuredly in my favor."

Why doesn't Father Michael want it returned? I thought to myself. *What is going on here?* Aloud I said, "I do not see what you mean. You don't have your relic, and you don't know where it is. It seems to me I have some bargaining power." I stared up at him from behind his desk.

"I will have it back, with or without your cooperation," he replied with an unnerving grin.

Standing up straight and putting on my most regal air I gambled. "You and what army? You know who I am. Though I don't use my title or family connections often, I am the beloved niece of the king. With one word from my uncle I would have the entire nation of France behind me."

Clément scoffed. "Child, I own the French court, and you overestimate your influence, uncle or no. You might have some bargaining power, but for one piece of information you lack. I have no need to kill you or silence you because you are already dead. Or as good as. The relic, you see, has its own protections and has for centuries. I will get it back eventually, one way or the other. When you stole it, you unleashed abominations unto the Lord; fallen Angels. Your fate is no longer in my hands. They will be coming for you. And they will kill you." His matter-of-fact voice sent chills down my spine, as my mind pulled the individual threads of what he was saying. *Who does he own at the French Court? What does he gain by using fairy tales to scare me?*

"You expect to scare me with some fairytale about fallen Angels? You're the Pope. That seems rather beneath you." The words were out of my mouth before I had time to think about them.

"You may not believe me now, but you will. Of course, if you return the relic then I can call them off and send them back to Hell where they belong. Assuming you live that long. This is not the first time they have appeared. They will not stop until their mandate is complete."

He was insane. That was the only explanation I could come up with for this crazy tale of fallen Angels. Abraham told me many things about the Miter, including the story of the existence of the demons, but it had to be pure fantasy. Nevertheless, the Pope's matter of fact attitude bothered me. This was one of the most powerful men in Europe. He had no need of fairy tales.

"So, you're saying essentially devils from Hell are coming to get me unless I return your property?" I asked putting as much skepticism into my voice as possible.

"You don't have to believe me now, but you will. Regardless I will have accomplished my goal. Furthering my power in Europe." He smiled, his cold eyes surveying me like a cog under a magnifier. "Such lovely hair you have. I understand that's how you transported the weapon that allowed you to escape from Charles."

The sudden change in topic confused me. I reached up and touched my hair, glancing at the display of wigs a finger of foreboding sliding down my spine. I loved my hair; it was one of my few vanities. "Hardly a weapon. It merely made him sleep for a time. A last defense, if you will."

"Sensible for a noble such as yourself. Though you flout it now, you would prefer to forget that you are the niece of the King of France. For now." He steepled his fingers and stared over them at me. My mind raced. Was my uncle in danger? Who did Clément 'own' close to the French throne? I wrenched my mind back to my own situation. My uncle had guards protecting him. Better to focus on my own problems at the moment.

"Tomorrow, after a long night spent in prayer and meditation, I will publicly announce you have confessed, and even though you refuse to return the sacred relic, I, His Holiness the Pope, out of the goodness of my heart, forgive you. Your identity as both the notorious captain of *The Indiana* and as a noblewoman, niece of the King, will be released to the public. The King of France will publicly owe me a favor for not executing one of his family members and a second favor for forgiving her of a high crime. My power there will be solidified. You, though you don't believe me yet, will do all that is in your power to find the relic and return it to me." He paused as another small earthquake rattled the building. When it subsided, he smiled.

"Your influences as an agitator in Europe will be considerably diminished with the public knowing that you are a noble. As an embarrassment to the royal family, it is unlikely any of the nobility will receive you. There will be very few places in Europe where you will be welcome. You have in fact backed yourself into a room with no doors, my dear."

My mouth gaped open in astonishment. "I admit, Sir, it seems you have outmaneuvered me." As I stood behind the desk I fidgeted with the various knickknacks, picking them up setting them down again in different configurations.

"Now, as I said before, if you return the relic, I will banish the abominations you have summoned. Call it incentive. If you don't, they will kill you, everyone you care about, and anyone who happens to get in the way. And they do not kill quickly." He seemed very confident, and I felt my own certainty slipping away.

"For my own curiosity, is there no way of defeating them? What if one of them should come upon me before I have a chance to retrieve the relic? Are they invincible?" It seemed a fair question to ask, though I doubted his sanity.

"Thinking ahead, I see. They will of course vanish when they have completed their mandate and returned the Miter. They can be killed, but the person who kills them then takes their place. Not a pleasant fate, I assure you."

No witty response came to me, so I remained silent.

"I can see that you doubt me. You may believe as you choose. And if you die in the interim, well, the Miter will show up again. We will find it." The sheer, matter of fact manner that he said these things rattled me to my core.

"Enjoy your last night as my guest. Beginning tomorrow you will be a shamed, outed, hunted woman. Tomorrow I shall send couriers to every airfield in Europe, as well as a message to the King of France."

"Something puzzles me. The charade you played out with Franco while Charles was here. What was that about?"

Clément chuckled. "Oh, that's a little side project of mine. Eventually Charles will do everything I say unquestioningly. Tomorrow I will make my announcement concerning you. You would be wise to immediately seek out my property and return it. Now go. Father Michael will see you to a room as befits your station, and the guards will see you do not leave it. Unless of course you prefer to return to the dungeon?" He smiled mockingly as he gestured to the door.

My thoughts were in turmoil as Father Michael showed me to a small suite with a bed, sitting room and bathing chamber. A dress of good quality, though not ostentatious, was laid out on the bed. "For your audience tomorrow, my child. Also, you must wear your hair loose and without adornment as befits a petitioner. Tonight, you must rest, pray, and thank God for His Holiness's mercy." Father Michael's hands were folded in the sleeves of his robe, and his face was serene.

"Father Michael, why did you help me before? Why did you betray me to bring me here?" I asked as he turned to go.

Looking back over his shoulder and smiling serenely he replied, "I helped you before to bring about this day. Helping you now does not suit my plans." He shut the door firmly and a welter of emotions boiled within me—fear, betrayal, but above all, anger. Anger at Clément for so casually destroying lives for political power, anger at myself for allowing greed to override my judgement, anger at Charles for failing to see the type of man he was working for, and anger at this mysterious Father Michael who had an unknown agenda.

While I had never been a fan of the Catholic Church, I had also never thought of it truly as evil. My research had shown that there had been good Popes throughout history – men who genuinely cared and tried to better the lives of their flock, and history had also shown a share of bad Popes. Clément was definitely the latter – not merely bad, but evil.

I bathed in a proper tub, taking time to wash out my hair, the luxury of hot water for once ignored in favor of my grim thoughts. Sitting in front of the small fire in my chambers I let my hair dry, running my fingers through to pull out the tangles of weeks.

Trying to set aside my anger and focus on what must be done was hard – there were too many loose threads in this tapestry that the Pope and I had woven. Though he revealed a great deal of information during our interview, he still held a great many cards. Clément struck me as the sort of man who, for his own amusement, would give his pawns just enough information to hang themselves with, while playing a much deeper game. I still held a few cards of my own – the Miter, Abraham's work on translating the scripture, my crew. I feared what I would be taking them into and what I might ask of them. There was a traitor in the French Court, and I needed to find out who. Politics and intrigue change people, and not in pleasant ways. What I faced on the morrow intimidated me, but not nearly so much as what was coming.

The next morning two guards led me to a dais in the middle of the square. A contingent of guardsmen circled the platform to keep crowds back. This was a familiar spectacle in Rome. A crowd had gathered, hissing and booing as I took my place. Clément, in full papal regalia, with Charles behind him came out to his balcony, and the crowd cheered.

"People of Rome! The woman who stands before you today has committed grave sins against the Church. She is Contessa Jacqueline de Valois of France. Also known as the notorious Pirate, Captain Jac. She has confessed to theft of holy relics, deceit, bearing false witness, and behavior unbefitting a woman." He paused and the crowd roared.

He raised his hand, quieting them. "People of Rome. She has stolen from the very house of God. I have spent many days in prayer, asking God if punishment or forgiveness was the better course of action. After much contemplation, he has guided me to forgiveness."

Looking out over the sea of faces, I blinked. For a brief moment I thought I had seen Niccolò in the crowd. I scanned, looking for other members of the crew, no longer listening to Clément. There! Standing up on the base of a statue I saw Niccolò. He was trying to signal me. My crew was near. Fear gripped me. God help them, if they tried to rescue me in this, they would be slaughtered. Better to play it out.

"Jacqueline de Valois, Contessa, it is customary for those seeking forgiveness from Rome to offer up penance for their sins. Something of personal value. Something that will then mark the petitioner as penitent." I listened with half an ear as Clément droned on.

I could feel the crowd around the platform turn their attention to me as I tried to signal Niccolò to stand down. The crowd was wavering on the border of maddened hostility. Whatever Clément had come up with, I would have to agree, or the crowd would tear me apart. The guards on the dais could feel it too and looked at each other nervously. This was more of a crowd than usual then.

"Such sacrifice must be made willingly and by the petitioner's own hands." One of the guards stepped forward with a pair of shears. I looked at him in confusion, dragging my attention back as Clément continued speaking. "As one of your crimes is behavior unbecoming a woman, and your hair is the most visible symbol of that status, you will be made to look less like a noblewoman. You must cut off all of your hair. This will also serve as a visible reminder of your penance to both yourself and to those around you."

"Your hair, my lady. You must cut it off. All of it." The guard held out the shears. "It will be collected and made into a wig."

I looked at him in anger and indignation, my hands moving up to my long flowing hair, worn loose today, as I had been instructed. Clément stood on his balcony, looking pleased with himself. Glancing at the crowd, I noticed many of those present had, themselves, closely cropped hair. The poor frequently sold their hair for pennies so that the rich could make their fantastical wigs.

The crowd was starting to get ugly and restless. "Look at the pretty noble, too afraid to cut her own hair!" a faceless voice yelled.

A piece of rotten fruit came sailing up onto the dais, missing me by a few inches.

"We'll strip her of her hair! And everything else, too!" another voice yelled, and I felt the crowd start to surge.

Anger smoldering in my eyes, I took the shears from the guard and turned to face the Clément. Grabbing a handful of hair close to my head I began cutting, watching the locks fall at my feet. A guard collected every strand that fell, gathering it in a purple velvet bag. Remembering the wigs along the wall in his receiving room I knew; this trophy was going in Clément's private collection. Refusing to let tears spill over I doggedly hacked at my thick hair while the crowd cheered. When I was finished, I turned to the guard, my voice trembling. "Is it sufficient?"

"There is one more step, my lady. Please stand still while we finish." Moving behind me and gesturing for me to kneel, he took out a long razor and began shaving off the last short vestiges of hair. He was done in a few moments, tipping my head this way and that to get the back of my neck and behind my ears.

My scalp was bleeding from a few places where he had nicked me, and the air felt strange and cold against my scalp. When he was done, he gathered a handful of hair out of the bag and held it up as a banner above his head. "Penance has been served!" he announced loudly to the crowd, and they cheered. Damn them all.

The guard nodded up to Clément on his balcony.

Numb, I touched my shorn head gingerly. I made eye contact with Clément as he stood on the balcony and he nodded, satisfied and gloating. "She has done her penance and been forgiven. She is free to go." I heard the pronouncement in stoic silence, head bowed; I wanted to glare up at him, but my life depended on appearing chastised. The crowd continued to catcall and heckle, and my anger began to swell. Staring out at the crowd, I asked the guard, quietly "Where should I go?"

"Anywhere you like, but I would stay out of sight as much as you can. The crowd in the square can get ugly after judgements. Particularly once he's no longer watching."

They quieted as I set foot on the stairs leading down from the dais, and a path opened. The jeers began again almost as soon as my foot touched the cobblestones, and rotten fruit hit my shoulder about halfway across the square. Once the first person was brave enough, the rotten fruit and vegetables fell like rain. The impact of something harder, a rock I think, against my ribs made me stagger, clutching my still recovering side. I made it to the edge of the square without falling. As soon as I was clear of the square I lifted my skirt and ran, ducking down side streets and out of the crowd. A few brave souls followed me but gave up after a few blocks.

When I reached a quieter section of town, where shops gave way to houses, I paused for a moment to catch my breath and run my hands over my scalp. I had never thought of myself as vain, but my hair had been my one beauty, and now it was gone. Tears streamed down my face for its loss, as anger and determination shored up my resolve. I leaned against a gatepost and closed my eyes for a moment to catch my breath and plan my next move.

"So that was a bit of a spectacle," Tyler's voice said in my ear. I jumped and glared as I whirled around. David, Tyler, Nina, Marie, and the rest of the crew stood there.

"Come on, Captain. Let's get back to the ship and get out of here." Nina took my arm, glancing at my shorn head, scowling. "And maybe get you a hat. Your head's going to get awfully cold at altitude."

Wiping my eyes, I chuckled softly. This was my family, and we took care of one another.

Onboard, while the crew prepared for departure, I collected my thoughts, staring out over the prow of the airship. Carefully, I examined my emotions, rage, fear, humiliation, love for my crew, and a deep and abiding determination to seek the downfall of Clément. I set aside those that wouldn't help with what was coming, closing them off so I could do what needed to be done. Clément had made a critical mistake; he threatened my crew. This was not the last he would see of me. Next time I…we… would be coming for vengeance.

Niccolò approached me tentatively. "Captain?"

"Yes, what is it Niccolò?" I asked, my mind still turned inwards.

He held up the velvet purple bag full of my hair. "I got you something." He paused, fidgeting. "I ... I didn't think we should let him keep it."

Startled, I laughed, and swept him up into an embrace, taking the bag from him. "You did good, my young friend."

Tyler shouted orders to launch, and suddenly we were rising back to the open sky where we belonged.

EPILOGUE

In a cave below the Vatican the earth shook for the final time, revealing an ancient, underground temple of pale stone. A great seal covered the floor, etched in the sandstone, with the markings highlighted in gold. The great seal rent down the middle with a horrific cracking sound. Dust and fire swirled through the temple. The head of a great beast rose, a misshapen scaly claw extended, pulling itself up and out. The beast was hideous. Pulsating skin the color of dried blood, stretched across a skeletal form. Curved horns jutted from his forehead sweeping back and curling behind his head. A skeletal face with holes for eyes, rose from the darkness, and the stink of sulfur and brimstone roiled off his dark form. When he stood, his horns brushed the temple's tall ceiling. Six more beasts followed him from the abyss, varying in shape, form and size. Each of them hideous, malformed creatures of the dark.

"My brothers and sisters, the journey to the land of the living was long. We have been awakened once again with a new mandate. Welcome back to the world of men." His voice boomed and echoed throughout the chamber and carried the scent of death. "Her name is Jacqueline de Valois, and she must die."

The End

Captain Jac and her crew will return in *The Second Sin*

If you have enjoyed this book, please consider leaving a review. Reviews help authors and readers alike!

To receive a free story download in the Adventures of Captain Jac, please join my mailing list!

Mailing list

ABOUT THE AUTHOR

Jessica Brawner grew up in the wilds of South Texas and plotted ways to spend her life traveling the world. She has been remarkably successful at that endeavor, attending school and traveling all over Europe at the age of eighteen, moving back to the United States to achieve two bachelor's degrees, and then moving to Central Asia for a time with the Peace Corps. Twenty years ago she discovered the wonders of Science Fiction and Fantasy conventions and the crazy, lovable, friends-are-the-family-you-choose mentality found there. She spent many years working and volunteering at conventions all over the country.

In addition to her convention activities, Ms. Brawner has developed and taught self-defense classes, worked as an event planner, an entertainment agent, a computer teacher, a personal assistant, and most recently works at an energy tech start up while pursuing her writing career.

You can find her online at www.jessicabrawner.com as well as on Facebook and Twitter @JABrawner

Made in United States
Cleveland, OH
25 July 2025